# NIGHT CREEPS 2

## AN ADULT HORROR STORY

## MICHAEL D'AMBROSIO

# TABLE OF CONTENTS

# CHAPTER I

# WELCOME TO PARMISSING VALLEY

Parmissing Valley is a small, reclusive town set within the beautiful Sierra Nevada Mountains. Since the alien incursion six months prior in the spring, the population, which was once about fifteen hundred, was now a scant fifty or so.

The cover story provided by the federal government about a rare strain of rabies that spread among many of the town's population, explained issues such as why the bodies were burned and why the evacuated survivors were quarantined for forty-five days afterward.

Conspiracies filled the internet because of the concurrent and unexplained explosions at an Air Force Base and over Graham's Mountain but, at this point, no one with enough credibility to open an investigation really cared. The problem was dealt with and the matter was considered closed as far as the authorities were concerned.

Like Sheriff Lamar Whittington and his deputy, Johnny Watkins, their nightmares about the creatures and what they did to their victims would scar them for life. What they didn't realize was that the spring event was just the beginning of something much more frightening.

On a clear, starry night in the valley, three small lights shot across the sky and vanished over Graham's Mountain. Lamar, now the interim mayor, exited the municipal building and paused to observe the lights. *Interesting*, he thought to himself and continued to walk the half-mile to his home.

It was rare that he worked into the evening, but he had four days, counting the weekend, to review applicable permits and codes associated with mining in the state and county. An ambitious company was anxious to start a mining project on Graham's Mountain and he wanted to understand all the requirements, both federal and state, before he gave them the okay to initiate the project.

Now that the town was his, he was determined to make it a model for other towns and possibly even cities across the country. This was his opportunity to make something good out of the horror that befell them.

As he strolled along the side of the road, he regretted how long it had been since he dated. He found it difficult for an African-American in a rural, predominantly white region, to find someone of his persuasion. Of late, he felt the emptiness inside and longed for someone to share his life with.

Johnny, now the interim sheriff, suggested to him several times that he ought to take a vacation on a singles' cruise, which was likely his best opportunity to meet someone compatible. Unfortunately, that wasn't Lamar's style. He preferred to meet someone naturally instead of seemingly arranged and let the chips fall where they may.

Taking notice of several of the empty buildings along the route, he assured himself that it was only temporary. Once the town's new reputation spread, potential residents would come from all over and repopulate the town - his town.

He noticed a poster in the window of the local hardware store, announcing the date and time of the town's barbecue on Saturday to celebrate his and Johnny's official swearing in to their new positions.

At times, Lamar found it awkward to replace the previous mayor, who died under horrible circumstances. He often wondered what he would do if someone he cared for became an alien creature. Could he pull the trigger and shoot them or would he, like his predecessor, shoot himself to escape the pain? That was a question he hoped he'd never have to answer.

After twenty years as a police officer and less than a year as the sheriff, he knew it would be tough to take on a bureaucratic job like mayor even in little Parmissing Valley. Lamar was always on the front line, fighting crime or aliens and mutants, for that matter. He also knew it would be tough to avoid interfering with Johnny when he needed to step back and let him do his job as the new sheriff.

Johnny convinced Lamar to join him at the gym regularly where they took out their anxieties from the incursion in the weight room. As a result, Lamar looked rugged at two-hundred and ten pounds instead of the blubbery two-hundred and sixty that he weighed when he first arrived in the valley last year. He owed Johnny more for that than anything else. With the weight loss, his self-respect and dignity returned. He hoped that one day he could return the favor and help Johnny overcome the effects of their horrific experience.

Lamar paused in front of his house and realized he was entering a new stage of his life. Many things would be different from here on out. He was now an administrative leader instead of a field expert.

*It can't be that bad*, he thought and entered the split-level rancher. Sometimes he had to admit that city life had its advantages. There was always someone around to talk to, friend or foe, and he missed that on many an occasion in Parmissing Valley.

After showering and changing into his pajamas, Lamar stared in the mirror at himself disappointedly. "Looks like another lonely night in the Whittington household," he grumbled cynically. He turned off the light and went to sleep.

***

At twenty-nine, Johnny Watkins took pride in his physical appearance for the ladies and, with a regular workout regimen, he was fit and trim in his tan sheriff's uniform.

Since the suicide of his girlfriend, Sally, three months ago, Johnny became more of a recluse, with Lamar as his only friend. He blamed himself for her death and often wondered that, if he took her away from Parmissing Valley, maybe things would have been different. Since then, Johnny found it difficult to even consider dating. He believed that he was a train wreck when it came to social skills and always would be.

Johnny expected that nothing much would change at the PV Police Station when he took over except that it was his to run as he saw fit. There would be, of course, the boring administrative responsibilities that come with the job but he figured that there couldn't be that much paperwork in a small town like this or could there be?

Then there was the issue of filling two deputies' positions soon. Johnny liked the solitude of having the station to himself and wasn't anxious to take on anyone new. He had the time to sort out details from the alien incursion and also his relationship with Sally. Perhaps one day he'd understand both.

Saturday arrived and forty of the townspeople gathered in the parking lot of the municipal building to celebrate the election of Lamar to mayor and Johnny to sheriff. Since the previous mayor's death earlier in the year, their positions were temporary until a formal election could be held. Now, it was official: Lamar was the mayor and Johnny was the sheriff.

A catering service came from the nearby town of Clearview to provide food and drink for the festivities since Parmissing Valley still lacked many of the basic services.

When the swearing in was completed, Lamar gave a brief speech at a podium on a decorated flatbed trailer and introduced Johnny as the new sheriff. As he stepped down off the trailer to the cheers of his supporters, he noticed a red Miata Mx-3 parked across the street in front of a small hotel. He thought it strange for a car of that caliber to appear in a small town like his. *Must be some hotshot business person*, he surmised. *Maybe even a future tenant.*

Another round of cheers filled the air as Johnny finished a short speech and left the podium to join him. The two sat down at one of twelve round tables and shared a beer.

"That was quick," Lamar remarked. "I thought you'd have a lot to say to some of those pretty ladies out there."

"Not much to say," replied Johnny with little enthusiasm. "I don't think we'll see much crime in this town for a while. Maybe a few cats stuck in the trees. That's about it, though."

Lamar pointed to an attractive, red-haired woman standing near the concession stand. She wore a skirt and short-sleeved blouse. "She could be the one, Johnny. All you have to do is …"

"All I have to do is nothing," Johnny responded curtly. "I'm not ready, Lamar."

"You never know when the action's going to find you," forewarned Lamar. "The key is to be prepared."

"Yes, father," Johnny replied cynically.

A young boy walked by them with a plate of chicken, mashed potatoes, and an ear of corn. Lamar eyed the chicken and glanced at Johnny.

Johnny knew that look. "All right, let's go get some. You'll pay for this at the gym tomorrow."

"Just one plate," Lamar suggested anxiously, "and maybe another beer, too."

"Now, you're talking." Johnny agreed heartily. They slapped hands in a high-five and then proceeded to the concession stand.

When the two men returned to their table, each had a plate of chicken, an ear of corn, potatoes, and a cold beer. They toasted to their first day officially at their new positions.

They joked at the idea of campaigning, especially when they were the only candidates for their positions. It was no surprise they received all forty-seven votes from the permanent residents.

"I feel like a Chicago politician," kidded Johnny. "You're guaranteed an easy victory when you're on the right team."

"Well, we *were* the only candidates in this case," countered Lamar proudly. "If we didn't win, I'd be real concerned."

Lamar sipped from his beer and looked past Johnny at the hotel across the street. A shapely, dark-skinned woman crossed the street and sauntered in their direction. He wondered if she was the owner of the Miata or just another tourist passing through. *Quite a looker*, he thought to himself as he ogled her.

Johnny interrupted, "What about our man-power issue at the station?"

A suspicious grin crossed Lamar's face and Johnny realized he was in trouble. "It's funny you should ask," Lamar replied slyly and took another sip from his beer. He was again distracted as the woman made eye contact with him. Lamar fretted as he realized she was heading in his direction.

"Something wrong?" asked Johnny, sensing Lamar's unease. "You didn't answer my question."

"I was …," he started to say.

The mysterious woman stopped at their table and ended his response. "Well, Mayor Whittington, I believe congratulations are in order for you and your sheriff," she declared while extending her hand to each for a congratulatory shake.

Hardly looking like someone in her early thirties, she wore a short skirt, white blouse with her hair tied up neatly in a bun. Her height at almost six-feet accented her brimming confidence and was intimidating, but her friendly mannerism convinced Lamar that he should be concerned.

Johnny was curious as to who the woman was and even more amused by Lamar's nervous reaction to her.

Enamored by the woman, Lamar tried to regain his composure. "Do I know you?" he inquired.

"If you don't, you will soon enough," she answered assertively. "We have a meeting tomorrow at eleven."

Lamar's eyes widened with surprise as he stammered, "Ah, you must be Ms. Bell from that, uh, magazine." He was embarrassed that his memory failed him at such a pivotal time.

"Yes, Mayor, I am from … that magazine," she chided.

Lamar strained to recall the magazine's name, while exhibiting a bit of humility. "I'm sorry, Ms. Bell. So much has been going on that I have to write things down anymore."

Johnny turned away to hide his smile. He enjoyed watching Lamar squirm in front of the woman. He recalled Lamar's advice to him earlier: You never know when the action is going to find you. The key is to be prepared. *How sweet it is*, he thought to himself as Lamar floundered. *So much for preparation.*

"Please, call me Sasha," she requested.

"Okay, Sasha. Once again, I'm really sorry for …"

"Don't beat yourself up, Mayor. I'll let you make it up to me tomorrow," she said coyly. "Good day, gentlemen."

The two men could only stare at her perfect ass and admire her as she walked away. Beads of sweat formed on Lamar's brow.

"Holy smokes!" uttered Johnny. "She is hot!"

"I can't believe I forgot the name of her magazine. I am such a moron!" he blurted as he wiped his forehead with a napkin.

Johnny reached into his pocket and handed him a tissue. "A little nervous, Lamar," he kidded. "You have to be ready when the action comes to you, huh?"

❖ ● ● ● ●

"There's no action with her. She's just here for …" Then Lamar wondered why she was there and what she wanted with him. "… something or other," he babbled cluelessly.

"I think she likes you," Johnny commented. "She gave you the 'look'."

"Ah, shut up," Lamar uttered playfully. "What do you know about the 'look'?"

"I'm no rookie, Lamar," Johnny remarked proudly.

The two men tapped their glasses together and drank.

"So, back to my question," Johnny continued. "What about our new hire?"

"Our new hire," he echoed smugly. "Let's see …"

A beat-up, blue Toyota pickup truck parked in front of the municipal building. Twenty-five-year-old Paula Mason stepped out and took a circular view of the mountains surrounding the little town.

With her shoulder-length, blonde hair waving lightly in the breeze, she savored the beginning of her new career away from the hustle and bustle of city life in Chicago. Paula was well-built for a petite gal at five-foot, four inches and a mere hundred pounds per her resume. Dressed in tight jeans and a pull-over sweater, she weaved through the small crowd with a lively gait to the concession stand.

Lamar spotted her and sat back in his chair, delighted by the timing of her appearance. Johnny noticed his demeanor and knew a trap was about to be sprung on him.

"What are you up to, my cagey friend?" Johnny asked. "You have a very suspicious look about you."

"It seems you know a lot about looks today, Johnny."

"You'd be surprised what I can tell from a look," he commented and scanned the area for an obvious clue. Unsure of what he was looking for, he turned his attention back to Lamar. "All right," he relented. "What gives?"

Lamar smiled and held up one finger. "Wait for it," he said giddily and closed his eyes, enjoying the moment.

"You'd better not screw me on this, Lamar," Johnny warned nervously.

Paula searched the crowd as she approached the booths. She questioned the caterer as he prepared a plate for her. He pointed to Lamar and handed her a beer. Paula thanked the man and approached their table.

Lamar opened his eyes and leaned toward Johnny. "You're about to meet her," he whispered cunningly.

"Her?" Johnny turned around and spotted Paula coming toward them.

"Yes, that's her," Lamar responded, pleased with his decision.

"You hired a woman?" Johnny questioned him, stunned by his choice.

"Yes, and a darned good one."

Johnny was shocked that Lamar would bring in a female after what he went through with Sally. He knew Lamar wanted him to open up to women again, but he wasn't ready. Johnny put his head in his hands dejectedly as he sensed nothing good would come of Lamar's ruse.

During the phone interview with Paula, Lamar felt a certain attachment to her when she mentioned her need to escape city life due to tragic circumstances. The two of them had that in common and he knew what it meant for him to get away. Hiring her seemed to be the right thing to do for another reason he couldn't explain. It was just one of those gut feelings you get as a cop.

Paula stood between the two men, beaming with pride, while holding her beer and a plate of food. "Good afternoon, Mayor Whittington," Paula said politely. She set her food on the table and shook his hand. "May I join you, gentlemen?"

"Of course," replied Lamar pleasantly.

The two men stood and Johnny politely pulled a chair out for her to sit.

"Thank you. You must be Sheriff Watkins."

"I am, ma'am."

"Johnny, this is Paula Mason, your new deputy from Chicago."

Paula and Johnny shook hands. "Welcome to Parmissing Valley," replied Johnny graciously. He gave Lamar a nervous glance as he suspected there was more to this hiring than just a pretty face.

The three of them sat down together.

"I didn't expect to see you until Monday, Paula," Lamar remarked.

"I was really excited about coming out here and getting started. I'm so grateful for the opportunity."

Lamar proposed a toast to their newest deputy. Immediately after, Johnny questioned Paula for twenty minutes about her qualifications. When he was satisfied that Lamar made a good choice, Paula then questioned him about his background and lifestyle.

Johnny was surprised by her boldness. For someone in a new town, she was neither nervous nor intimidated.

Lamar's mind wandered to Sasha during their conversation and what brought her from New York City to a small town like his, nearly on the other side of the country.

Music interrupted their conversation as two local country-western singers took the stage and entertained the crowd with cover songs. Six couples got up in front of the stage and danced energetically to the music.

As Johnny watched them, Paula noticed his interest in the music and the hopeful gaze in his eyes.

Johnny glanced at her and smiled.

Paula responded as a joke, "Sorry, I don't dance, Sheriff."

Johnny was surprised by her remark and countered, "Neither do I. I just like the music."

"Touché," she replied, pleased.

A Dodge Ram drove past the gala, towing a long, unmarked trailer. A U-Haul truck and an Escalade followed.

*That's odd*, Lamar thought.

Paula noticed his perplexed expression. "Something wrong, Mayor?"

"No, just some new visitors in town."

"Anything unusual going on?" she inquired. "That's a strange combination of vehicles."

Lamar was surprised that she took notice of them without exhibiting a glance and countered. "You saw them, too, huh?"

Johnny turned around to see what he missed but the vehicles were out of their sight by then.

"I rode in behind them on the interstate," Paula admitted. "They're from Nevada.

Lamar liked her confidence. He held his beer up to her as a sign of his approval and drank to her.

"I don't miss much, sir," she assured Lamar and then winked at Johnny.

Johnny became annoyed with Paula's bubbly enthusiasm and brimming confidence. He took a sip of his beer and focused on a middle-aged woman standing in front of the stage. She wore tight jeans and a blouse tied at the midriff.

Paula again noticed his interest and teased, "Cougars are a dangerous sort, Sheriff. Sometimes they leave a nasty bite."

Lamar burst into laughter and enjoyed the challenge she posed to Johnny. Unfortunately, Johnny wasn't thrilled by her audacity and set his glass of beer down with authority.

"Look Miss Mason," he said sternly, "you don't come in here and start critiquing your boss the first day you meet him."

Paula looked down sheepishly as Johnny stared her down. "I'm sorry. I didn't mean anything by it, Sheriff," she replied innocently. "I was kidding with you."

She was relieved to see that Lamar enjoyed their showdown and didn't see any harm in it.

Johnny eyed Paula and asked, "Have you ever had a cougar before, Miss Mason?"

Paula was shocked by his question. "Of course not! What kind of girl do you think I am?"

"Well, neither have I," he continued sarcastically.

"Then maybe you should," she replied defensively.

"Maybe we both should," he responded callously.

The two locked eyes as each waited for the other to blink. Paula refused to back down and kept her eyes glued to Johnny's.

Lamar was intrigued by the surprising turn in the conversation and quickly interceded. "I have a meeting tomorrow afternoon with a representative from a company that wants to mine diamonds on Graham's Mountain."

Paula was relieved to turn her attention to Lamar. "Strip miners?" she asked.

"No, they have something new and improved for their mining process."

"I'd like to hear more about them when you have time."

"I can do better than that. You and Johnny will deliver the permits to them when I'm finished with the paperwork."

"That'll be great!" Paula finished her beer and stood up.

Johnny stared at the band on the stage and pretended to ignore her. She was embarrassed that Johnny wasn't thrilled with her presence and fretted the idea of starting her knew career off on the wrong foot.

Scrambling for something positive to say, she informed him, "Don't worry, Sheriff, there's a lot more of me to like than meets the eye. I won't disappoint you." Then she realized how clumsy that sounded. *Paula you are such an idiot*, she thought to herself.

"We'll see," he said disinterestedly and finished his beer. Johnny winced at the idea of having her as a partner. He envisioned her talking his ear off about how he should live his life and how things were in Chicago.

"You're leaving already?" asked Lamar, concerned that he let things get too far out of hand.

"I'm sorry, Mayor. I'd like to stay," she replied with a pleasant smile, "but I have to meet a realtor about an apartment."

Lamar and Johnny stood and shook hands with her again.

"Welcome aboard, Paula," said Lamar. "We're glad to have you."

Lamar glared at Johnny and nodded for him to acknowledge Paula.

"I'm looking forward to working with you," replied Johnny unconvincingly. "Just be cool. This isn't the big city out here."

"I know. It's cougar country," she kidded once more, but immediately wanted to kick herself for the slip.

"Miss Mason," Johnny answered back, growing more annoyed, "I warned you once already."

Paula responded apologetically, "Sorry, boss. Thank you both again for the job. I'll see you tomorrow." She left them and dropped her plate and glass off at the clean-up booth.

Johnny stewed as he didn't appreciate her remarks, regardless of how innocently she meant them. He already struggled with self-confidence with women and didn't need someone to remind him of it.

Lamar was concerned by Johnny's defensive attitude. "She's only messing with you, Johnny. That's what friends do." Johnny bit his lip and refrained from responding.

The two men ogled Paula as she walked away, eyes glued to her small but shapely ass. "Damn, she's got a hell of a walk, eh, Johnny?" Lamar sighed as she got into her truck and drove off. Johnny remained silent, wishing that she'd keep going and never come back.

"Well, Johnny, I hate to leave but I have a few calls to make. I hope you enjoy your new partner," he added with a chuckle.

"You're not right, Lamar," Johnny replied cynically. "You just aren't right." Johnny was used to Lamar playing jokes on him and became more suspicious of Paula's selection for his new deputy than at first. He grabbed Lamar by the wrist and asked, "What's the catch with her? I know you all too well."

Lamar smiled at him. "Why would you think there's a catch? She's a wonderful girl. Just give her time to get acclimated."

When Johnny released his hold on him, Lamar patted him on the back and suggested, "You need to relax, man. Everything's gonna be fine."

"Just what I need around here," Johnny complained. "Another city cop telling me what to do." Then he recalled that Lamar fit that same description and he laughed. "Must be a special on city cops these days," he quipped.

"Ah, you and she are going to be a nice match," Lamar assured him. "Both of you have excellent perceptive abilities. Remember how you and I started?"

"Yeah, we didn't hit it off too well at the start either," he recalled. "I guess I should thank you that we got over it."

"It's my pleasure," Lamar replied giddily and left Johnny floundering.

• • • ◆ • • •

The police station was a simple modular building with a kitchenette, restroom, small supply room, sleeping area and the main living area. Four desks were centered in the middle of the room. A thirty-five-inch TV sat on the counter in front of the window. Blank forms were stacked sloppily in piles on either side of the TV. Files, empty energy drink cans and food wrappers were scattered across the desktops and three overflowing trashcans next to Johnny's desk made for a congested area. The station was a real mess.

Johnny arrived the next morning at the station feeling tired and miserable. He didn't sleep well and considered seeing a doctor for prescription sedatives. Tonight was his night to go to the gym with Lamar but he needed sleep. Lamar would surely torment him when he asked him to skip a night.

He dropped into his seat at the desk nearest the front window and TV. After rubbing his eyes and yawning, he turned on Sunday wrestling on the TV set. A fly buzzed near his left ear and annoyed him as he watched the feature match between the number two and three contenders for a shot at the wrestling championship. He swatted the nagging fly with a tattered swatter and sipped from a leftover can of Red Bull.

When the commercial came on, Johnny muted the TV and peered out the window at an empty street. He wondered if people would ever return or would it continue to be something just short of a meaningless ghost town.

Johnny appreciated the effort that Lamar put in to help restore the town's population. After three trips to the state capitol, Lamar convinced the politicians to offer incentives to draw people back to the town. With the state's backing, he hoped to dispel any lingering fears and rumors of plagues, rabid creatures and mysterious deaths. Johnny felt guilty for not sharing his friend's enthusiasm but catastrophes like they had don't fade away easily. The wrestling match returned and Johnny turned off the mute on the TV.

Paula's pickup truck raced into the parking lot and skidded to a stop between Johnny's Jeep and the police SUV. She hopped out and retrieved her gym bag from the Toyota's bed. Feeling anxious on her first day at work, she took a deep breath and walked to the small patio at the entrance. She wholly expected to be welcomed by Johnny with at least a 'good morning', but when she entered the station, she immediately recognized that he was in a dour mood. She greeted him politely and waited for his response.

Glancing at the clock and then at Paula, he remained frigid toward her. "Not bad, Mason," Johnny commented coldly. "Fifteen minutes early, but it's Sunday. Why are you here?"

Paula tossed her bag on a vacant desk in the corner and shifted in front of him, blocking his view of the TV. He displayed no emotion over her presence and nonchalantly gestured with his hand for her to move out of the way.

Paula glanced back at the TV and stepped aside. "Sheriff, I'm ready to work."

"Not now," Johnny replied in a monotone voice. "The winner of this match gets the championship match next week."

Paula was confused by his coldness and pulled up a chair next to him. "Good morning, Sheriff Watkins," she announced with a tad of attitude in her voice. "As I said, I'm ready to work."

A commercial came on the TV again. "Damn it!" he complained and muted the voice.

"Sorry if I interrupted your show," she responded cynically.

Pointing to the last desk in the corner, he replied, "You can have that desk if you like. Uniforms are in the closet next to the kitchenette. The mayor suggested that you wear kid sizes."

Paula stood in front of him and proudly stuck her chest out. "Do these look like kid sizes to you, Sheriff?" she mocked him.

Johnny was surprised by her boldness and held his hands up. "I'm only kidding, Miss Mason. You can stand down."

Johnny became nervous as he sure didn't want a sexual harassment charge against him on her first day at the station. He focused his attention once again on the TV.

Paula sat down in the chair next to his desk and inquired, "Do you have something against women, Sheriff?"

"Not at all," he replied without taking his eyes off the TV.

"Is it my age?" she taunted. "I can understand if you prefer older women."

"If I hear one more reference to older women, cougars, or anything of the sort, you'll find yourself going back to wherever you came from. Got it, Mason?"

Johnny turned off the mute when the wrestling match resumed. He was determined to put an end to the cougar remarks.

Paula glared at him and responded, "Fine. I won't mention your ..."

Johnny glared at her and waited for her to say it.

Perplexed, Paula went to the closet and picked out three shirts and pants. She studied them for a moment and glanced back at Johnny. It was time for her to make a statement. With a devious grin, she took her uniforms to the desk and removed her shirt. Johnny remained focused on the TV, which frustrated her even more. She unbuckled her jeans and tossed them on the desk.

Johnny glanced over and was stunned to see her standing there in a pink bra and panties. "Whoa there, Ms. Mason, there's a rest room for changing."

"Since you're ignoring me, I figured I'd change right here," she responded defiantly and donned the department's tan shirt and chocolate brown pants. "You just go back to watching your near-naked boys on TV."

"They aren't naked boys, damn it!" Johnny shouted at her. He was clearly distracted by her appearance.

"Oh, I'm sorry. Your near-naked men."

Johnny muted the TV in frustration. "I guess you want boots, too."

Paula sat on the desk and wiggled her toes. "No, I think I'll just work barefoot," she commented. "Should I be pregnant and stay in the kitchenette, too?"

"No! Damn it!" he shouted. Realizing he crossed a sensitive line, Johnny took notice of the size of her feet and reached under the desk for a shoe box with a pair of women's Wolverine boots inside. He set the box on the next desk and turned his attention back to the TV.

Paula opened the box and ogled the new boots. She glanced at the side of the box and complained, "These are size seven. I asked for a six."

Johnny sighed and turned off the TV. He realized that he wasn't going to enjoy the show today and maybe never again, so long as she was there. Maybe this was Lamar's idea of a joke – someone to tantalize him.

"They run a little small," he explained. "I thought a size seven would be easier on your feet."

"Ah, you do care about me," she teased.

"I didn't say that," he grumbled. It was convenient that Jeanie didn't need the boots during the few months she worked with them and her feet were small, too.

Paula smiled at him and took a pair of socks from her gym bag. "Regardless, it was very thoughtful of you, Sheriff," she replied as she slid the first boot on. "This feels really comfortable. Good call."

Johnny felt aroused as he tried not to look at her. The image of her standing there in a bra and panties was stunning. He grabbed the keys to the police SUV and went to the front door.

"Where are you going?" she asked, surprised.

"Got some stops to make. I'll be back later."

"What should I do?" she asked, baffled by his decision to leave.

"Johnny looked around the station and shrugged his shoulders. "I don't know. Do whatever you think a deputy should do." He stepped out the doorway and drove off in the SUV.

Paula studied the messy police station and decided to tidy things up a bit. She became concerned that her new job wasn't going to be what she hoped for. Thoughts ran through her head as she recalled how she left her last job in the city because of bigots and chauvinists. Unfortunately, Johnny already seemed like a real pain in the ass and likely was just another male pig.

*Perhaps,* she thought, *I can fix him. Maybe he just needs a woman's touch.*

After another look around the messy station, she felt the need to make a difference and create a more professional environment.

Paula bagged much of the trash and emptied the cans. She swept the floor and was amazed at how Johnny managed to work through such a mess.

When six o'clock arrived, Johnny still hadn't returned. Paula felt alone with no one to talk to all day. Dejectedly, she closed up the station and went home to her apartment.

She hadn't eaten all day and felt tired. It would have been nice to have lunch with her new boss and get to know him better. Instead, she wasted her time and waited for nothing.

As she drove away from the station, horrible flashbacks of her boyfriend being beaten to death by thugs three years ago haunted her. She arrived at the apartment and hurried inside. The emptiness sent chills down her spine. Her hopes of putting the incident behind were crushed with nothing positive to look forward to at Parmissing Valley after all.

Several times, she stared out the window at the empty street while heating canned chicken noodle soup. When she finished eating, she pushed the bowl away and plopped on the couch. "I'll go crazy if I don't find something to keep me occupied," she grumbled aloud.

After a hot shower, she lay down on the bed and became restless. With the window open, she could hear the sounds of animals in the nearby forest. A cool breeze blew in off the mountain and the curtains flapped gently. The serenity of the night air relaxed her and she finally nodded off.

⋅⋅◆⋅⋅

The next day, Johnny returned to the station and took a seat at his desk in front of the TV. He turned on the Monday morning news and twisted the cap off a bottle of orange juice.

A few moments later, Paula's truck pulled up outside the station. She pondered what grief she'd receive today from him. When she entered the station, neither spoke to each other. Paula set her gym bag down on the desk and went to the kitchenette.

Johnny grew irritated as she rattled around in the cabinets. He turned up the volume and continued watching the news.

Paula stepped out of the kitchenette with a spray bottle of cleaner and paper towels. "I waited until six o'clock for you to come back," she announced sarcastically.

"What for?" asked Johnny. "I can't pay you overtime for that. Hell, I can't even pay you straight time. You'll have to book it for comp time."

"Look at this place!" Paula shouted at him, bristling with her hands on her hips. "You boys sure didn't clean up much around here," she complained. "I never worked in such a pigsty before."

When a commercial appeared on the screen, Johnny lowered the volume. *Damn, she's just like Jeanie. Nothing's ever right.* Then he realized the irony in his thought. *Perhaps that's why Lamar hired her.*

He turned toward her and explained, "You have to understand some things here, Paula. We went through a terrible spell with the outbreak and all. After it ended, the mayor and I were quite busy recovering from the catastrophe, corpses and the federal inquisitions that followed. Ergo, things are a mess."

Paula stared coldly at Johnny. "And I see you're doing a good job of restoring order around here," she chided. "I guess watching TV is part of your daily regimen."

Johnny grew weary of her nagging and went to the rest room. Jeanie used to nag him, but it was all in fun. They tormented each other like a brother and sister. Paula was … Well, that he wasn't sure of yet.

When he returned to his desk, Paula entered the restroom and sprayed the toilet seat with Lysol. She figured that two can play at this game.

Johnny did a double-take when he saw what she did. He jumped out of his chair and rushed to her. "Leave the cleaning alone, damn it!" he barked at her. "I'll hire a service to take care of it." He returned to his chair and raised the volume again on the TV.

"That's pathetic!" she countered angrily. "You can't keep a simple place like this clean on your own? What kind of sheriff are you?"

Johnny ignored her and raised the volume higher on the TV. His blood pressure rose as he resented her questioning his authority. She grew flustered as well with his stubbornness and returned to the kitchen.

Too aggravated to enjoy the news, he relented and turned off the TV. After watching Paula toil in the kitchen, he felt some remorse. Maybe there was no catch to her. Perhaps Lamar hired her because she was qualified and would fit in with their rural environment if he'd just give her a chance.

Johnny stared out the side window toward the mountains. Dark clouds formed over one of the peaks, indicative of an approaching storm. He recalled the events that led to the alien invasion of Parmissing Valley that fateful day. It was a warm and humid day just like this one. The cable had no signal and the radios went dead. Then the bodies turned up. Soon after, the locals became mutants and attacked in packs. It was horrible, like something out of a horror movie.

Paula peered out at him from the kitchenette and noticed the sadness in his eyes. She suspected that there was more to the story that Lamar told her during the interview than an outbreak of rabies and she was eager to know what really happened that would affect two strong-willed men like Lamar and Johnny.

Hoping for a thaw in their relationship, she leaned against the doorway and explained, "I'm sorry, Sheriff. Please understand, it means a lot for me to fit in here."

Johnny sipped from his bottle of orange juice and replied somberly, "You will, Paula. Just relax and give me time. I've got my own demons to deal with right now and I'm not sleeping well." He tossed the empty bottle at the trashcan and missed. The bottle rolled across the floor. He glanced back at Paula. She frowned at him.

"Sorry about that," he said apologetically and then picked up the bottle.

"I appreciate that," she said. "It shows that you respect me."

Johnny tossed the bottle in the recycle can and returned to his seat. Feeling her eyes upon him, he turned to her and explained, "Of course I respect you, Paula. It's me I have a problem with. That damn outbreak really screwed things up around here and it screwed me up even more."

Growing more curious over the 'outbreak', she pulled up a chair next to him and requested, "Would you tell me about this outbreak that you guys dealt with?"

Johnny looked away from her and said nothing. Paula grew frustrated and returned to the kitchenette. He considered revealing the details of the alien incursion to her but he was still uncomfortable about sharing his experiences. Baffled about what to do, he entered the kitchenette and leaned against the counter. Now he had to say something of interest to her.

Paula glanced back at him and then inserted a plastic bag into the trash can. Johnny hoped that she would say something first, but she ignored him and continued her task of cleaning the kitchenette.

"To be honest, Paula," he started sheepishly, "it was more than an outbreak."

"No kidding," Paula quipped without looking back and opened the freezer. "I already figured that part out."

She frowned at the frozen contents. A package of ground meat had thawed and refroze during a power failure some time ago and the meat looked grossly discolored. She tossed it into the trash can.

At a loss for words, Johnny found himself in an awkward moment. Paula stood with her hands on her hips and insisted, "How about some details? After all, I am a member of your team. Perhaps you should start treating me like one." She turned back to the freezer and continued to remove spoiled meat.

While considering her words, Johnny took notice of Paula's shapely figure from behind and had to remind himself to be professional about their working relationship.

"Well," she said wryly.

"You wouldn't believe me if I told you," he began, still distracted by her ass.

Paula sensed that he ogled her and was pleased that he finally took notice of her. She had her own demons to deal with and hoped that, if she had the right man in her life, she might be able to put the past behind her. Three years was a long time for any woman to be alone.

Another awkward moment passed and she turned to him. "Try me. I might surprise you," she prodded and gazed at him with her brown eyes.

Johnny noticed the coyness in her tone and the innocence with which she looked at him. Despite his rudeness toward her, she kept trying to be civil toward him. "Do you believe in aliens?" he asked uneasily.

"Not really."

"Then you'd better start," he replied sternly as he became emotionally charged. "You'd better start believing in a lot of things because monsters and aliens … they're real."

Paula stood up and got in his face. "Don't screw with me!" she warned with a cold stare. "I'm not stupid."

Along with her fire, Johnny saw her passion. Something about that look turned him on. They both were locked in a frozen moment in time until he turned away. Perhaps, he considered, it was better not to reveal the truth about the alien incursion right now. Flashbacks of Sally's death robbed him of his courage to speak further.

"Stick to the outbreak story," he advised. "That's all you can handle."

Paula wasn't sure if he mocked her or if he was that scarred but, in either case, she refused to be treated like a child. "Oh, no, Sheriff. Don't stop there." she insisted. "Let's hear it."

"Just leave it alone."

"Look, I'll decide what I can handle and what I can't."

"Forget I ever mentioned it," he said dejectedly. Johnny wanted so badly to share his feelings about what he went through but who would listen without thinking he was insane. With his luck, Paula might shoot herself, just like Sally did.

Paula floundered for words to encourage him to continue his story. This was a critical point in building trust between them and she had to break through to him.

Johnny reached past her and opened the refrigerator. He took out a Red Bull off the shelf and left the kitchen with his head down.

Paula paused and called to him, "If you're serious, I won't doubt you, but if you're trying to make a fool out of me, I won't play very well either."

"Not today, Deputy," Johnny replied, then sat quietly at his desk. He tapped on the desktop nervously with a pencil and rubbed his forehead.

Paula thought better of pursuing the conversation and ruining what little progress she made with him. Frustrated, she resumed the dubious task of cleaning the freezer.

The last item she retrieved was a plastic bag, containing an odd sausage-shaped piece of meat with a flared end on it. Unbeknownst to her, it was an alien tongue, stored there by Lamar during the incursion and forgotten. She innocently wondered if it was Jeanie's poor attempt at home-made kielbasa that went awry.

*Maybe my cooking could help improve things between us,* she hoped. Without another thought, she tossed the bag with the tongue into the trash can.

Once the bag was full, she struggled to remove it from the trash can and lugged it outside the station to the trash receptacle. As she did, she recalled the interview with Lamar. He told her so much about Jeanie and her impact on the team during their phone call. He honestly believed that a female is vital to their chemistry and she would be that missing piece.

Paula sensed the camaraderie that Lamar and Johnny had for Jeanie and was determined to earn that same respect. More importantly, she needed to belong somewhere, someplace, and to someone for her own sanity.

Johnny glanced at a picture on his desk of him surrounded by Lamar, Jeanie and Sally, taken right before Sally's death. They were happy for a brief period over their success against the aliens but then things changed. The nightmares started. Sally's suicide made things all the worse. Then Jeanie suddenly left to be with her boyfriend in another town. She was really spooked by Sally's death.

*What if the aliens return again?* he often asked himself. This time he'd be responsible for taking action the way Lamar did before. He recalled last year how he disrespected Lamar and treated him as a coward when they first met. Lamar came from out of nowhere and took the sheriff's position right out from under him. Then, when the event started, he realized that Lamar was the right man for the position. They developed a mutual respect for each other and an even better friendship. Now, it was Johnny's turn to lead if things ever went bad.

When Paula returned, Johnny remained in the same position at his desk, still bitter. She lifted a second green trash bag from the plastic can and hauled it out of the kitchenette. This one was much heavier than the first bag. Pausing by the desk, she waited for Johnny to offer some assistance. Without even a glance at her, he left his desk and walked out of the station.

Aggravated, Paula dragged the heavy bag outside and heaved it inside an aluminum trash receptacle underneath a steal overhang. She angrily kicked the lid away and cursed when she jammed her big toe through her boot in the process.

*If this is how it's going to be, I won't be staying here very long,* she decided. "He's such an asshole!" she complained to herself disgustedly.

Johnny debated making the call to Lamar. Something about today gave him the creeps. He sensed the evil that preceded the last alien incursion was returning once more.

When he looked up, he saw Paula standing at the front door of the station with her hands on her hips, looking pissed. "This isn't right," he mumbled to himself. "She doesn't deserve this."

Paula shook her head at him disappointedly and went back inside the station. Johnny rubbed his eyes in frustration and tried to make sense of his life. *Maybe I should tell her what happened*, he contemplated. It was times like this that he really appreciated having Jeanie around.

"Pull up your man-panties!" she'd shout at him. "I'm not your babysitter."

A smile returned to his face as he recalled the good times. Maybe one day Paula could fill her shoes if he gave her the chance. The difference between the two is that Jeanie was in a relationship with someone else. Johnny knew from the beginning that he'd never have her. Paula, on the other hand, was single, according to Lamar.

Johnny went back inside the station and leafed through several proposed zoning revisions.

"Feeling better?" Paula asked icily from the kitchenette.

Johnny looked up and tried to ascertain her meaning. "Are you concerned or just mocking me?" he asked.

Paula stood in front of him and spoke sarcastically. "Let me rephrase that: Are you done acting like an ass?"

Johnny was embarrassed and apologized. He picked up a yellow envelope with the permits for the mining company and left the station.

Paula was more puzzled than ever. She took a broom from a closet in the kitchenette and swept the floor, all the while wondering if Johnny was insane or just seriously screwed up. Either way, he was a mess.

---

Johnny drove the police SUV down the highway toward Graham's Mountain. His mind was filled with frightening images of mutants and aliens as they attacked the town during the first incursion. Then, he imagined Paula standing in front of him at the station in her pink bra and panties. *Damned girl's got a hell of a body on her,* he thought to himself. Then he considered where their relationship could go if he learned to get along with her.

Johnny tossed the envelope with the permits in the back seat and parked on the side of the road. "That cougar shit's got to stop, though," he muttered and then chuckled over the absurdity of the topic.

His imagination took over and he again imagined Paula scantily clad. Then she unhooked her bra and ... "What the hell am I doing?" he bellowed as he snapped out of his daydream.  He placed the SUV in 'drive' and continued on.

As he cruised along the Pomona Trail near the top of Graham's Mountain, he noticed a charred section of grass and bushes about six-feet in diameter. He stopped and inspected the burnt foliage, wondering what could have caused it.

When he knelt near the blackened soil, he noticed a conical depression in the ground about three feet deep, as if there was an impact from some object. There was no sign of what might have caused the depression so he attributed it to a bolt of lightning or even a meteorite.

In the trees above him, an alien creature with wings, an Ardonean, watched him with keen interest. The creature resembled a dragon with a patch of short tendrils across its chest. The alien remained motionless and was unnoticeable in its stance among the branches.

Johnny took his camera from the SUV and snapped pictures of the area, including the trees around him. Perhaps there was something he missed that would show up on the computer when he downloaded the pictures. He returned to his vehicle and sat for several moments, contemplating what to do next. He wanted to deliver the permits, but it would be wrong to do it without Paula. He remembered how interested she was in the mining project and seeing the new technology.

His thoughts turned to Paula again, standing in front of him in a bra and panties. A smile crossed his face as he imagined her wrapping her arms around him and pressing her body against his. "Stop it!" he hollered to himself and drove off.

When he arrived at the station, he was relieved to see that Paula had gone already. He felt guilty that she waited the previous afternoon for him to return and really didn't want to roil her any more than he already did.

- - - ◆

Johnny placed the camera on top of the empty desk next to his and retrieved his gym bag from underneath his desk. With nothing more to be accomplished, he turned off the lights and left the station.

Outside, he paused to send Lamar a text that he would be at the gym if he cared to join him. He peered up at the peak of Graham's Mountain and cringed. "I hate that fucking mountain," he groaned as he climbed into his vehicle and drove off.

# CHAPTER II

## LONELY HEARTS

In the second-floor office of the Parmissing Valley municipal building, Lamar sat in a plush, leather chair behind an oak desk. While marking up copies of existing zoning codes for land development in the valley, he peered out the window and was pleasantly surprised.

In front of the municipal building parked the red Miata Mx-3 and Sasha stepped out. She glanced up and down the street as if looking for something, before walking up the cement steps to the municipal building's entrance.

Lamar refused to be distracted by her allure as he watched from the window. His gut told him that she had an ulterior motive for coming to his town and would no doubt try to persuade him to give her something.

*Not many African-American women in these parts, especially ones who drive sports cars,* he thought suspiciously to himself. Then he pondered how she fit those long legs inside a small car like that.

The circumstances surrounding his last job made relationships difficult for him and, like Johnny, he had little, if any, self-confidence. The only woman he ever had feelings for was the young sister of his former partner in New York City. He was too close a friend to the family to risk dating the woman he truly wanted. Those feelings might as well never have been after the humiliating events that drove him from the city to Parmissing Valley.

His phone buzzed and he read the text from Johnny. "Damn. Looks like I'll have to pass on the gym today." He responded with a text explaining that he had Ms. Bell's appointment and stowed the phone.

A few moments later, the door opened and Sasha peeked in. "Good morning, Mayor. Can I come in?"

Lamar greeted her and invited her in. Smitten by her beauty but still wary, he politely pulled out a chair for her across from his.

"I'm Sasha Bell, senior editor for Oddity Magazine," she announced proudly, "just in case you forgot to write that down".

"I do remember you… and your magazine, Ms. Bell," he lied. "What can I do for you?"

Sasha folded her arms and leaned on the desk. With a determined stare, she informed him, "I want the story on the aliens – all of it."

Lamar chuckled and inquired, "What makes you think there's a story about aliens?"

"Look, Mayor Whittington, I did my homework and I probably know more about you and Parmissing Valley than you do. What you don't know is that I came here for something and I won't stop until I get it."

Lamar picked up the phone and requested two lemonades from his intern. He leaned back and folded his hands behind his head. "What if there is no story?" he asked with an amusing grin.

"Then I'll settle for something else," she responded coyly. "But only after I'm convinced that you're telling the truth."

He grew nervous and contemplated what 'something else' was. "There really isn't much to tell about the rumors. Just a bad outbreak of a rare strain of rabies," he explained. "Sorry you wasted your time."

Sasha gazed confidently at him. "I hardly think it's wasted. This is a town that's going through a rebirth," she reminded him. "I understand there's a mining company interested in Graham's Mountain; you've got a lot of empty farm country to the east; and Vegas isn't all that far to the west."

"And your point is?" queried Lamar curiously.

"My point is that there are a lot of exciting things in the making here and I'd like to be part of it."

Lamar laughed at her. "Why would anyone come to a place with a track record of death?" he commented cynically, "Especially a senior editor from New York."

"I'm not just any senior editor from New York. I'm the best thing to happen to you in a long time."

Lamar had the feeling that he should know her or did know her once before, but he couldn't fathom from where. "There's nothing exciting happening around here and that I can assure you. Furthermore, I'm not sure how, but I wish you were the best thing to happen to me. Not a whole lot happens around here these days."

A young Hispanic man entered and placed two glasses of lemonade on Lamar's desk. "Anything else, sir?" he asked humbly.

"No, Pedro. This will be fine."

Pedro nodded and left the room. Lamar pushed one of the glasses toward Sasha but she pushed it back. Lamar was puzzled by her reaction.

"So, what do you say, Mayor?" she pressed.

Lamar chuckled and briefly considered her request. "I don't even know you and you expect me to give you all the details of a story that, if it were true, would be highly classified."

"Is that a problem?" Sasha asked.

"It would be, but there isn't a story to be told."

She reached across the desk and took his hands in hers. "Look, Mayor, this is really important to me. I need to be here right now."

Again, Lamar was confused by her references. *What did she mean she 'needed' to be there?*

Lamar considered what harm there would be in revealing some of the details to her but then decided against it. Just like Johnny, he was dying to tell his story to someone and bare his damaged psyche. Maybe then he would begin to heal. Unfortunately, that was too risky. If details of the event ever got out, especially to a magazine editor, the feds would put him away forever.

"There were a lot of tragic moments," he explained cautiously, "because of the outbreak and, even more so, because of the casualties that occurred." He sighed and looked away from her with sadness in his eyes.

"That's it," Sasha complained bitterly.

Lamar pulled his hands away from hers. "All I can say is that I hope it never happens again. Now please accept that as my final answer, Ms. Bell."

Lamar walked to the door and held it open for her to leave. She approached him with a seductive smile and gently pushed the door closed.

"I'm not done yet," she said coyly. "Why don't we get together, at least as friends? I'm new in town and I wouldn't mind sharing a dinner with you."

He was amused by her offer and countered, "Why do you think this warrants a date?"

"You're alone. I'm alone. I like your style. You have a job, a place to live and people respect you."

"So that explains why you've come all the way out here for a story that doesn't exist," he concluded suspiciously and returned to his desk.

"You are so naïve, Lamar." Sasha folded her arms in frustration. She walked around the desk toward him and repeated determinedly, "I always get what I want. I won't go away so easily."

Lamar broke a sweat when she stroked his cheek, still unsure of Sasha's real intentions.

She was amused by his shyness and wore a sly grin. "Don't worry, Mayor. I won't eat you," she teased and stepped out the door.

"Wait, Ms. Bell!" he blurted.

Pleased that he responded, she returned to the desk and waited for him to continue.

At a loss for words, he studied her face, now even more unsure than before of what her game was. His indecisiveness was obvious.

Sasha read him like a book. "Alright, Mayor, we'll go slowly. Let's try dinner tonight," she suggested. "Just friends. No obligations."

"I am free tonight for a change," he responded and forced a smile. "I won't be finished until seven though?"

She stopped at the door again and looked back at him. "I'll pick you up. Oh, and don't back out on me. I will come after you."

Lamar was impressed by her determination. "Clearview has some nice restaurants," he suggested.

She paused halfway out the door without looking back and replied, "Your place is fine. I'll cook."

*Damn, girl*! he thought to himself. "You're on," he replied excitedly.

Sasha closed the door behind her. She smiled contentedly as she descended the stairs to the lobby.

Lamar stared out the window and watched until she got into her sports car. He guzzled one glass of lemonade and thought giddily, *The woman cooks and drives! Maybe there is some potential here.*

After Sasha's car pulled away, he anxiously tackled his paperwork with renewed enthusiasm. His mind wandered repeatedly as he tried to recall if and when he met Sasha before. Then the phone rang and jarred him back to reality. He glanced down at the display and saw 'J Watkins'. Eagerly, he picked up the phone and took a seat.

"Hi, Johnny. Sorry I had to pass on the gym." After a brief pause, he continued, "How's things?" After listening to Johnny's response, he inquired, "How's Paula working out?" He was amused by Johnny's response. "No one can nag like Jeanie. Speaking of which, have you heard from her?" He cracked a smile and chuckled. After a brief pause, he asked, "Nightmares again, huh?"

Lamar frowned as Johnny told him of his uneventful visit to Graham's Mountain. "I could have told you there's nothing to see up there," he chided. "The feds' Sweep Team made sure that every shred of evidence was erased, one way or another."

Then Johnny revealed how he found the charred ground near the peak of the mountain. Lamar recalled the three lights he saw earlier in the week.

Inside the police SUV, Johnny tapped the dashboard nervously and suggested, "How about a few beers later?"

Lamar blushed as he thought about his date with Sasha. "Sorry, Johnny, I have a ..."

Johnny sensed his hesitation and chuckled. "Not a date!" he blurted playfully. "Come on, Lamar. Where are you going to get a date?" Then Johnny remembered Sasha's visit at the barbecue. "You dog! You have a date with the magazine lady!"

"Yeah, I do."

"How did you swing that?" he asked in disbelief. "I'm impressed."

"You wouldn't believe me if I told you. I have some errands to run and I have that dreaded file with the proposed building code revisions for you to look at. How about I stop by this afternoon and drop them off?"

"I'll be back at the station in a little while after I get a quick shower. Some of us still go to the gym, you know."

"Yeah, I owe you one for that. How about we get together tomorrow night for beers and maybe, just maybe, I'll give you the steamy details about my date."

"You're on," responded Johnny excitedly. "This I've gotta' hear."

"I also need you to sign off on the license for our mining friends as well. I'll drop them off on my way by."

Johnny groaned as he disliked the administrative portion of the job and recalled that he still had the environmental permits in the back seat of his SUV.

"I still haven't finished with the zoning codes," he complained.

"I'm sure you'll get to it when you have a chance," Lamar replied confidently. "See you later."

Johnny hung up and debated his next course of action with Paula. Again, he fantasized about her removing her bra and panties in front of him. It worried him that his imagination almost seemed real. He had the same fascinations with Sally but something went terribly wrong with their relationship. Somehow his fascinations had an impact on her.

Lamar beamed as he hung up the phone. Like a young boy, he grew giddy over Sasha's interest in him.

*It's almost too good to be true*, he thought and walked to the door. *It probably is, with my luck.*

The phone rang again and halted his departure. He pushed his thoughts of Sasha aside and answered it. The contractor involved with the diamond mining project on Graham's Mountain called to inquire about permits and a pre-job site inspection. After the three-minute conversation ended, Lamar left the office.

Pedro intercepted him at the stairs and requested, "Sir, I'd like to pack for my hiking trip tomorrow. Would it be okay to take the afternoon off?"

Lamar placed his hand on Pedro's shoulder. "Of course. Just be careful out there."

"Yes, sir. I have my cell phone in case of an emergency."

"Good boy. Where are you hiking at?"

Pedro thought for a moment and then answered, "I think I'll try the Pomona Trail. I've heard it's very scenic."

Lamar shuddered as he recalled the hikers on the trail who were among the first casualties of the alien incursion. He also recalled that Pedro lost his family to the mutants as well.

When they exited the building, Pedro noticed his grim expression and became concerned. "Are you alright, Mayor?"

Lamar hesitated and rubbed his chin uneasily. "I still harbor some bad memories from up there," he explained.

"I understand but I think this is a good way for me to put mine behind me."

"Well, be careful up there," Lamar cautioned.

"Will do," replied Pedro enthusiastically and he hurried off.

A strange feeling in the pit of his stomach left Lamar feeling edgy. He tried to dismiss it as nerves over his involvement with Sasha but it gnawed at him. Like Johnny, he felt as though something evil was happening and he wasn't aware of it. Without further delay, he climbed inside his king-cab truck and drove off. He turned up the music to settle his nerves.

Lamar appreciated rural life in a mountain community compared to his days as a police officer in the city. With the exception of the 'event', life in the mountains was peaceful and relaxing.

The police station was a short five-minute ride from the two-story municipal building on the main highway, but in a small town everything was close.

Johnny exited the station as Lamar stepped out of his truck.

"How's administrative life treating you?" Johnny kidded.

"Boring as hell," he replied as he handed Johnny the file. "How's Paula treating you?"

Johnny rolled his eyes and grumbled, "She's a neat freak."

"Could be a good wife for you one day," Lamar joked.

"She's crazy, man! She cleans everything."

"Oh, come on. She can't be that bad."

Johnny placed his hands on his hips and looked down in embarrassment. "She sprays the john with Lysol every time I use it. How's that for crazy?"

"Maybe she's trying to make a good impression," Lamar suggested. "Kind of like auditioning for ..." he paused briefly with a sly smile and then continued jokingly, "... your wife."

Johnny frowned at him. "That's not even funny."

Lamar patted him on the back sympathetically.

"I guess I shouldn't complain. She's a good kid," Johnny confessed.

Lamar went on to explain, "I'm meeting Joe Fama at the drill site tomorrow for the site inspection and I need his paperwork ready. He wants to move on this mining project like yesterday

"I can handle it, if you like," Johnny offered.

"No, I want to check this out personally. It sounds almost too perfect and I'd like to make sure we're not getting snowed."

Johnny commented somberly, "I guess it's time to take our new careers seriously."

"I'm afraid it is. Things are changing and we have to be ready to handle them."

Johnny was about to comment when the station door opened and Paula stepped out with her spray bottle and paper towels. "Well, hello,

Mayor," she interrupted cheerfully. "Thank you again for hiring me. It means so much to me."

Johnny frowned at Lamar, who grinned innocently.

"Not a problem, Paula," he replied.

Paula smiled coyly at Johnny. "I'm sure Johnny's going to forget all about Jeanie before long," she remarked confidently. "Well, boys, I'd love to chat but I've got a lot of work to do. Have a great day, Mayor."

"You too, Paula."

Lamar poked Johnny playfully as they watched Paula wipe down the outside windows of the station.

"Damn, that girl's got a body on her," commented Lamar, once again.

"Yes, she does," replied Johnny as both men ogled her.

"On that note, I'll leave you two lovebirds alone," Lamar said giddily as he climbed back into his truck. "See you tomorrow evening."

Johnny waved half-heartedly and entered the station.

Lamar noticed that Paula stopped cleaning and eyed Johnny from behind. She seemed focused on his ass and looked quite pleased with it. He chuckled as he drove off. *So, Johnny's got his guardian angel. Now who's going to be mine?* he questioned himself. *Perhaps it'll be Sasha one day.*

⋅⋅⋅◆◆◆⋅⋅⋅

The skies darkened and a thunderstorm rolled over the mountains. Inside the police station, Johnny sat down at his desk and opened the file. Inside was a list of building code revisions for fire exits. His thoughts were disrupted as he recalled the bar where he first encountered the mutants. There were only two exits and the windows provided very limited egress. The mutants easily trapped and slaughtered everyone inside.

He drifted into a daze and recalled the first time Lamar saved his life. As he knelt over a dead mutant, gazing in awe of the horrible creature, another charged at him from behind. Lamar targeted the creature and killed it with a clean shot to the head just before it reached Johnny.

A clap of thunder jarred him back to reality. The rain fell in torrents and the wind shook the windows.

Paula stored her cleaning supplies and took out two more bags of trash. When she returned, she was drenched.

"It's really coming down out there," she complained. "That's the last of the trash to go out."

The sound of her voice aroused Johnny again. He imagined Paula performing kinky acts for him and falling madly in love with him. *I can't keep doing this*, he chided himself. "Thanks, Paula."

Paula took off her boots and set them next to her desk. She peered out the front door at the pouring rain and then removed her wet t-shirt, revealing a white sports bra. With the shades of her large nipples clearly defined, Paula was an image of beauty that Sports Illustrated would die for.

As she glanced back, she noticed Johnny's distant gaze. "What are you thinking about?" she asked, curious. "It must be good since you have a little smile on your face."

"You wouldn't believe me if I told you," Johnny replied, somewhat embarrassed.

"Maybe I already know," she kidded. Paula approached him from behind and massaged his shoulders. "I'm sorry if I snapped at you before," she said apologetically. "I was afraid you were making fun of me."

Johnny was pleased by the massage and put the file down. For the first time, he seemed to relax around her. "Now why would I do that?"

"At my last station, they never took me serious."

"How do you know?" he inquired. "Maybe it was just your perception."

Paula appeared embarrassed and explained, "They had degrading nicknames for me because I was blond and big-chested. They always played annoying jokes on me. I think that makes it pretty obvious."

"Did you report it?" he asked.

"Of course, I did. My Captain advised me to have thicker skin or else it'd get worse. That's why I left and came out here."

"I have more respect for you than that. To me you're Deputy Paula Mason."

Paula continued to massage his shoulders and requested, "How about if I'm Paula, your friend, first?"

"Alright, friend Paula, we'll skip the formality. Call me Johnny, not Sheriff."

"Deal. You know, I'll listen to you if you ever want to talk," she offered, "now that I know you aren't screwing with me."

Johnny reached back with one hand and held hers. Each felt something magic develop between them when they touched.

Johnny suddenly imagined himself making love to Paula in different positions. He caught himself and nervously yanked his hand away.

Paula was disappointed by his reaction. She felt something stir in her when they touched that aroused her – something special.

"Johnny, if you feel like I don't belong here, please tell me and I'll leave. I don't want to come to work every day on pins and needles, wondering if we're going to get along."

Johnny turned and faced her. "Look, Paula, it's not you. I swear."

"Then talk to me," she pleaded. "Tell me what's going on that creates such a problem for us."

"I wish my experiences that caused this weren't real," he explained uneasily. "I saw things I never imagined could exist, even in horror movies."

"Then tell me about it. Get it off your mind."

"Are you sure you want to hear this?" he asked uneasily.

Paula took a seat across from him. "Yes. Please tell me about it," she urged him. "I really want to know what happened to you and the mayor out here."

Johnny reluctantly started from the beginning and related everything that they went through. Three hours later, he finished and looked drained. Despite that, he felt relieved to have the burden of secrecy off of him.

Paula was amazed that something of that magnitude could really happen and very few people knew about it. Then she noticed a tear in Johnny's right eye. She moved alongside him and nestled his head against her bosom. She rubbed his hair gently and promised that she would be there for him. They both felt a peace that neither had in a long time.

Paula gently pushed him away and stood up. As she prepared to put her t-shirt back on, something came over her. She suddenly imagined doing things with Johnny – naughty things. She gazed proudly at her breasts and teased, "I guess there's no point in showing these off."

Johnny finally took notice and remarked, "Damn, Paula, they are impressive."

"You finally noticed! I was beginning to think you were only into half-naked men," she ribbed him.

"That's real funny, Miss Mason. If it makes you feel better, you can wait until the shirt's a little dryer before you put it back on."

Paula knew he was staring at her nipples through the sports bra but felt daring. "Let me know when you've seen enough," she kidded and set the shirt on the desk. Johnny chuckled over her remark. "If you don't mind me asking, when was the last time you were with a woman?" she inquired and sat down again next to him.

"Four months ago. I thought Sally and I had something special. Unfortunately, she struggled more with the nightmares than I did. The sleepless nights took their toll on her."

"She split on you?"

Johnny looked at her sadly and replied, "She killed herself. She was depressed by what happened and being with me made it worse."

"Jesus!" blurted Paula.

"What really hurt was that she did it in front of me. She blew her brains out - with my gun – in my house – right in front of me."

Paula was stunned by his misfortune. "Well, I don't plan on killing myself," she assured him. "So, let's get this shit behind us and move on."

Johnny appreciated her enthusiasm. "What's your story?" he asked curiously.

Paula looked away briefly and then suggested they save it for another day. She responded, "This is my day to make you feel better. Next time I'll tell you and it'll be your turn to give me an attitude adjustment."

Paula kissed his forehead and retrieved her tan shirt. Johnny watched disappointedly as she put on the shirt with her back to him and buttoned it. She knew he was eying her and was excited by it.

Now that they had a rapport, Paula felt a desire to have Johnny. She couldn't remember being so impulsive before but this attraction to him when they touched was different than any she recalled with other men. Unfortunately, working together could create problems in a physical relationship.

The wind howled and thunder rocked the station. Paula peeked out the window at the rain and suggested, "How about I get us a six-pack and some snacks? Maybe there's something on the TV."

Johnny leaned back in the chair and considered her offer. He didn't want the evening to end yet and hoped that something more would develop between them. "Sure, why not?" he replied.

"I'll be back shortly," Paula announced and left the station.

Johnny wondered if he made a mistake in revealing the details of the alien event to Paula. She was right, though, that she was part of his team now and he needed to trust her.

He surprised himself by straightening his desk top and pushing in the chairs to the other desks. Paula was already having a positive influence on him.

Johnny downloaded the pictures from his camera onto a laptop on the counter. Their desktop computers were confiscated by the federal agents for 'cleansing' after the event and never returned. Lamar brought in used laptops until he purchased new computers for the station.

He scanned the pictures until one caught his eye. It was a picture of the trees on the mountain and what appeared to be a winged creature hidden among the branches. Johnny rubbed his eyes in disbelief and attributed the illusion to fatigue. He closed the laptop computer and stowed it in his locker.

The wind gusted and the window panes rattled disturbingly louder. Johnny entered the kitchenette and pulled out a jar of popcorn kernels. He poured them into an old popcorn popper and waited patiently for the kernels to pop.

The office lights shone through the window onto the trash cans outside of the station. A coyote crept from the trees and paused under the aluminum overhang near the cans. With drenched fur, the skinny animal trembled, frightened by the storm. It perched on its rear legs against one of the trashcans, water dribbling from its fur onto the cement pad. When the coyote pushed against the lid, the trashcan fell over with a bang.

Inside the station, Johnny was startled by the noise. Instinctively, he drew his pistol and approached the door.

The coyote tore into one of the trash bags and greedily devoured the spoiled meat until it reached the plastic bag with the alien tongue. The thawed tongue pulsed with life as it sensed a living presence nearby. When the coyote tore open the plastic bag on the cement, the rain water invigorated the tongue and it changed from pink to deep red in color. The severed end of the tongue closed over and sealed shut as if it were healing itself. The flared end had flaps that curled open like a Venus Flytrap.

Three bulges formed inside the tongue and one of them slithered toward the tip. When the coyote sniffed at the flared end of the tongue, the flaps wrapped tightly around its snout. It forced the creature's mouth open and wedged itself firmly inside.

In a panic, the coyote tipped over the other trashcans and struggled to free itself. The first of the three bulges, each one a small alien entity known as a *churlis*, passed from the tongue into its mouth. The coyote gagged and rolled frantically across the ground.

Paula returned from the deli at the end of the highway and parked in front of the station. The headlights from her truck glanced off the crazed coyote and caught her attention. Johnny, waiting by the front door, was relieved when her lights flashed across the office wall through the window.

Paula got out of her truck and hurried to the end of the porch to investigate the creature's strange behavior. She stood by the corner of the building, dripping wet, and watched the coyote as it quivered erratically.

Johnny peered out the window and panicked when he saw no sign of her between the truck and the station entrance. He burst out the door with his gun drawn. Paula was startled when she saw him behind her and nearly dropped the bag with two six-packs of beer in it. The coyote froze for a brief second and then vanished into the trees.

"Jesus, Johnny!" she exclaimed. "Put the gun away."

Johnny stowed his pistol and breathed a sigh of relief. "I'm sorry, Paula. I thought …"

"Relax. I'm okay," she assured him. "Let's go inside before we both get pneumonia." She glanced back at the trash, which now littered the ground, but the coyote was gone. Paula shook her head at him in disbelief and went inside. Johnny scanned the trees once more and followed her.

Once inside the station, Johnny locked the door with one hand while his other hand still rested on the handle of his pistol. Paula set the bags down on the desk and stared at him with a worried look.

"You really are spooked," she remarked with a concerned tone.

"Yeah, I guess I am," he replied, looking somewhat embarrassed. After stowing the pistol in the top drawer, he turned on the TV set. Sheepishly he asked, "Did you see anything unusual out there? I heard the trashcans fall over."

Paula took the cans of beer out of the bag and popped the tops off two of them. "Just a coyote that got into the trashcans," she explained. "Guess I should've put the lids on tightly this afternoon."

Johnny looked relieved. "I'll clean it up in the morning," he offered and went into the kitchenette. "I'm surprised a coyote would be scavenging for food in a rain storm."

"Maybe it's hungry," Paula suggested and pulled two chairs together in front of the TV set. When Johnny returned with a bowl of popcorn, she was surprised. "I'm impressed. You aren't completely helpless after all."

"I hate to admit it but having you around does rub off on me."

Paula was pleased by his compliment. Perhaps they could have a normal relationship. She handed him a beer and held hers up for a toast.

Johnny raised his can and asked, "What to?"

"How about a toast to our new friendship?" she suggested.

"To our friendship," he repeated and tapped her can. They each took a sip and sat down. Paula unbuttoned her wet shirt and started to remove it. This time, Johnny took notice.

"This is getting to be a habit," he joked.

Paula froze for a second and then replied, "My pants are damp, too. Should I take them off?"

Again, Johnny felt embarrassed. "I haven't figured out when to take you serious yet."

"Sometimes you have to take a chance and find out," she replied playfully.

Johnny tried not to stare while she hung the shirt over the back of the chair but didn't fare too well.

Paula noticed but wasn't offended. She removed her pants and laid them over another chair to dry as well.

Johnny felt an animal magnetism draw him to Paula. He wanted to find out what was under her bra and panties so badly. "I wasn't kidding when I told you about Sally," he reiterated nervously.

"Maybe I can help with that," she suggested coyly.

For a moment, they both nearly embraced, dying to make that first kiss. Johnny backed away, much to Paula's disappointment.

"So how about you?" he asked. "I sense that you haven't dated in a while either."

"Yeah, well it's a really sad story," she replied. "One I'll never forget."

"Now it's my turn to make you feel better," Johnny informed her. "Tell me what happened to you."

"Isn't this ironic?" she remarked, amused. "Now I'm the one who needs to open up to you."

"We can skip it if you prefer," offered Johnny," but I'd really like to hear about it."

Paula slid her chair closer to Johnny's and she placed her arm around him. "The short version: My drunken boyfriend picked a fight at a football game and got his head bashed in on the sidewalk. His attacker's friends held me back while I watched him die." She grew teary-eyed and drank from her beer. "I know what it's like to watch a loved one die."

Now Johnny was stunned by her misfortune. He leaned against her and sipped from his beer as well. "Aren't we a pair?" he commented sadly.

Paula picked up the remote on the desk and flipped through the channels. Together they watched a classics channel with old movies for four hours. They enjoyed each other's company and their friendship grew.

When midnight came and the movie ended, Johnny was disappointed as he held the last empty beer can and complained, "I guess the party's over."

Paula stood and put on her nearly dry uniform. "Don't worry, there'll be more," she promised. "All I expect from you is respect."

Johnny smiled and tossed the can into the trash. Paula kissed his cheek affectionately and left the station. He turned off the TV and wondered if maybe Lamar was serious with his comments about her. It seemed that she was so right for him after all. Perhaps she really was auditioning to be his wife. *Nonsense,* he thought. *She's just here for the job.* He turned off the lights and left the station.

The rain fell lightly with occasional thunder and lightning. A cool wind left him chilly as he hurried inside his Jeep and drove home.

When he parked in front of his two-bedroom rancher, he sat and wondered what it would be like to make love to Paula. He thought about how good it would feel to caress her body and feel her respond to him. As he became excited, he thought about the noises she would make when she climaxed.

"Oh, shit!" he groaned when he became aroused. "This is way out of control." He hurried through the light rain across the walkway and inside his house.

There was a distinct calmness in him now that he told Paula everything that happened last spring. There was even hope that they might have a relationship because of it. For once he felt as though he'd get a good night's sleep.

Lamar waited anxiously at the entrance to the municipal building as the storm raged around him. He stared at the outline of Graham's Mountain during a flash of lightning and a chill ran down his spine. Then he saw a small light drop from the sky onto the mountain, just like the ones he saw earlier in the week. He couldn't be sure if it was an illusion created by the lightning or maybe the water in his eyes.

"Something just doesn't feel right," he muttered to himself. "I can sense it."

The headlights from Sasha's Miata startled him as she slowed to a stop in front of the building. Lamar hustled down the steps toward the car and opened the door.

"Get in, Cowboy," she invited him.

Lamar was concerned about how he'd fit his big frame into such a small car but, once he slid inside, it wasn't so bad. There was a bit more leg room than he imagined and once he noticed Sasha's long legs and short skirt, he forgot all about the car's design.

"Looks like it's going to be a miserable night," he commented. "Sorry if I got your seat wet."

Sasha cast him a seductive glance and remarked, "I don't think the weather will be an issue for us." She expertly shifted gears and the Miata sped away from the police station at a high rate of speed. "Besides, I hope the seats aren't the only thing getting wet tonight," she joked.

Lamar was speechless over her comment. When she glanced over and noticed his wide-eyed expression, she quickly replied, "I meant having a few drinks, you dirty man."

Lamar covered his face with his hands. "I guess I walked into that one," he admitted, red-faced.

Chuckling at his innocent behavior, Sasha enjoyed his naivety and looked forward to the evening ahead. The Miata did a short power slide and straightened out on the side road. She expertly shifted gears again and gained speed.

"Damn, you drive like my ex-deputy Jeanie!" he quipped.

"A fast car requires a faster driver," she remarked proudly. "It's all about control."

"Please save it for a day when it's not pouring rain," he requested nervously. Lamar was dazzled by Sasha and her ambitious approach to him. It bothered him that this was likely a façade for something else that was bound to disappoint. "Look, Sasha, let's be adult about this," he said tersely. "What's your game?"

Sasha rubbed his thigh and replied. "My dear Lamar, you are every bit as good as they said you were," she commented and cut the steering wheel hard to the right. The sports car slid around a corner and slowed to a stop in front of Lamar's split-level rancher.

He was taken aback by her comment and asked nervously, "Who said what about me?"

"I told you I did my homework on you. I'm a bit of a detective myself, but not for law enforcement."

Lamar grew agitated. He pointed his finger at her and warned sternly, "If you don't stop with the games, our date ends right now."

She was hurt by his reaction. "I'll explain everything over dinner," she promised. "It's nothing to get excited about."

The rain stopped but the storm was far from over. A clap of thunder broke the brief silence.

"Fine," he relented, "but you're on thin ice, young lady."

"Please, Lamar. I'm not here to hurt you," she assured him. Sasha was perplexed by his defensiveness when she popped out of the car. This wasn't the reaction she expected from him.

Lamar pulled himself out and leaned on the hood. "Anything I should know about 'before' dinner?"

She regained her confidence and opened the trunk. "I'm glad you asked. Can you help me with the grocery bags?"

"I suppose I could."

She lifted two bags out and passed them to him. Lamar politely took the bags from her and went to the porch to unlock the door. They entered the house just as the rain started again.

The sound of thunder shook the house and flashes of lightning lit up the inside of the house for seconds at a time. The lights flickered but remained on.

Sasha took note of the living room as she walked through to the kitchen. The house was neat and the decor was simple. Candles were placed randomly around the house.

"Lose power much around here?" she asked, curious.

"Quite often," Lamar replied. "It usually takes a while to come back on, too. The utility workers have to come all the way over from Clearview, so we're low on their priority list."

They set the bags down on the kitchen table and unpacked them. Inside the first bag was pasta, tomatoes, garlic and four bottles of wine.

Lamar picked up one bottle of Cabernet and read the label. "Boy, you're ready to party," he commented.

Sasha filled a pot with water and set it on the stove. "Two of those are for my other boyfriend," she kidded.

"So, now I'm your boyfriend," he remarked.

"Not yet. You're still being evaluated," she teased.

Lamar appreciated her humor and took two stemless wine glasses from the cabinet. Sasha tossed him a corkscrew. "Why don't you do the honors?"

He caught the corkscrew and opened the wine bottle. "So how about you tell me what's going on?" he asked and poured the wine. "I know you're priming me to get a story for your magazine."

Sasha didn't respond but opened a box of ziti and poured it into the pot. She uncapped two jars of tomato sauce and emptied the contents into another pot.

Lamar stood and handed her a glass of wine. She held it up for a toast and suggested, "How about we drink to our new relationship?"

He studied her eyes, hoping for a clue to her real motive. "How about we drink to truth and friendship?" he suggested. "Then we'll work on the relationship part of it."

"I wouldn't have it any other way."

They tapped their glasses and sipped. She returned to the stove and checked the ziti. "I guess you want the short version."

Lamar sipped again and replied, "I'll take any version at this point."

"I heard from a friend what really happened out here and I had to find out for myself."

"What friend?"

"One of your 'casualties' – Pam Slater."

Lamar was shocked as he never considered any of Suzie Beauchamp's friends could have sent a message about the alien presence in the valley.

Sasha noticed the surprise on Lamar's face and continued, "Pam sent a text just before things went to hell up there. I didn't receive it until after communications were restored several days later."

Lamar recalled that Pam was one of the three women that mutated into hybrids. He shuddered at the memory of what her corpse was like when he inspected it.

Sasha noticed his discomfort and knew she hit a nerve. "Pam was a friend of mine who moved to Parmissing Valley seven years ago. She was looking for a new beginning since her husband abandoned her. Now, she's dead."

"You heard wrong," Lamar answered defensively. "As I told you before, there is no story."

Sasha leaned against the counter and faced him. "I have to know how a small-town sheriff like you was able to defeat a whole alien army with just one deputy. That's pretty damned impressive."

Lamar blushed and sipped from his wine. He knew she was baiting him into revealing what happened. He wanted so badly to tell someone that it was more or less a miracle how they overcame the aliens and their mutants. Despite his overwhelming urge to explain the events, he knew he couldn't risk that there would be repercussions from the government. He and Johnny had explicit instructions not to discuss the events with anyone or they would be incarcerated for something or other.

Sasha took a knife from the drawer and diced the garlic into tiny pieces. She slid them into the pot of tomato sauce.

"You didn't use any fancy weapons," she continued. "Just brains and pistols."

Lamar thought back to some of the creatures they encountered and recalled the spaceship he destroyed. "Since it didn't really happen, does that lower your expectations of me?" he asked.

"Not really," Sasha replied confidently and lowered the heat under the tomato sauce. "I'm just disappointed."

"What did you expect? Should I give you some cock and bull story just to get laid?" he responded gruffly.

Sasha slammed the knife down on the table and glared at him. "Is that what you think is going to happen?"

"I don't know. You seem to have all these secrets." Lamar finished his wine and poured another glass. He sat down and pondered what to say next. Perhaps he was too abrupt.

Sasha turned off the stove and walked out of the kitchen. Lamar panicked as he had to do or say something fast or risk losing her. "Wait!" he shouted and rushed into the living room. "Don't leave."

Sasha stopped and glared back at him. "Why? So you can insult me again? I'm no whore, you know."

"I'm sorry. I didn't mean what I said."

Sasha folded her arms and contemplated what to do. Lamar knew he hurt her and conceded that he blew it. "I understand if you want to leave, but I really am sorry." Lamar returned to the kitchen and sat dejectedly at the table. He stared at the contents of his wine glass and became teary-eyed.

To his surprise, Sasha returned. She sat at the table and explained, "Good men are hard to find these days. When you're a popular public figure, everybody wants to be your friend. New York ruined my attitude that way."

"That also makes you an easy target when things go wrong," he added.

"You and I have much more in common than you can imagine. I promise you that I won't do anything to hurt you."

Lamar was humiliated now. Sasha sounded so sincere and he felt like the biggest ass in the world.

"You and I can have a really nice relationship if you just give it a chance. I'm not here for just a story."

"Then I owe you a chance to prove that to me," he replied earnestly. "I'll try to be a friend to you and not a city cop."

Sasha was relieved and took his hands in hers. She stared into his eyes and explained, "All I'm asking for is one chance. I'll prove to you that our friendship is real."

Lamar realized that, for the first time, she was totally sincere. No acting could hide the honesty in her eyes. "I guess that's not asking too much," he relented. "Can we start over and call this a date?"

"I think so." She turned the burner back on to heat the pot. "I could really use a friend right now."

Unaware of the underlying meaning of her remark, he promised, "You can trust me. I just can't help being the suspicious cop looking for the ulterior motive."

"And maybe that explains why you've been alone for so long."

Without comment, Lamar fretted that she really had been digging into his past. "Don't feel bad. I've gotten used to the lonely life as well." she explained. She took a long, crusty roll from the bag and sliced it up.

"Then relationships haven't been good for you either, I presume," he remarked cautiously.

"No, not at all," Sasha responded. "I had a man once. A competitor used him to get to me – through my heart."

"I'm sorry," Lamar responded compassionately.

"Out here, everything is real," she continued. "There's no drama, no competition. All I want is a simple life with a good man."

"And you're ready to leave New York City just like that?" he quizzed her.

"In a heartbeat. Since Oddity magazine is fiction, I'd love to write a 'fictional' story in a made-up location about what *may have* happened out here. Kind of a swan song I can dedicate to my lost friend on my way out of the business."

"That's an interesting idea. Perhaps we can make something together," he suggested.

"I'm sure we can make a lot of beautiful things together if we work at it."

Lamar's heart pounded as he imagined having Sasha to himself. He couldn't believe that she actually wanted him. Sasha stood and gazed at him with wanting eyes.

Lamar thought, *What the hell have I got to lose?* He stood and stepped toward her. Her eyes remained focused on his. He placed his hands on her hips and pulled her close to him. They embraced and became lost in their first kiss. It was slow and steamy as they showed their hunger for each other.

A moment later, the boiling water interrupted their moment. Sasha blushed and hurriedly turned down the flame under the pot of ziti.

Lamar sat down and watched her prepare the dinner. When she turned her head sideways, he noticed something familiar about her. Unsure what it was, he mentioned curiously, "I have an odd feeling that you and I have met somewhere before." Sasha smiled without comment and stirred the ziti.

Lamar inquired, "How did you know who to contact about my past in the police department?"

Sasha turned to him with a smile and folded arms. "You worked with my brother there," she revealed. "We met a few times over the holidays and then one night you and I ..."

Lamar's eyes widened with surprise as he recalled that night. "Your brother?"

"Uh-huh. The two of you would sit in front of the house on your nights off and drink Elderberry wine. I used to watch you from my bedroom window."

"You're Beanie, Jimmy B's little sister!" he exclaimed in utter surprise. "I can't believe it!"

"I always had a crush on you," she replied sheepishly. "That night you kissed me, I fell in love with you. And then we never spoke again."

"I never meant to hurt you, Sasha. I felt so terrible for that." Lamar never knew her real name was Sasha and was shocked by the turn of events. "I'm so sorry," he continued. "I was afraid of what your family would say if they found out how I felt about you."

Sasha seemed lost for a moment in her thoughts. Then she continued, "When mom passed away last January, I decided to chase my dream. I realized that I always wanted to be your girl. The only way to find out if it was possible was to come out here and see what happens."

Lamar was both impressed and flattered. "How is Jimmy?"

"He died a few months after mom in a crash. It was so tragic."

They were silent for a long moment. Finally, Lamar inquired, "Did Jimmy tell you why I left?"

"He did. After you were gone, he discovered the truth about the shooting and why it was covered up."

"Covered up?" he asked, curious.

"The shooter in the store was the police chief's kid. You were the fall guy."

Lamar felt his blood pressure escalate. He recalled all the humiliation he went through over that incident. "Those sons of bitches!"

Sasha placed her hands on his shoulders and gazed affectionately at him. "That's all behind now for both of us. Let's try and start over, shall we?"

Suddenly everything made sense to him. He felt as if a burden had been lifted that dogged him for so long. After all these years of wondering what went wrong and what could have been. Now, here she was, the girl he always wanted but couldn't have.

"So why did you wait so long to tell me?" he asked in a puzzled manner.

"I wanted to make sure that you were still the good man I once knew. Kind of a way out if I needed one."

"And …"

"And I think you are."

"And …"

"And I'd like to think that we can be together like we should have been back when."

"I suspected you were hiding something. I hope you don't mind that my police instincts are usually right."

"Not at all. I'm really glad to be here."

They conversed eagerly as Lamar opened up to her about his past before Parmissing Valley. By the end of dinner, he understood that they both had more in common than he could ever imagine. Then, as if on cue, the lights flickered and extinguished.

"There's our loss of power," he proclaimed.

"Maybe it's an omen," Sasha remarked giddily. "This is kind of romantic."

"It does create a better mood for …," he started and paused briefly.

"…our date?" she finished.

"Yes," he agreed, feeling satisfied with a broad grin on his face. "Yes, our date," he answered contentedly.

Lamar took a book of matches from the drawer of an empty china cabinet and lit several of the candles. As Sasha stood, he embraced her and kissed her again. He had an overwhelming desire to have her but remained a gentleman. They moved into the living room and sat together on the sofa.

"I've been alone for a long time," he admitted. "Don't take it personal if I'm a bit rusty."

"I haven't been with anyone in a while, either. Time to dust off the cobwebs," she kidded playfully.

Flashes of lightning illuminated the room from time to time. The two kissed passionately and finished their wine. They nestled together on the couch and slept in each other's arms.

# CHAPTER III

# BUDDING RELATIONSHIPS

When morning came, Lamar awoke and was surprised to be alone on the couch. *That's strange*, he thought. There was no sign of Sasha. He entered the kitchen and was stunned. It was immaculate. "Damn!" he exclaimed. "This neatness thing is contagious."

"Sasha," he called out, but there was no answer. On the table was a note. "Just great," he muttered dejectedly. "I should've seen this coming." The note read: Thanks for a great night. You're the best.

His cell phone chimed and distracted him. He answered and spoke with a female from the diamond mine project. After the call, he trudged up the stairs to the bathroom for a shower.

As he lathered himself with soap, he fretted over what happened with Sasha. *Did I do something to upset her?* he asked himself repeatedly. After rinsing himself, he turned off the water. He feared that his earlier remark about getting laid ruined what could have been a beautiful thing for them. "Damn!" he shouted and punched the wall. "I'm such an ass!"

---

Jo Fama, thirty-eight years old, dressed in jeans and a flannel shirt with thick-rimmed sun glasses, leaned against the front of a dirty Escalade and studied an E-sized drawing. Her long, dark hair hung down across her shoulders and onto her back. Two male interns in their early twenties unloaded equipment from the trailer and the Dodge Ram pickup truck.

Jo approached the men and placed her arms around both of their shoulders. "How long before we're up and running boys?" she inquired anxiously with a distinct southern drawl and a seductive manner.

The first intern, Gino, replied confidently, "By this evening, Ms. Fama."

"We're right on schedule," her second intern, Adam, reassured her.

"That's why I love you both," she said coyly and kissed each on the cheek. "You always give me what I want."

The U-Haul truck was parked nearby with the rollup door raised halfway. Inside was a state-of-the-art drill assembly the size of a John Deere tractor. Jo gazed proudly at her creation and reveled in the success she anticipated to follow.

When Lamar's truck appeared, coming up the road, Jo returned to the Escalade and laid out her drawings again.

Lamar parked his truck alongside the Escalade and stepped out. "Good morning, ma'am," he greeted her pleasantly. "Is Joe Fama around?"

The woman removed her glasses and extended her hand in a gesture of friendship. "Mayor Whittington, it's a pleasure," she replied politely.

Lamar was surprised when he realized Joe was a woman. He shook her hand and responded, "My apologies. I didn't realize …"

"Jo is short for BettyJo," she interrupted. "How about we get right down to business? I have a lot to do before we start drilling and I'm sure you do, too."

"Your proposal sounded straight forward but I'd like to hear from you exactly what you'll be doing up here."

Jo showed him a series of photo images taken of the mountain both above and below ground using specialized equipment from an aircraft. "This is what makes your mountain so appealing to me," she explained.

"You guaranteed me this would be a small operation. How is that possible?" he questioned her.

Jo removed her glasses again and gave him an intimidating stare. Finally, she explained, "I left Tri-star Diamond Exploration to free-lance. I can run a small operation at low cost with minimal man power and no threat to the environment."

"You make it sound so easy," he remarked.

"It's all about understanding geology. You see this cavern inside the mountain," she indicated on the drawing. "The makeup of the surrounding terrain and the depth of certain types of strata make this an ideal location for diamond growth. All I need is one tunnel in. Nature already did the hard part."

Lamar glanced at the map and then at Jo. "This all sounds fine and dandy but I hope you don't mind if I have my sheriff and his deputy drop in occasionally to keep an eye on things."

Jo placed her sun glasses over her eyes and turned her focus back to the drawing. "So long as they don't get in the way, I don't care what they do."

"Then you have my blessing, Ms. Fama." He handed her an envelope and explained, "Here is your license, plus an outline of what your tax and liability responsibilities are. I think you'll find them reasonable."

Jo shook his hand. "Thank you, Mayor. I assure you, there will be no problems."

Lamar smiled and returned to his truck. Something bothered him about Fama. She seemed like she knew her stuff but her type stops at nothing to get what they want – just like Sasha and Suzie Beauchamp. He watched her briefly as she meticulously marked off an area with stakes. Content that nothing was amiss, he drove back to town.

·⁺⁺◆⁺⁺·

In the woods, about a mile from the police station, the coyote lay on its side panting heavily. Its stomach swelled and blood streamed from its mouth onto the mossy ground.

Branches snapped a short distance away and the coyote frantically struggled to stand. It stared alertly and then hobbled toward the source.

Hidden among the bushes hovered a small, metallic ball. The coyote approached and eyed it curiously. The ball, a communication device from its alien world, hummed briefly and a probe extended to the coyote and touched its forehead. The coyote's eyes went blank for several seconds until the probe retracted back inside the ball and then it trotted away with renewed vigor. The ball darted away into the Earth's atmosphere and vanished. The alien presence inside the coyote had received its instructions.

◆····

50

In a nearby clearing, a deer innocently emerged and nibbled at berries on a bush as the winged Ardonean watched from overhead in the trees. Content that there were no threats in the area, the alien flew down from the trees and tackled the deer from behind. It bit into its flank and then perched on a fallen tree nearby, waiting patiently for its army to form.

The coyote observed from a distance with a fearful look in its eyes. It sniffed at the air and appeared panicked as it nervously paced back and forth.

The foam from the crippled deer's mouth emitted a chemical with an aroma that attracted other animals. It struggled to stand upright but was unable to flee. Its face contorted and, within an hour, it mutated into a grossly disfigured creature.

The Ardonean sensed the coyote was nearby and then spotted it in the trees. It hissed and took flight in pursuit. The coyote fled from the area and, after several fruitless passes, the Ardonean returned to its perch and focused its attention back to the wounded deer.

Soon after, two wolves arrived, sniffing excitedly for the source of the aroma. When they reached the deer, it lay on its side panting heavily. The wolves pounced on it and hastily fed on the dying creature. They tore into its belly and gorged on it. The helpless deer emitted two brief yelps and died.

A bear lumbered from the trees, also attracted by the aroma from the chemical in the saliva and growled at the wolves as if warning them away. After each tore off another piece of flesh from the deer's flank, they fled. The bear then fed off the deer carcass.

A second and much larger bear emerged from the trees and approached the first. The smaller bear snarled and resumed feeding. The second bear also fed off the remains. When they devoured all the accessible meat from the carcass, the two disappeared into the forest. The Ardonean was pleased with the predators that showed to feed on the deer. It took flight again and disappeared in the sky.

Later, the alien returned with a dead crow in its mouth and surveyed the remains of the deer. It absorbed the DNA from the crow as it did with the deer through its mutated tongue. Its eyes glowed red as it eagerly waited for more creatures to feast. Now, with the crow's DNA in its system, it summoned an additional cast of creatures to join its growing army.

A murder of crows quickly descended from the trees on the carcass to pluck at the remains while the alien creature perched calmly nearby, observing and waiting.

The Ardonean dropped the dead crow on the ground and took off into the sky. Several of the crows fought each other for the little bits of flesh that the dead bird's carcass offered.

Lamar parked in front of the police station and pondered last night's experience with Sasha. Selfishly, he fretted that he allowed her to play him over her true identity. Still convinced that the story took precedence over her desire for him, he wondered how to handle their situation. Should he track her down or just let it go as another sorry chapter in his life?

He then recalled the old days with Sasha's brother, Jimmy. Whenever he joined their family for dinner, he had difficulty keeping his eyes off of Sasha or Beanie as she was called then. Every time he looked at her, her eyes were on him as well. *Maybe she just wanted me to know about Jimmy and fulfill a childhood dream at the same time*, he concluded. *Regardless, she's gone and my sorry life goes on.* The idea of leaving a note roiled him.

Inside the station, Johnny sat at his desk and leafed through a binder of material on zoning codes. He peeked out the window and saw Lamar's truck. A sly grin crossed his face as Lamar entered the office.

"Hey, Johnny," Lamar greeted him in a subdued manner. He pulled up a chair and sat across from him.

Johnny set the binder down, folded his hands and stared at Lamar. "Well, good morning, Romeo. What brings you here this early?"

"Just a social call," he replied and peered around the station. Where's Paula?"

Johnny looked up at the clock. It was ten forty-five. "She'll be here soon. We worked late last night and she had comp time from Sunday."

Lamar laughed. "You dog! I thought it'd take a lot longer than this for the two of you to bond."

"We straightened the place up a bit," he replied defensively. "Nothing else, I assure you."

Lamar peeked in the trashcan and noticed empty beer cans and a bag with popcorn kernels. He glanced up at Johnny and chuckled again. "Anything going on that I should know about?" he questioned playfully.

Johnny knew he was caught. There was no way he'd talk his way out of this one. "Nah, just friendly chit-chat and a few movie classics," he explained and fidgeted.

Lamar leaned back in his chair and folded his hands on his lap. He was amused by Johnny's sensitivity over Paula. "Don't worry. I'm not going to lecture you about ethics in the work place. After what we went through, you do whatever you think is right with your deputy."

Johnny was somewhat relieved by Lamar's remarks. He didn't want Lamar babysitting him because of Paula.

"I'll take the permits from you. I want to check them out once more."

"Why are you so jumpy about this?" Johnny asked as he retrieved the envelope from the drawer.

"Just want to be prepared for the activists if they come. Besides, I don't want Jo coming to my door at two in the morning looking for them."

"Sorry about that, Lamar. I knew that Paula wanted to go so I put it off until she could join me."

"No worries. You and Paula can see her operation later; that's if you two are still buds." The two men laughed.

"How about you, Inspector Clusoe?" Johnny queried, eager to change the topic. "What about your big night?"

Lamar looked disappointedly at the ground. Johnny immediately realized that things didn't go well for his friend and regretted asking about it.

"It was nice," Lamar replied unconvincingly, "until I found the 'dear Lamar' note this morning."

"You mean women still do that?" Johnny asked, surprised.

"Obviously they do," he answered cynically. He took a plastic cup and went to the freezer for ice. It was empty. "Where's everything at?" he asked edgily as he stared inside.

"Paula cleaned the whole kitchen yesterday - even the freezer," Johnny replied with a note of sarcasm in his voice. "I told you she's a fanatic about cleaning, didn't I?"

Lamar nervously returned to the desk and sat. "There was something in there that I …" He hesitated and glanced out the side window. Perhaps, he thought, he should forget that the tongue was ever in there. It was surely harmless after all this time.

"What in the world would you have in the freezer after all this time that's so important?" Johnny asked giddily. Then Johnny recalled the contents of one of the plastic bags. "The alien's tongue!" he exclaimed as he leaped to his feet and hurried out the door.

"Wait up!" Lamar shouted and hurried after him.

Johnny scrounged through the trashcans on the side of the station. The plastic bags were shredded and there was no sign of the tongue.

The two men stared at each other uneasily. "You don't think …," started Johnny.

"Don't even go there," warned Lamar. "It was frozen for so long; it's got to be dead." With an ashen face, he got into his truck and drove off.

Johnny fretted and kicked at one of the trash cans. "Damn, Paula! You couldn't leave well enough alone!" he blurted to himself. Just the thought of a new alien incursion caused him to have a rapid heartbeat and break a sweat.

As if on cue, Paula arrived in her small pickup. "Hi, Johnny," she called to him as she got out of the truck. "What's going on?"

Johnny tried to bite his tongue but couldn't refrain. "One of those bags from the freezer had something very important in it."

"You're kidding! That stuff was all rotten."

"There was an alien tongue in there," he informed her. "Whittington saved it from one of the creatures he killed."

Paula's eyes lit up with excitement. "You mean that sausage-looking thing was a real alien tongue?"

"Yeah, it was," he answered dejectedly.

She thought for a moment and then replied, "So what? It's dead, right?"

"We certainly hope so," he fretted. "What if it spreads some kind of disease or starts making mutants again?"

Paula rubbed Johnny's arm. "Think about what you're saying."

He threw his arms up in despair and groaned, "This is why I have nightmares, Paula. It's never gonna end!"

Paula led him by the hand into the station and nudged him into his seat. "I'll make you a cup of hot coffee and we'll talk about it," she offered.

Johnny buried his face in his hands in near panic. He had to do something to put the issue to rest quickly. This time, it was his responsibility to handle things and not Lamar's.

Paula brought a wet towel and dabbed the beads of sweat from his forehead. "Trust me, Johnny. Things will be alright," she promised him.

Johnny looked up at her like a frightened child. "You weren't there," he reminded her. "You can't imagine what we went through."

Paula knelt down in front of him and placed her hands on his cheeks. "Johnny, it's not happening again. There are no aliens out there."

"You don't know that for sure," he argued adamantly.

"Stop it right now!" she ordered and stood with her hands on her hips. "It was just a dead piece of meat. Nothing bad is going to happen."

Johnny shook his head at her. "I hope you're right. I don't think I can handle another mess like that again."

Paula hugged him compassionately and asked, "Have you considered psychiatric counseling? It might help put your mind at ease."

Johnny pushed her away and snapped, "They'd lock me up in a straight jacket if I told them what I know."

"But look at you! You're a basket case."

Johnny stared regretfully at her and stood up. "You don't get it, Paula," he grumbled and walked to the door.

"Wait," she called to him.

Johnny paused at the door and looked back. She wanted to speak but was lost for words. He turned away and opened the front door.

Paula was frantic and rushed to him. She threw her arms around him and hugged him tightly. "I'll help you through this," she promised him. "Don't walk away from me."

Johnny returned her affection and embraced her. The feel of her body against his felt so good: her hips against his; her breasts pressed against his chest. Suddenly, he became aroused and thoughts of perverse sexual acts with Paula flooded his mind.

Paula felt overcome with passion and then felt the overwhelming urge to make love to him. She also knew that if she moved too fast, he might think of her as a goofy whore and lose respect for her. *Patience*, she told herself. *He wants you, too.*

"I can help you," she continued as she embraced him. "I know I can, if you just give me a chance."

"Why do you care so much about me?" he inquired apprehensively as he ran his hands down her back toward her ass, pausing just as he reached her belt.

"Because I want you to …" she stammered, hesitated for a moment and then continued confidently, "Because I need you. I need you to help me through my ordeal, too. We can help each other."

"And how's that gonna work?" he asked, unconvinced.

"If we can build a trusting relationship, I know we can beat this."

"And you think we can make everything all right," he remarked cynically.

"No, you jackass! But if we can't, we can face it together. I don't want to be alone anymore and neither do you."

Johnny was shaken by her words. Then, as if on cue, they kissed softly. Now the barrier was gone. Paula felt uninhibited and was ready to stake her claim to him.

Johnny lifted her in his arms and set her on his desk in a sitting position. He pushed his files to the floor and maneuvered himself between her legs. She eagerly unbuttoned and removed his shirt. Johnny closed his eyes and imagined where this was going as she anxiously lifted his t-shirt, all the while kissing his chest.

"Are you all right with this?" he asked uncomfortably.

"Of course, I am!" she replied confidently. Then she placed her hands on his chest and pushed him away. "No, wait," she blurted. "This isn't right."

After a moment of uncomfortable silence, Johnny asked, "Was this a mistake?"

"Do you think it was?" she countered.

"No, but I do want it to mean something."

"Then let's be patient and see where things go," she suggested. They stared at each other, knowing the lust they felt for each other.

Johnny leaned forward and kissed her, softly at first, and then hungrily. Paula welcomed his affection and savored the warmth of a man. She wanted him so bad and returned his passionate kisses. An inner urge drove an animal instinct in her. She nibbled on his lips and inadvertently bit him. Johnny lurched back and they suddenly lost their balance, falling off the desk.

"Oh, shit!" groaned Johnny as he helped her to her feet. "I need a bigger desk,"

Paula noticed blood on Johnny's lip and fretted. "Johnny, your lip!"

Johnny touched his lip and saw the scant bit of blood on his finger. "Wow, that must be the animal in you coming out," he kidded.

She scrambled off the desk and snatched a tissue from a dispenser. "I'm so sorry!" she exclaimed and dabbed it gently until it stopped bleeding.

Johnny appreciated the attention and embraced her. Paula fed off his desire and was anxious to accommodate him. But now, she was more concerned that she bit him. That couldn't happen again.

"Really, Johnny, I'm sorry," Paula repeated, quite upset over the incident. "I lost control."

"Can you do me one favor?" he requested innocently.

"Anything."

"Can you lock the door before someone comes in? I'd hate to explain this to the mayor." Paula burst into laughter and locked the door.

Again, Johnny admired her cute ass and was overcome by a renewed surge of energy. She asked innocently, "Do you like what you see?"

Johnny growled at her and she eagerly embraced him.

⋅⋅⋅✦⋅⋅⋅

Two young Ardoneans appeared in the sky. They circled the area, studying the terrain around the mountain. Throughout the forest on the east side of Graham's Mountain, the two Ardonean creatures joined a third and attacked several deer, much like the earlier prey and left them wounded. Soon after, wolves gathered and fed on the helpless creatures, unaware that the dying creatures were infected and that the alien DNA would cause them to mutate as well into something else – something alien.

The Ardoneans, with glowing red eyes, again admired their growing army of mutant animals from a distance as the wolves took the same bait as the earlier creatures.

On the west side of Graham's Mountain away from Parmissing Valley, a coffin-shaped slab of green rock, smoldered next to a stream. The rock crackled and broke away, revealing a gray, metallic pod. A hissing sound from the disintegrating green rocks was replaced by a low-pitched hum. Other animals emerged from the forest, already mutated from the infected deer carcasses. The crows arrived in large numbers and settled in the trees around the pod. Wolves came and gathered on one side. Four bears settled on the opposite side.

Four healthy coyotes arrived with the sickly one but they kept their distance from the pod, as if spying on the creatures.

An antenna-like rod extended from the pod and pointed at the mountainside. A bright, red light shot from the rod and lasted until it burned a hole through the mountain, creating a four-foot round entrance to the cavern. The sides of the tunnel were amazingly smooth as the searing heat from the laser vaporized the rock. When the rod retracted, the pod rose above the ground and glided into the tunnel.

From a distance, the swelled coyote was disturbed by the appearance of the pod and paced frantically. When it raced off into the woods, the other coyotes followed. Meanwhile, the infected animals settled outside the tunnel and waited patiently for their orders.

+·+◆+·+

Lamar returned to Graham's Mountain later that afternoon in a desperate attempt to quell his fears. He recalled the falling lights and wondered if there was any significance. Later, he would check Johnny's pictures and try to validate if there was anything to be concerned about. *It's all okay. There's nothing to worry about*, he reiterated to himself over and over again, hoping for reassurance.

In a small clearing at the side of the road, three wolves eyed him as he drove by. "That's strange," he uttered to himself. "Never saw them in broad daylight like this before."

Had he looked closer, he would have seen that they were mutated with significant deformation occurring in their faces and paws.

Lamar drove along the rough mountain road toward two cabins, located about a mile apart from each other. Campers and tourists were restricted for a year from the area to ensure there wasn't any evidence left to indicate the alien event ever occurred. Nature would see to that foliage grew over anything that might have been missed.

After three hours of searching the woods around the cabins with his binoculars, Lamar felt satisfied that nothing was amiss and drove toward Jo Fama's drill site. He pondered why he didn't encounter the charred plot of ground that Johnny discovered.

When he arrived at the site, Jo had set up her drilling equipment. The drill, mounted on a crawler was already positioned near the mountainside. Her two assistants, Adam and Gino operated a generator on the back of the pickup truck. Two thick cables, one for four-hundred-and-sixty-volt power and another for one-hundred-and-ten-volt control power ran from the truck to the control panel of the drill assembly.

The two young men were college interns looking for summer money and credits for on-the-job-experience. Jo handpicked them and trained them on the setup and operation of the drill assembly in a warehouse outside of Las Vegas. When she felt 'her' men were ready, she brought them to Graham's Mountain for the real operation.

She enjoyed a unique relationship with her 'boys' and took care of them in more than the usual ways for their loyalty and support. Her ex-husband Leon had his share of harlots over the years so she believed that she was entitled to her boy toys as well. Now that she had the power of owning her own company and a technology that everyone else would desperately want, she controlled her own destiny.

The diamond-tipped drill was a state-of-the-art device that fit in the back of the moving van. With four lasers mounted alongside it, the drill assembly was designed to soften or fracture the rock so the drill bit could easily power through at a much faster speed than standard drills.

Lamar pulled up in his truck and stepped out with a yellow envelope in his hand. He was impressed with the drill assembly as he walked around it. *So, this is Jo's big invention*, he thought to himself. *Very impressive.*

Jo approached and shook hands with him.

"Good afternoon, Mayor. I didn't expect to see you this late in the day."

"Good afternoon, Ms. Fama," he replied and handed her the envelope. "I had a few stops to make while I was out this way."

"On a mountain? That hardly makes sense for a mayor," she commented dryly.

"It's a long story," he replied sheepishly.

Jo peeked inside the envelope. Pleased to have the permits, she affirmed, "So we're good to go, I presume."

"You sure are," he answered. "By the way, I noticed a few wolves down the road. They seemed a bit brazen for the middle of the afternoon. You got something for protection, just in case?"

Jo walked to her Escalade and reached inside. She took out a belt with an H&K .45 caliber pistol holstered, and then strapped the belt on. "I do now, and a permit to carry as well. Thanks for the heads up."

"Call me if you have any problems," he instructed her and climbed into his truck.

"When will your sheriff be around?" she inquired. "I have a little problem I'd like to discuss with him."

"Possibly tomorrow afternoon, Ms. Fama. I don't know what his schedule looks like."

"I'm staying at The Given's Hotel if that's convenient for him."

"I'll be sure to let him know," Lamar promised.

Jo glanced once more at the envelope's contents and waved to him. She tossed the envelope on the passenger-side seat inside her vehicle and returned to the drill assembly. Lamar got in his truck and drove off, considering his next course of action.

Adam came to Jo with a broken connector and suggested repairs with parts from the hardware store in Clearview. She agreed and sent him on his way.

Lamar drove down the mountain trail and reached a fork in the road. He stopped and noticed in his side mirror that the three wolves appeared again on the road behind him. Chills went down his spine as he considered what could alter their behavior like this. Then Adam pulled up behind him and honked the horn.

Lamar was startled and nearly jumped out of his seat. "Holy shit!" he exclaimed. When he looked in the mirror and saw the Dodge Ram, he turned up the trail and allowed Adam to pass. He glanced again in the rear-view mirror but the wolves were gone.

Sasha took advantage of Lamar's busy schedule to do her own investigative work. She had already arrived at the campsite, eager to find some clue that the alien story was more than just a myth.

At the site, where Pam Slater and her friends were attacked, Sasha searched everywhere for clues.

Lamar's truck parked next to her car and the door slammed. Startled by his appearance, she wondered if he'd be angry over her presence there or just passive if her efforts were for naught. She stepped out of the trees to greet him.

Lamar already looked annoyed to see her there. He approached with a purposeful gait. Glaring, he asked, "What the hell are you doing up here?"

She replied hurtfully, "Well, good morning to you too, Lamar."

"Save the pleasantries. I asked you a question."

Sasha sat on a fallen log and patted the spot next to her, suggesting he sit with her. Reluctantly he complied.

"How did you find out about this site?" he questioned her with an attitude.

"I told you that Pam was a friend of mine. I was supposed to make the trip with her and the others."

Lamar realized she was more observant than he gave her credit for.

Sasha grew frustrated with him and responded irritably, "I'm going to get to the bottom of this little mystery of yours, with or without your help."

Lamar lost his patience with her and warned, "It's dangerous out here. Wild animals roam the mountainside and you have no protection. This stops here."

"I can see we're getting nowhere," she complained disappointedly.

"Oh, yes, we are. We're getting out of here now." He took her by the hand and led her to her car. "Go back to your hotel or wherever you're staying. Don't let me catch you up here again."

Sasha bristled with anger. "You can't tell me what to do!"

"I can when it endangers your life."

She responded defiantly, "You're not the sheriff anymore. You push pencils, not people. Get used to it." She slid into her car and drove off, spinning wheels in the dirt and launching stones all around him.

Lamar clenched his fists and stormed back to his truck. Something told him she'd come back to the campsite again.

When he returned to town, he stopped by the police station, but no one was there. Disappointed, he drove back to the municipal building and went to his office. This late in the day, the town was eerily quiet. No one came out except to visit the bar at the end of the street, and even then, only a few contractors frequented the establishment.

Lamar turned on his laptop computer and searched the internet for information on Sasha. Everything he researched about her career with Oddity Magazine was accurate. He found a news story about her being at the center of a valentines' scandal between two public relations CEOs. So far, everything made sense.

He searched for information on Pam Slater. Not a lot came up, although it did mention she was a writer for hire who started her own company. Perhaps Pam did call her that night about 'the story'.

Curiosity got the better of him and he searched for information on Jo Fama. To his surprise, Jo was much more popular than Sasha. She went through a high-profile divorce from Leon Bartok, the president of Tri-Star Diamond Exploration, and received one heck of a buyout for her share of the company.

At issue was an invention she developed in a separate location to reduce the time it took to drill through rock. Her ex-husband felt that he was entitled to it as much as she was. The court felt differently since it was funded by her own money on her time and on her own private location after her separation from Tri-Star and Leon. Then, when she successfully completed the drill assembly with the additional money she received from the divorce settlement, her ex-husband vowed to get even with her in an interview.

*That never goes well*, he thought. Ms. Fama was a good-looking woman for her age and surely would have no trouble finding a man, assuming she wanted one.

With nothing more to do, he locked up the building and left. On the way home, he stopped by the Given's Hotel to speak with Ms. Fama. He was concerned that her ex-husband might come looking for her if he found out she was in Parmissing Valley.

The hotel was more of a bed and breakfast with an old-time atmosphere. Lamar spoke with Mr. Givens at the desk and learned that Jo specifically requested the third floor since there was just one room up there and that only she and her two assistants would access it.

When Lamar reached the top of the stairs and stood by her door, he heard a woman's intense moaning, possibly as a result of being assaulted and in pain. His first instinct was to grab his gun but, since he became mayor, he kept his gun in the truck and no longer carried it with him.

The moans grew louder and he panicked. "Ms. Fama, are you okay?" he shouted. When the moans continued uninterrupted, he kicked open the door and was shocked by what he saw.

Jo Fama was indulged in a threesome with both her young assistants. Sitting on Adam's lap and being mounted from behind by Gino, she looked to be in total ecstasy. His presence in the doorway, though, literally brought them to a grinding halt.

Jo looked exhausted and asked wearily, "Did you come to join in, Mayor. There's always room for one more."

Lamar was embarrassed beyond belief. "I'm so sorry, Ms. Fama. Carry on." He fled down the steps.

*Carry on! What kind of idiot says that?* he thought to himself.

As he passed the desk, Mr. Givens was concerned and asked, "Is everything okay, Mayor? I heard a crash."

Lamar opened his wallet and gave the man a twenty-dollar bill. "The door might need a little fixing," he said, embarrassed. "Sorry about that." He left the hotel and raced home. Mr. Givens looked at the twenty and stared out the door, wondering what had happened.

Lamar sat alone in his living room and brooded over the day's events. He considered that Sasha might be right. Perhaps he should stick to pushing pencils and not people.

In the morning, he decided he would find her and apologize. He also figured it was a good idea not to send Johnny to the hotel. Surely nothing good would come of it.

Inside the huge cavern there were now five pods. Three were empty. One had the charred remains of an Ardonean that died while passing through the atmosphere. It was responsible for the charred patch of grass that Johnny stumbled upon. The more recent pod was larger and housed the alien leader.

The pod opened and an adult Ardonean with wings, talons and a red plume on its head emerged. It had folded wings behind it and hundreds of tiny tendrils on its chest. Immediately, it took flight to the top of the cavern. After circling twice, it exited through a narrow opening in the ceiling. Once outside, it perched on the rocks above, where it overlooked the growing mutant army below.

When the smaller Ardoneans settled in front of the mutated creatures, the adult creature glided down and landed between them. Pausing in front of each creature, two tendrils extended from its belly, attaching briefly to either side of the animals' heads. With tiny incisions, it injected a foreign substance into each creature's brain until their eyes glowed red. The ritual proceeded until all of the creatures were given a crude telepathic ability that allowed them to communicate among themselves and their benefactor.

---

Adam left the hardware store in Clearview and climbed into his truck. He texted Jo and informed her that he purchased the necessary parts to repair the connector and was on his way back.

As he returned to Parmissing Valley on the remote highway, he noticed a dark Crown Victoria approaching from behind at a high rate of speed. When he pulled onto the shoulder to let them pass, the sedan pulled behind him and three men jumped out. They drew their pistols and rushed toward him. "Don't move or you're dead!" shouted one of the men.

Adam held his hands up in compliance. The men dragged him out of the truck and beat him repeatedly. When he was unconscious, they tossed him in the trunk of the sedan. The Crown Victoria then raced toward Clearview, away from Parmissing Valley. One of the men remained behind and drove Adam's truck toward Parmissing Valley.

---

The next morning, Lamar stopped by the hotel. Immediately, he noticed that Sasha's car was gone and knew that she returned to the campsite. At first, he was irate, but then realized it would be better to work with her and maybe, just maybe, he could salvage their relationship.

Meanwhile, Sasha did return with a camera and tape recorder. She was determined to gather enough evidence to do her story without Lamar's help.

After one last look and finding nothing unusual, she decided to search along the trail. When she exited the woods, hundreds of crows covered the ground between her and her car. In a panic, she rushed up the trail to a cabin and slammed the door. Frightened, she retreated to the rear bedroom.

Another murder of crows was perched in the trees outside the cabin. Their caws sent chills down her spine as she peered out the window at them. Suddenly, the crows swarmed toward the cabin.

Sasha frantically raced to the closet. She hesitated before closing the door and watched fearfully as the crows crashed through the windows. Seven fell to the floor with broken necks while the others stormed through the broken window, quickly filling the room.

She slammed the closet door shut and cowered in fear. The crows beat against the door until their sounds became deafening. She searched her pockets for her phone and panicked when she realized it was in her car.

The crows relentlessly pecked at the door. As she huddled on the floor like a frightened child, she saw pieces of wood chips piling up on the floor through the small gap under the door. The crows were shredding the door and soon they'd get to her. She realized that she should have heeded Lamar's warning. Now she would die just like others before her.

⸺ ⸱⸱◆⸱⸱ ⸺

Lamar stopped the truck at the base of the mountain and considered giving Sasha her space for the story. Unfortunately, his gut feeling was that something was amiss and the area wasn't safe. Perhaps if he discussed with her what happened that fateful night, it might allay his fears and make her understand his concerns.

Once he made up his mind to confront her peacefully, he continued up the mountainside. When he reached the dirt trail road, he noticed the smaller tire tracks from Sasha's Miata and grew anxious. Further up the trail, he saw that she took the left trail. Sasha didn't return to the crime scene at the campsite after all.

Anger overtook his calmness as he again became upset with her for leaving him like she did and now for sneaking up to the cabin against his wishes. Forgetting his prior thoughts about reconciliation, he raced up the trail intent on venting at Sasha.

As Lamar drove, he recalled that his investigation was the campsite only. The feds assured him that they took care of the area so he never searched the cabin. That was the least of their concerns in the earlier battle. Thoughts of what evidence she might find made him uneasy.

In front of the cabin was Sasha's Miata. Right away, he heard the caws of hundreds of crows. He scanned the area but only saw a dozen or so on the porch. Then he realized that the sounds came from inside the cabin.

Frantically, he rushed to the front door. When he opened it slightly, he was overcome by the ear-splitting sounds of the crows swarming about inside the bedroom. Panic set in as he realized Sasha could be injured or dead.

"Jumping Jesus! What the hell is this?" he shouted.

Lamar checked his pistol and pushed the cabin door open. When he burst inside, Sasha's hoarse screams were barely discernible through the caws of the crows. The living room had about twenty crows flapping about, but on the other side of the bedroom door; it was mayhem.

Lamar took a quilt from the sofa and used a lighter to set it on fire. He barged through the bedroom door and tossed the burning bedspread on the floor. The smoke engulfed the room and spewed into the living room. The crows evacuated the cabin, crashing into the walls in a desperate attempt to find fresh air.

Once the last of the crows fled the smoke-filled cabin, Lamar rushed into the bedroom and dragged the burning cover out to the porch.

When he returned to the bedroom, he heard Sasha's sobs inside the closet. His anger abated as he turned the latch and opened the rickety, splintered door. "Fancy meeting you here," he commented sarcastically.

Sasha looked up at him with tear-filled eyes. She stood and embraced him tightly. "What took you so long?" she cried. "I thought I was going to die." She kissed him repeatedly and hugged him.

Lamar was more confused than ever. "Let's get you out of here," he said calmly and carried her in his arms to her car.

"Aren't you supposed to carry me over the threshold going *into* the cabin?" she kidded through tears.

"This is serious, Sasha," he replied tersely.

She kept her arms tightly around his neck and nestled her head against his chest.

"Are you okay to drive?" he asked in a concerned tone.

"I think so. Thank you for saving me."

"That's what I do best." He set her down next to her car and pondered his next words. His stubbornness kicked in again and he informed her, "When you decide to tell me what's so important about your damned story, then we'll talk. I can't have you risking your life prying into things you know nothing about." He marched away from her toward his truck, desperately trying to contain his rage.

"Wait!" Sasha called to him.

Lamar paused but didn't turn around. She rushed to him and hugged him from behind. Tears still streamed down her cheeks.

He turned around and brushed the hair from her moist eyes. "Look, Sasha, I can't help you if I don't know what you want. Is it me, the story, or something else? Help me out here."

"Don't leave yet," she pleaded. "I need to talk to you … about this place."

Sasha took his hand and led him back to the cabin. Lamar kicked the smoldering quilt on the front porch away from the doorway and returned to the living room.

She explained sadly, "I was supposed to join Pam and her friends on that camping trip. My boss decided to take a leave and put me in charge of the magazine until she returned or I would have been here too. It was a chance to show I could handle the job of a full-time magazine editor."

"I see," Lamar said half-heartedly as he wondered if she really knew what happened to the women.

"Suzie was a friend of mine as well. I knew all their little girls, too. It's a tragedy that they died and I know it wasn't from rabies."

"Why didn't you tell me?" he asked sympathetically. He didn't realize the extent of her relationship with the women and their daughters.

"I need to know the truth. Pam texted me after the girls were killed. She told me some things …" Sasha's eyes filled with tears as she paused, "… some horrible things. I should have died with them."

"What things?" Lamar quizzed anxiously. He thought it strange that Pam had an opportunity after the girls' deaths to text before she fully mutated into the frightening creature she became.

Sasha stared at dark blood stains on the wooden plank floor and continued sadly. "She told me about alien creatures and mutants. She said that they killed the girls and mutated Suzie."

"And you believed her?" Lamar asked, knowing this wasn't going to be easy.

"At first, no. I tried to come up here to find out the truth but the area was already quarantined by the military."

Lamar was speechless. Everything seemed like it was covered up so neatly with no loose ends and now Sasha showed up, knowing way too much. Something strange was happening as evidenced by the crows and she was now a part of it whether he liked it or not.

The cabin was strangely quiet until a large crow crashed through another pane of glass and nearly struck Sasha. She screamed as the crippled bird shuddered and died.

Lamar pulled her away from the window and tried to calm her. The crow had no feathers on its belly, just mutated scaly tissue. More glass shattered as two more crows burst through another window and fell to the ground, badly wounded. Lamar and Sasha grew more uneasy.

Lamar stomped on the wounded birds until they were dead. "Let's get the hell out of here," he urged. "This place gives me the creeps."

He escorted her back to the Miata and opened the door for her. She sat inside and gazed up at him. "I'm so sorry," she said apologetically.

"Where do we go from here?" he asked somberly. "Do you have a letter for that, too?"

"A letter?" she replied, looking baffled. "Christ, Lamar, nobody does that anymore."

Lamar placed his hands on his hips and turned away in embarrassment. "I'm such an ass," he grumbled. "I don't know what to think about us or any of this for that matter."

"I really meant what I said about us yesterday," she assured him, "but I need to know what happened here for my own sanity."

"Then I'll see you back at my place," he instructed her. "We'll talk there."

"Thank you, Lamar," she said humbly.

"Please don't go anywhere without me in the future. As you can see, it's dangerous out here."

"Where else can I go?" she blurted tearfully. "You're all I have."

Lamar was touched by her words. "I'm serious, Sasha. I want you to go straight back to my place. If you need to see anything else, I'll go with you."

Sasha smiled appreciatively. He closed the car door for her and she drove off. Curiosity pushed him to examine the cabin more closely.

When he reached the porch, the sickly coyote stared at him from the trees. Lamar drew his pistol but the coyote disappeared. Before he could close the cabin door, three more crows crashed through windows and again rattled him.

"Well kiss my ass!" he shouted, while pointing his pistol in several different directions defensively. "This place is sure going to hell in a hurry!" He rushed out to his truck and sped recklessly down the trail.

When he reached the intersection where the dirt road met the stone road, he stopped and parked. Something wasn't right and, once again, his curiosity got the better of him. With his pistol again drawn, he stepped warily out of the truck and eyed the forest around him. He was being watched. Perhaps it was the wolves, the coyote, or something worse.

⋯✦⋯

Three miles away, Pedro and a friend, Jorge, hiked along the Pomona trail. As they neared the peak of the mountain, they came upon a deer's carcass. Upon closer inspection, they were horrified by the grossly contorted features of the animal. What remained of the partially-eaten carcass was transformed into something grotesque.

Pedro warned his friend to stay away from the dead animal while he called the police station with his cell phone.

⋯✦⋯

Back at the station, Johnny jotted notes in a file on one of the proposed revisions for another of the local codes. He already grew frustrated with the administrative burden associated with being sheriff.

Then he recalled his earlier encounter with Paula. He hadn't been free from the horrible memories of the incursion in months and now things

⋯✦

were better - much better. Then he questioned himself about the origin of the nightmares. *Was it really the aliens or was it Sally's death?*

Johnny recalled explaining to Sally some of the things that happened to him and how he changed during the incursion. At times he felt that he could manipulate her mind with his thoughts.

One day, Sally realized it was more than a coincidence. Believing that he was an alien, she freaked out and locked herself in the bathroom. After becoming impaired from sleeping pills, she calmly left the bathroom, picked up Johnny's pistol off the table and blew out her brains all over his living room wall.

The sight of her head with the gaping hole in it never left him. He contemplated whether or not he should feel guilty for it and wondered if he could have prevented it. Then he considered Paula's change in behavior after learning about the incursion and how supportive she was. She responded to his thoughts and feelings in a positive manner that pleased him. The guilt he felt over Sally was gone. The phone rang and interrupted his thoughts.

"Here we go again," he complained and answered the phone. His face grew somber as he listened to Pedro. After Pedro finished his rant, Johnny instructed him to stay put and wait for them. He hung up the phone and peered nervously out the window at the mountain. The peak grew more ominous as the sky took on an eerie, gray tint from the clouds.

"Just fucking great," he grumbled.

Paula entered the station with a brown bag, seeming pleased with herself. "Look what I found in the trees out back," she announced proudly. "You're alien tongue!"

Johnny looked distracted for a moment, not wanting to say what he thought for fear it was true.

"What's wrong?" she asked apprehensively.

"Get your gun," he ordered her. "We're heading up on the mountain."

"And what should I do with this?" she asked, displaying the bag disappointedly.

"Throw it in the back seat. I'll see what Lamar wants to do with it." Johnny opened the desk drawer and took out his pistol and holster. He stowed two loaded magazines in his shirt pockets and strapped on the gun belt.

Paula retrieved her pistol and holster from the cabinet and strapped on her belt as well. Urgently, they rushed out the door.

"Will you please tell me what's going on?" she requested impatiently.

"Lamar's aid, Pedro, called. It seems they found a deer carcass on the Pomona Trail."

"And what's so urgent about that?" she asked.

"It doesn't look much like a deer."

"Obviously not, if predators got to it."

They hurried into the police SUV and drove off.

She grew concerned by Johnny's silence. "So, what does it look like?" she asked, curious. "It must be something special if we need to see it."

"Don't know. I guess we'll find out soon enough, though."

"Well, at least it's not a mutant," she joked.

Johnny ignored her remark and remained strangely quiet as they pulled away from the station. Paula sensed his anxiety and placed her hand on his thigh for assurance. He forced a smile and rubbed her hand affectionately.

When they reached the base of the mountain, Sasha's Miata was about to turn onto the highway. Johnny and Paula recognized her and turned on the flashing lights. Sasha parked, rolled her window down and waited as they pulled up next to her.

"What are you doing here, Sasha?" Johnny asked. He promptly noticed her tear-streaked face and she looked exhausted. The worst thoughts crossed his mind.

"We, Lamar and I, were at the cabin and…, well…, you'd better talk to him about what happened."

"Is he still up there?"

Sasha looked back up the narrow road but saw no sign of him. "He was supposed to be behind me."

Johnny glanced at Paula and then instructed Sasha, "Go on back. We'll make sure he's okay."

Paula got out of the SUV and walked over to Sasha. She placed her hand on Sasha's arm and asked, "Are you okay? I can ride with you if you like."

"I'm fine. Thank you, deputy."

Paula realized that something frightened Sasha and she did her best to hide it. "Drive slowly. It'll be all right," she assured her and returned to the SUV.

Sasha forced a smile and drove away. Paula stared at Johnny uneasily as he drove up the mountain road.

"She's scared to death," Paula said somberly. "I felt her arm. She was trembling."

"You were very thoughtful back there. Thanks."

"I was concerned about her. Did you see the look in her eyes?"

"Yeah, and I should've been more considerate. Instead, I was thinking about what might have happened up there."

Paula held his hand affectionately. "That's what a good partner does. You can't think of everything."

Johnny smiled at her. She really did make a difference in how he saw things.

Half way up the mountain, they spotted Lamar's truck. When they pulled alongside the vehicle and stepped out, Lamar was focused on the trees with his pistol aimed and ready to fire.

"You lost, Mayor?" kidded Johnny. "You should be behind a desk in town."

Lamar held his hand up for silence. Johnny and Paula glanced at each other and drew their pistols. Standing with Lamar for what seemed like an eternity, they waited but nothing happened. Finally, they lowered their guns, content that the threat had passed.

"What are you doing up here?" Lamar asked.

Johnny and Paula stared in silence. Lamar was perplexed by their expressions and put his hands on his hips in resignation. "All right, what's wrong?"

Paula walked away from them, granting them privacy. Johnny placed his hand on Lamar's shoulder and explained, "We've been friends for a while. Whatever is going on between you and your lady friend, I think you need to be with her."

"She's just a little scared, Johnny. We were …"

Johnny interrupted him and urged, "Go to her. She needs you."

"And what about you?"

"Don't worry. We'll handle it. I'm the sheriff, remember?"

"Have you been up to see Fama yet?" Lamar inquired.

"Not yet. We'll take care of it. I promise."

Lamar looked concerned that he hadn't been there yet and recalled that Jo requested to meet with Johnny over some other issues.

"The crows: watch out for them," he warned suspiciously.

"I got it, Lamar. I'm sure Fama's doing just fine, too."

Lamar looked down at the ground dejectedly. "I'm having a hard time with all of this, Johnny. I feel like I've been put out to pasture."

"You earned the right to control what happens to this town. You're going to make it better than it ever was."

Lamar man-hugged Johnny and thanked him.

"You once told me that I needed someone to bring stability to my life," Johnny reminded him. "Paula might be the one. Maybe Sasha's your stability."

Lamar bit his lip. He fought back the tears as he realized Johnny was right. "I'll be at home if you need me."

"I'll call you later and we'll have a few brewskies," Johnny promised.

Lamar nodded and walked sadly to his truck. He decided that he would go to Sasha and make things right. Her presence brought something that made him feel alive but he wasn't quite sure what it was. Staring at the trees once more, he reluctantly drove off.

Paula joined Johnny as they watched Lamar's truck disappear down the mountain road.

"Is he okay?" asked Paula.

"I hope so."

Two wolves emerged from the trees and stared at them with red eyes.

"Oh, shit, Johnny!"

The wolves darted toward them. Their heads were larger than that of a normal wolf and their fangs were much more obvious.

Paula fired one shot and staggered the nearest wolf. Johnny quickly drew his pistol as the second wolf lunged at him. He dove aside and landed face down in the dirt, barely avoiding it. Paula fired four rounds into both wolves and killed them.

Johnny stood up and dusted himself off. He was about to thank Paula when two more wolves burst out of the trees behind her. "Duck!" he shouted and fired three rounds. One of the wolves tumbled and lay dead.

Paula went to one knee and fired twice. She struck the remaining wolf as it lunged and toppled her. Time seemed to stand still as she lay motionless, frozen with fear, with the dead wolf on top of her, coldly staring into her eyes. Then, before she could react, a tear drop fell from the dead wolf's eye and landed in hers. Stunned by the fear that a single tear drop from the wolf could infect her, she closed her eyes and prayed that it wasn't the case.

A sharp pain in her side jarred her back to reality and she panicked. As Paula reached down, she realized she lay on a tree branch and it dug into her back and side. What she didn't realize was that the sharp inner claw on the wolf's paw jabbed her in the same area. It was more of a talon than a claw and left a short, jagged cut in her side.

"Paula!" cried Johnny as he rushed to her and rolled the dead animal aside. When Paula arched her back and yanked out the tree branch, he breathed a sigh of relief.

"Are you alright?" he asked in a panicked state, while lifting her into a sitting position.

"I'm fine," she replied, her voice trembling. Johnny put his arms around her. "I thought I lost you."

Paula's eyes welled with tears as she thought about how close she came to dying.

"Did you get bit or scratched?" he asked, concerned.

She checked her arms and hands for any wounds. "No, I don't think so."

Johnny inspected the wolves and their mutated features. Including their enlarged heads, their paws were wider than normal with talons instead of claws. Chills ran down his spine as he feared that this meant a new alien incursion.

"Let's get Pedro and get the hell out of here," he instructed Paula.

Paula scanned the trees with her pistol ready to fire. "I'm all for that," she replied and hurried into the SUV.

"What happened to those wolves?" she asked. "They looked really sick."

"The damn things are mutating!" Johnny groaned. "It's happening again."

Johnny took one final look back at the dead creatures and then climbed inside the SUV. He looked distracted as he drove onto the Pomona Trail toward Pedro's location.

Again, Johnny's silence haunted Paula. "Talk to me," she pleaded.

Johnny grimaced as he tried to articulate the thoughts running through his mind. "I hoped that the missing tongue would explain what's going on with the wildlife," he began. "Since that doesn't seem to be the case, we have a different problem. It could be worse, much worse."

"Let's see what Pedro's deer carcass looks like. Maybe that'll explain what's going on."

Johnny calmed down and placed his hand on her thigh. "Nice shooting back there," he complimented her. "You were so calm and in control while that wolf was bearing down on you."

Paula was pleased that he would complement her when warranted. She also took note of his reaction when the wolf landed on top of her.

"You really thought you lost me and you were upset," she remarked in a pleasant tone. "You just made me feel… special."

"You are special," he responded sincerely. With his eyes focused on the road, he confessed, "I think… I think I'm falling in love with you, Paula. I know it's a bad idea with us being working partners and all, but I can't help it."

Paula was elated. "I already fell in love with you and I think it's a great idea."

"Lamar's gonna have a canary," he said with a sly grin.

"He's lucky if that's all he has," she kidded. "I think he'll have his hands full with his new lady friend."

They both chuckled. Johnny liked that she could regain her composure so quickly and that she shook off the attacks. He developed a trust in her that he could rely on, no matter what.

Pedro and his friend, Jorge, stood over the partially-eaten deer carcass and studied it. Claws had grown out of the deer's hoofs and its tail seemed much too long.

Branches snapped and startled them. Pedro instinctively stepped toward the trees but a low growl quickly changed his mind. He backtracked away from the trees to the middle of the trail.

A large, black bear emerged from the trees and eyed the deer carcass. The chemical from the deer's saliva was like honey and the bear wanted it badly. When Pedro and Jorge fled down the trail, another bear emerged from the opposite side of the clearing and challenged the first bear for the carcass. The two fought briefly but then paused as if by command. Then they took notice of the two young men and stalked them.

The police SUV appeared, racing up the trail. The two young men frantically rushed toward it. Johnny slammed on the brakes, barely avoiding them, and leaped out of the truck.

Pedro and Jorge screamed to him for help as the bears closed on them.

"Get in the truck!" Johnny ordered and took aim with his pistol at the bears. He fired two shots into each bear but only wounded them. They charged at him with the same glowing red eyes that the wolves had.

Paula stepped out and fired two rounds into each of the bears as well, but they relentlessly continued toward them.

As soon as Pedro and Jorge were seated in the back of the truck, Johnny and Paula got in and locked the doors. Johnny punched the accelerator with the truck in reverse. The SUV whirled in a half-circle, now facing the down side of the trail. The vehicle lurched as one of the bears lunged against the rear of the vehicle and smashed the window.

Johnny quickly shifted gears and pulled away from the bear. The SUV sped down the trail and onto the mountain road.

"What's wrong with those bears?" asked Pedro. "They looked really weird."

Paula glanced back at their frightened faces and explained, "The bears are sick. They are suffering from something we don't understand right now."

Johnny appreciated her calming effect and how she handled the young men. He became aroused by her 'take charge' attitude and soothing voice.

"What are you gonna do about them?" asked Jorge. "You can't let them loose like that."

This time Johnny answered. "You're right. We're going to come up with a plan to put them down before they hurt anyone. In the meantime, we need to keep everyone away from the mountain."

"You don't have to tell me twice," said Pedro convincingly. "I've seen enough."

Paula questioned the boys about the appearance of the deer carcass and took notes.

# CHAPTER IV

# THE HEART OF THE MATTER

Johnny dropped their passengers off at Pedro's home and returned to the police station. Once he and Paula were inside, he locked the door. Paula chided him, "You aren't that scared, are you?"

Johnny smiled at her and replied, "Not at all. I've got something else in mind." He pushed her against the wall and pressed himself against her. They kissed each other hungrily.

When they paused, Paula commented seductively, "That's the animal I want to see." The two undressed each other in a chaotic frenzy.

Suddenly, she felt a sharp pain in her side. When she ran her hand over the area, she felt a small cut. A chill swept through her body as she feared it was from the wolf.

Johnny noticed her tenseness. "Are you okay?"

"Yeah, just a cramp," she lied. "Keep going, my little monster!"

Johnny crept on top of her, aching to be inside of her. He lapped at her breasts as she arched her back, overcome with pleasure.

"Now, Johnny! Now!" she cried.

Johnny slid himself inside of her and locked his mouth onto hers, their tongues entwined together, in a surreal rush. Johnny ground his hips against hers as he pushed himself inside her. Then, reaching their moment of ecstasy in unison, they gripped each other tightly, draining every ounce of energy from their rigid bodies. As if on cue, they exhaled together and their bodies relaxed.

Johnny rolled over and lay next to her on the desk. They stared at the ceiling, panting and wanting more. He leaned on her and nibbled at her neck.

Paula pushed him away gently. "We have to start using a bed. One of us is going to get hurt on this desk."

"Hazards of the job," he kidded.

"And who's going to file that report?" inquired Paula giddily. "Not you, I'm sure."

Johnny sat up; sweat dripping from his brow and down his chest. "You're right," he replied. "You deserve better than the top of a desk."

"Thank you, Johnny."

Paula stood over him, proudly eying her man. Johnny laid motionless and exhausted, arms dangling off the desk.

"Damn, girl, you are something else," he uttered, nearly breathless.

Paula went into the restroom and washed up. She raised her arm and examined the wound on her side. It appeared much smaller than it felt. She panicked as she fretted whether or not the branch inflicted the wound or the wolf's claws. *No*, she convinced herself. *A claw couldn't cause me to mutate*. Then she wondered, *Could it?*

Inside the cabinet was a first aid kit. She removed a tube of Neosporin and dabbed it on the cut. *It's probably nothing*, she assured herself.

As soon as she stowed the kit and closed the cabinet door, Johnny entered and wrapped his arms around her from behind. "Everything okay?" he asked.

"Never better, but I hope you came in here for a reason," she chided and then leaned against the sink. When she spread her legs, Johnny immediately rose to the occasion and mounted her from behind.

Paula looked up at the mirror and watched Johnny's euphoric gaze, but then she saw her eyes briefly turn red.

Johnny pressed firmly against her and erupted inside her. The two tensed and then, for a brief second, Paula thought she noticed Johnny's eyes flash red as well in the mirror. She lost interest in their encounter and felt as though she would unravel.

As Johnny ran his hands along her arms, he noticed that she was tense again. "What's wrong?" he asked.

Paula turned around and hugged him. "This is just… just wonderful. I've never felt anything like this before."

"Me, too. I feel like I can't get enough of you."

Paula couldn't tell Johnny that she might have infected him. She grew fearful that they would mutate into something horrible and be put down for it. She also feared that their ravenous craving for sex and unusual stamina could be a side-effect of an alien infection. *What if it's true and I did infect him?* she tormented herself. *Johnny will hate me forever.*

They returned to their desks and dressed. Paula looked up at the clock. It was seven o'clock. "It's getting late, Johnny. Are you going to call Lamar?"

Johnny buckled his pants and replied, "In a while. I'm hungry right now."

"We can order out from the deli," she suggested.

"Let's see what Lamar and Sasha want to do," he responded.

They left the station and went to his house. Johnny paused at the door and texted Lamar: "Come by the station at eight o'clock. Beer, too."

Paula looked over his shoulder at the message and nestled against him. "Beer sounds good to me," she remarked. "I'm parched."

Johnny opened the door and stepped aside in a gentlemanly manner. "After you, my dear."

She nodded in appreciation and entered. Johnny gazed at her ass and became hot for her again. *Damn, that ass looks so good*, he thought to himself and hurried inside after her. He didn't understand what happened to him since that first encounter with Paula but every time he got close to her, he felt the urge to make love to her. He was more amazed that she appeared to feel the same. Recalling what happened with Sally, he considered that perhaps he did have some sort of influence on her thoughts. He also contemplated what the potential was if this was true.

✦

Lamar arrived at his home where Sasha waited in her Miata on the street. He parked in the driveway and pondered what to do about her. As he leaned his head against the steering wheel in frustration, she opened the passenger door and startled him.

"Talk to me," she urged. "What's going on between us?"

Lamar leaned back in the seat and complained. "Your 'dear Lamar' letter?" he answered.

Sasha giggled at him. "Oh, Lamar, you are so naïve," she teased. "I told you, no one does letters anymore."

Lamar was both confused and embarrassed. "That's funny," he replied, embarrassed. "Johnny was under the same impression."

"All I meant was that I had a great time. I really missed being held by a caring man. What did you think I meant?"

Lamar groaned and answered humbly, "I thought you changed your mind about me and moved on."

"I'm not going away that easily unless you want me to," she assured him and kissed his cheek.

He didn't respond and looked dejectedly down at the floor. Sasha threw her hands in the air in frustration. "All right, Lamar, I get it," she responded sadly then backed away with moist eyes. "I really thought we could build something good."

Lamar's mind spun as he tried to rationalize what he should do. Sasha walked away disappointedly.

"Damn it!" he blurted out angrily. "Why are things so friggin' complicated?" He watched her get into her car and became frantic. He wanted to stop her but couldn't. The red Miata pulled onto the highway and drove off slowly.

Lamar banged his head three times on the steering wheel and he realized he couldn't let Sasha go. He started the truck and raced after her.

Sasha glanced in her mirror and was surprised to see his truck rapidly gaining on her. She pulled off to the side of the road and waited, curious about his change of heart.

Lamar parked behind her and got out of his vehicle. Sasha played it cool and lowered the window half way. When he paused at the window, she inquired with a serious tone, "Are you giving me a ticket or something, Mayor? I don't think that's in your job description anymore."

Lamar put his hands in his pockets and replied, "I can't, I mean I don't do that anymore. I just wanted to say …" He hesitated and looked away, embarrassed by his ineptitude with her.

Sasha put the car in 'drive' and said, "Call me when you remember."

Lamar grabbed her arm gently. "Please, wait a minute, Sasha."

Sasha grew impatient but put the car in 'park' again. She stared at him and tapped the steering wheel impatiently.

◆••••

"Can we start over?" he asked. "I don't want you to leave."

"Was that so hard?"

"For me it is," he answered as he regained his composure. "Look, I know I have to trust you if this is going to work. It's the cop in me that says you're holding something back and I have to turn that off."

"And I feel the same way about you. I need to know what's on your mind. How about we try dinner again?" she suggested. "Seafood, perhaps?"

Lamar leaned inside the door and kissed her on the lips. "Whatever you want?"

"Now that's more like it. I'll race you back to your place."

Lamar was pleased with the outcome of things and hurried back to his truck. When they returned to his house, he escorted Sasha to the door and stopped. "Tell me once more that you weren't bailing on me yesterday," he asked, seeking reassurance.

"I swear to you, Lamar, I wasn't going anywhere. If I were, I wouldn't have done your dishes."

"I guess I suck when it comes to women," he relented.

"I'm sure I can help with that," she said coyly.

They engaged in a long, romantic kiss. When they separated, Lamar opened the door for Sasha and they entered.

Sasha sat on the sofa and waited eagerly for his next move. He sat next to her and placed his arm around her. "I really do want this to work," he reiterated.

"So do I," she replied, "but you need to make me feel like I'm needed instead of a suspect who's under investigation."

Lamar's phone buzzed briefly for a text but he ignored it. They again embraced and engaged in several moments of passionate kissing.

Lamar glanced at the text on his phone and groaned. He leaned his head back against the wall and complained, "Damn! I have to meet Johnny at the station at eight."

"I understand," she replied, somewhat disappointed.

"We can do dinner after that, if you don't mind," he suggested.

"Is that an invite for me to come with you to the station?" she asked naively, "Or should I wait here?"

Lamar glanced up at the clock. It was seven-thirty. He considered whether or not he wanted Johnny to meet his 'date' and whether or not it was a good

••••◆

idea in light of the earlier attacks on them by the crows. "Oh, what the heck!" he responded enthusiastically. "Sure, you can come."

After twenty minutes of making out on the couch, Lamar glanced at his watch and sighed.

"Come on, big boy," urged Sasha as she checked her watch, too. "It's time to go."

"My timing always sucks," he complained.

---

Johnny and Paula returned to the station at eight o'clock with two cold six-packs, a bag of chips and a jar of cheese. Johnny noticed that the front door was slightly ajar and drew his pistol.

"Did you leave the door open, Paula?" he asked suspiciously.

"Of course not," she replied, wondering why he asked.

"Then we have a visitor," he replied, suspicious.

The two entered the station and set down the groceries. They quickly searched the station but no one was there.

"Did you leave out anything important?" Paula asked.

Johnny noticed that the camera was missing off the desk next to his. The files on his desk were shuffled as if someone had rifled through them.

"You didn't put my camera away, did you?" he asked uneasily.

"No, it was there when we left."

Johnny leafed through his files but nothing was missing, just the camera.

"What was on the camera that someone would steal it?" she asked, curious.

Johnny thought for a moment and then explained how he came across the burnt section of ground up on the peak and took pictures of it.

"That makes no sense, Johnny. Who would give a hoot about something that insignificant?"

"I don't know." Frustrated, he dismissed the incident as another mystery, like the burnt patch on the mountain.

Paula tidied up the area around the desks while Johnny placed the beer in the refrigerator and microwaved the cheese for their chips. He leaned against the counter and pondered why someone would take the camera and nothing else.

Paula slipped into the kitchenette and ran her fingers along Johnny's butt while cuddling against him. "Think we have time for a quickie?" she teased.

Johnny turned and embraced her. "I was thinking the same thing."

Lamar's truck pulled up in front of the station and the doors slammed shut. Johnny and Paula frowned at each other. Paula backed away reluctantly. "I guess a rain check is in order."

"Yeah, I suppose so," he replied disappointedly.

Lamar and Sasha entered the station and appeared quite happy. Johnny noticed right away and was pleased that they seemed okay.

"Thanks for coming," Johnny announced as he left the kitchenette.

"I hope you have something worthwhile to tell me," complained Lamar. "Now that I'm only the mayor, I feel like I've been banished from the island in 'Survivor'." He pulled up two chairs, one for Sasha and one for himself. They sat down across from Johnny's desk.

"I'm sure we do. How about you? Anything good to tell?" Johnny pressed him and winked.

"Yeah, you need to stop up and visit Fama tomorrow at the site and only at the site."

Johnny was perplexed by his insistence to see Fama only at the site but dismissed it for now. "No problem," he replied. "I'll take care of it."

"Do not go to the hotel to see her," Lamar instructed him sternly. "Take my word for it."

"I got it, buddy," answered Johnny suspiciously. "Tomorrow - at the site."

"Fama has an issue she needs to discuss with you and she expected you sooner."

"I doubt she did much at the site with all the rain we've been having. We'll go first thing in the morning."

Paula brought out a bowl of chips and another with melted cheese from the micro-wave. "How are you feeling, Sasha?"

"Better than before. Thanks for your concern."

Johnny brought out four cold beers and gave one to each of them.

"We had a little experience we wanted to share with you," Paula started. "We were attacked by wolves."

Johnny interjected, "and we rescued your boy Pedro and his friend from bears."

"Both the wolves and the bears had freaky red eyes and really bad complexions," Paula remarked cynically.

"We had a bad experience with crows," Sasha responded. "It's a good thing Lamar showed up when he did."

Lamar considered what the attacks could have in common. "Something's not right with these creatures," he mused. "The crows that attacked us back at the cabin were disfigured as if they mutated." He went on to relate the story about what happened to them.

"Rabies?" suggested Paula.

"We can only hope," answered Lamar. "I passed the wolves on the way up. They stood impudently by the roadside and stared at me."

"You're giving me the creeps, Mayor," Paula uttered nervously.

"Well, I already have them," he confessed.

"Your boy Pedro found a deer carcass," Johnny explained. "He said that we really needed to see it."

"And?"

"We never got to it. The bears showed up and I didn't want to risk Pedro or his friend getting hurt."

"Paula, you found the tongue, I understand."

"Yes, Mayor."

"Please, call me Lamar."

Johnny interceded, "The tongue is in the back of the truck. Probably smells a little rank right now, too."

"I'll go get it," offered Paula. She got up and left the station.

"We have to be sure the tongue had nothing to do with this," Lamar emphasized. "Once we're sure of that, then we know all bets are off and this is a new phenomenon."

"Are we talking something alien here?" inquired Sasha, "or is this the bizarre consequence of rabies?"

Lamar grew frustrated with her and chided, "You aren't going to stop riding me about this, are you?"

Sasha put her arm around him and asked, "Is that so bad?"

Lamar promised, "You'll know everything that goes on so long as it stays confidential."

"I promise," she said contentedly.

•·•◆·•·

When Paula retrieved the bag from the back seat of the SUV, a strange sensation came over her as if someone was talking to her but in a different language. She looked across the parking lot and then at the trees on the side of the station.

"Who's there?" she called out but no one answered. She returned to the SUV and closed the door. Again, she heard something. This time she saw the coyote in the trees watching her. When she approached with one hand on her pistol, the coyote fearlessly trotted out onto the gravel lot and stared at her. She heard a voice, this time loud and clear. "I … will … help … you."

Paula reluctantly lowered her pistol. There was something to be gained by this encounter and patience seemed the smarter choice right now. She studied the creature and noticed that its sides bulged as if something was growing inside it.

"What do you want from us?" she asked warily as she realized it was communicating telepathically.

"The tongue," she heard and then the coyote trotted into the trees.

Johnny called out from the door to her. "Are you okay out here, Paula?"

Paula glanced back at him. "I'll be right in."

Johnny closed the door, leaving her alone again. She wondered how she had the ability to communicate with the coyote and feared what was happening to her. She wondered what the coyote meant by 'it will help us'.

Then she recalled the image of Johnny's eyes like hers in the mirror. When she thought about the cut on her side, shivers went down her spine. She recalled the tear from the wolf that landed in her eye. If it wasn't the cut, then the tear surely would have infected her. Now, it was just a matter of how far she was going to mutate.

"Get control of yourself," she whispered. "This isn't happening." Regaining her composure, she went back inside the station.

Everyone stared at her expectantly as she handed the bag to Lamar. "We were getting worried about you," he remarked, concerned.

"I thought I saw something in the trees, but it was nothing."

When she glanced at Johnny, he winked at her as if he knew something. *Maybe he heard the coyote, too,* she thought to herself. *That's it. He must have heard it, too.*

Lamar took the bag from her and peered inside. Convinced that it was real, he dumped its contents on the table.

Johnny was horrified. "What the hell, Lamar? That's my desk!"

"This is more important than your desk, Johnny." Lamar took out his pocket knife and slit the tongue open.

Johnny covered his eyes in disgust. Paula and Sasha both watched anxiously as he pushed apart several flaps of tissue until he uncovered two small fleshy objects.

When he poked one with the point of his knife, four tendrils shot out and wrapped around the knife. He flexed the knife down against the tendrils and cut them off.

"They're alive!" Johnny exclaimed. "After all this time, they're still alive!"

"This is unbelievable!" Lamar uttered in sheer horror.

Johnny opened his desk drawer and took out a hammer. "Not for long," he said and raised the tool.

Paula thought she heard the coyote plead for the tongue. This was no time to raise the issue with her peers. They would surely become suspicious of her.

Lamar grabbed Johnny's wrist. "Not yet." He pushed one of the foreign bodies into the brown bag and quickly slit the other one open. Inside, were miniature organs that oozed from the fleshy bulb onto the desktop. Gray liquid seeped out of the exterior layer of flesh onto the table. The tendrils lay limp and secreted brown blobs of fluid.

"Holy shit!" exclaimed Sasha. "What the hell is that stuff?"

"Looks like instant alien in a pod if you ask me," remarked Lamar sarcastically.

Paula felt an intense high pitched sound ring in her head as if they were hurting the alien objects. She looked away and grit her teeth to suppress her reaction. When the sound faded, she peered down at the remnants of the tongue. "You think they breed like this?" she inquired curiously.

"If it's not breeding, then it's some kind of biological transmitter," surmised Lamar.

"You think this is what made Suzie Beauchamp become what she was?" inquired Johnny.

"At this point, I don't know what to think. What amazed me about Suzie is that she could transform from human to alien and back at will."

"That's pretty amazing," Sasha remarked. "How would you know if you terminated all of the mutants like Mrs. Beauchamp if they could look human?"

"Deductive reasoning," Lamar replied. "We concluded that we got them all based on conversations with Mrs. Beauchamp and the others."

"They must have been real interesting conversations," she remarked cynically.

"Lamar was onto her right from the beginning," Johnny announced proudly. "He played her better than she played us."

Paula gulped as she compared Suzie's circumstances to hers. Johnny was quite relaxed, although, by the look in his eyes, he was concerned.

Lamar pushed the alien pieces into the bag and took them out to the parking lot. The others followed and watched him set the contents of the bag on fire.

Paula felt a shrill sound like screaming in her head again and covered her temples in a desperate attempt to control the pain. She went inside the station before the others could notice her anxiety.

Johnny felt the same ringing pain in his head that Paula felt. He squinted and rubbed his temples.

"Are you alright?" asked Lamar.

"Yeah, just a migraine." He placed his hands on his hips and shook his head in frustration. "So, this tongue could have implanted one of those things in the coyote after all."

"It's possible but we won't know until we kill the coyote and open it up."

"Then we could be in deep shit," Johnny commented. He picked up a stick and stirred the ashes to make sure the appendage and its contents were completely incinerated.

"I'm afraid so," replied Lamar. He turned to Sasha and informed her, "Looks like you're going to get to write part one *and* part two of your story."

Sasha shuddered at the thought of what they were getting into. "This isn't what I had in mind, Lamar. I'm not a reporter."

"You wanted to know what happened," he calmly reminded her. "Welcome to our world." He then placed his arm around her affectionately.

"Remember I told you about the pictures I took on the mountain," Johnny mentioned. "Well, someone broke into the station and took the camera I used. They also paged through all the current files on my desk."

Lamar considered whether Johnny just misplaced the camera but inquired, "Did you have anything else besides the charred area on the camera?"

"No, it's the first time I used the damned thing."

Lamar glanced at Paula. She shrugged her shoulders and had no response. He glanced at the broken door jam and weighed out why someone would break into a police station and steal a camera. It made no sense to him.

"I did download the pictures onto the laptop if you care to look at them," Johnny offered.

"Let's see them," Lamar requested.

Johnny pulled the laptop out of the file cabinet and set it up.

Lamar explained some of the issues they encountered with the previous alien incursion to the women while they waited. When the pictures came up, Johnny turned the laptop toward the others and they inspected them.

The first two pictures showed the burnt patch but nothing more. When they inspected the third and fourth pictures of the trees surrounding the area, they noticed something peculiar in the trees.

"Any idea what that is?" inquired Lamar.

Johnny recalled the image that resembled a creature in the tree and replied, "Looks like some kind of a creature hiding behind the branches."

"If it is, it's pretty friggin' big to be hiding up there,"

Paula and Sasha leaned over the men and browsed at the pictures.

"It might just be an illusion from the sunlight on the leaves," suggested Sasha.

Paula pointed to a portion of the picture and commented, "Those look like wings. Maybe that's how your creature got up there."

Lamar punched the table and stood up. "If that's a creature in the picture, it's not Earth-born. We have another alien outbreak." Everyone grew silent and stared at him.

"We'd better call it a night," he suggested. "This is going to get a whole lot worse before it gets better."

"It's my watch," Johnny announced confidently, "I'll handle it."

"And we'll help in any way possible," Lamar assured him. He and Sasha climbed into his truck and drove off.

Johnny entered the station and found Paula scrubbing the desktop with cleaner. She looked frantic as she tried to remove the residue from the wood.

Johnny grabbed her arm and stopped her. "It's all right, Paula. We'll get through this."

Paula wondered if he knew what happened to her. His words sounded so understanding.

"I'm fine," she replied and threw the scouring pad into the trash. "This isn't quite what I expected tonight."

"Yeah, well, I'm not convinced the tongue is our only problem."

Paula froze and asked nervously. "What do you mean?"

"The red eyes on the creatures; that's new. The mutants worked together before so I can accept that. This makes no sense at all, what we're seeing."

Paula was relieved that he wasn't referring to her.

Johnny took her in his arms and asked, "Do you feel okay? You've been acting really uptight lately." He rubbed her back affectionately and kissed her neck.

She pushed him away and chastised him, "I will never make love to you on that desk again. It was sentimental and now it's ... contaminated."

Johnny burst into laughter. "So that's what this is all about."

Paula bristled at him. "Let's go to my place before I change my mind and beat you."

"Whatever you say, Sweetheart." He followed her out to her pickup.

Paula knew they were being watched. She could tell that three coyotes were in the trees across the street. *How the hell can I know this?* she questioned herself. *What do they want?* When they reached the Toyota, she tossed the keys to Johnny. "You drive…please."

Johnny sensed there was more to Paula's discomfort but figured it best to give her space. They would talk more in the morning.

When they arrived at Paula's apartment, she stopped Johnny at the door and apologized for being a bitch. They backed into the room and she kicked the door shut. The apartment was a small studio, simple and neat. Paula's three suitcases were still unopened by the door.

Johnny unbuttoned her shirt but she went for his pants right away. She felt an immediate need to be satisfied and fumbled with the belt before unbuckling his pants and dropping them.

As soon as Johnny balanced himself against the sofa, Paula dropped to her knees. Johnny was stunned by her insatiable hunger for him. He became excited and was soon spent.

Paula returned with two beers. She handed one to Johnny and chugged the other.

"You were really thirsty, huh?" quipped Johnny.

"Just a little chaser for your good stuff."

Her bold language and sexual aggression turned him on. After making out and fondling each other, Paula pushed him onto his back across the couch and climbed on top of him.

"You have to slow down," Johnny urged her. "You're gonna kill me."

"I'd never do that," she said coyly, while stroking him. When she felt him regain his stamina, she straddled him, eager to have him inside her.

Paula gyrated on him madly while squeezing his nipples until he squealed in pain. She leaned forward and licked his neck before kissing him again.

Johnny moaned again, this time in pleasure. She sucked on his neck like a starving animal. As they climaxed together, she bit into his shoulder, gently, but enough to draw blood. Together they fell onto the floor and passed out from exhaustion.

When morning came, Johnny sat up and rubbed his eyes. The sunlight hurt and his back was sore from the wooden floor. Paula still slept next to him. He got up and hobbled into the bathroom.

While rinsing his face at the sink with water, he looked up and noticed the small wound on his shoulder. *Jesus, that girl's an animal! That's twice she bit me.*

He dismissed any further thought of it and stepped in the shower. The hot water streamed down his back and felt good. He lathered himself and thought about how lucky he was to have Paula. She became more than a friend and now he was in love with her. As if on cue, the shower curtain slid back and Paula stepped in. He found that more than ironic. "Fancy meeting you here," he remarked cheerfully.

Paula inspected his neck and was embarrassed. "I'm really sorry, Johnny. I have to stop doing that." She slid against him as she stepped under the hot, streaming water. "When I'm with you I just lose control. It's like you're my soul mate and, together, we're like fire and gasoline."

Johnny placed his hands on her hips and guided her toward him. "Come here and I'll show you what happens with fire and gas," he kidded as he became aroused.

"I see you're an early riser, too," she joked as she lathered herself.

"Only since you came along," he replied proudly. "I was never like this before."

Paula was pleased by his comment and felt special. She ran her hands down his sides. The water streamed down their faces until Johnny reached past her and turned it off.

They embraced and kissed for what seemed like eternity. Finally, Johnny reached for a towel and dried their faces off.

Paula reached for a second towel and dried Johnny's body off, beginning with his shoulders and, dropping to her knees, his legs. Again, as if on instinct, she was overcome with an insatiable desire to have him. She felt so naughty and excited when she recalled how virtuous she had been, compared to her friends in New York. They all swore she'd become a nun one day. Now, she was Johnny's girl and then, as she maneuvered him in and out of her mouth, she felt like a slut - a very happy slut.

Johnny was amazed at her spontaneity when it came to oral sex or any other sex for that matter. She was like a machine that just kept giving. She became everything he wanted and then some.

Paula heard his thoughts and grew giddy, knowing that it pleased him. When she finished with him, she dabbed her lips clean with the towel and then knelt down to wipe off her trophy. In her eyes, Johnny was more than enough to please her. Then it struck her that she heard his thoughts.

Johnny leaned against the shower wall and slid down into a sitting position. His strength was already drained and it was only eight in the morning. Paula leaned toward him and kissed him.

There was something in her kisses that drove him crazy. She licked his lips and her breathing quickened until she was nearly panting. Through all this, she never broke eye contact with him. Her lips locked over his and her tongue flitted with his, faster and faster until they both lost control. Each time, their emotions would run higher. Unfortunately, the tub was not conducive to their desires and they wisely backed away from each other.

When they stepped out of the tub, Paula brushed her hair in front of the mirror. Johnny stood behind her with his head resting on her shoulder. "What's happening to us, Paula?" he asked.

She was taken aback by his question and set the brush down on the sink. "What do you mean by that?"

He answered hesitantly, "I feel like we've evolved into something more than we were. It's like … It's like we make love on a higher plane."

"Is that a bad thing?"

"No, but I almost feel like we aren't human anymore."

Paula grew unnerved by his words as she fumbled for a response. "Maybe we've become better than human," she suggested. "I hope I'm not disappointing you."

Johnny hugged her tightly. "I don't think you'd know how to."

"That's so sweet," she replied and embraced him. "I'm not the perfect little woman you think I am," she confessed. "I have my share of issues."

"And I swear that I'll never let them come between us."

"Do you really promise?" she asked, hoping that he'd understand her situation.

"Of course," replied Johnny. He couldn't imagine what could be so bad that he'd feel otherwise.

Paula knew he would learn of her 'changes' soon enough and dreaded what his reaction would be. She pondered if he would embrace the new Paula or would he exterminate her out of fear. Then she considered that she already infected him and he was just like her. *Boy did I fuck this up*, she thought to herself.

As they dressed, Johnny gazed at her and could see her thoughts running through his mind. He knew that Paula had become infected and she *was* just like him. Their intense sexual hunger for each other seemed more than human to him and, now, he began to read her thoughts more clearly.

Paula was so caught up in her own ideas about what would happen if the others found out about them that she didn't realize Johnny was in her mind. His thoughts were clouded from her by her own emotions, leaving her oblivious to his talent. Each time she looked back at him, he seemed so contented with her and just smiled.

"Hungry, Babe?" she asked.

"I'm famished. Are you cooking this morning?"

"No food here yet. How about we get something to go from the café across the street?"

"Works for me."

Paula suddenly fretted that Lamar would want to kill her if he found out about her. *But what about Johnny?* she thought. Would that change Lamar's opinion of the situation?

Johnny rubbed her shoulders and assured her that things would be okay. Again, she worried that he might already know. His choice of words seemed to have a double meaning. They finished dressing and left the apartment.

⋅⋅◆◆◆⋅⋅

Lamar and Sasha sat at the dinner table, discussing the alien tongue and what the aliens did to their victims during the incursion. They shared a bottle of red wine as he opened up to her on his thoughts and feelings about their alien situation.

Sasha took notes and tried to correlate what they saw with the information Lamar gave to her. She reached out and held his hand. "Thank you for trusting me."

Lamar gazed into her eyes. All he could think about was her beauty and how lucky he was that she wanted him.

"You aren't even listening to me, are you?" she asked, disappointed.

Lamar smiled at her. "Of course, I am. I'm just considering how much better my life is since you arrived."

Sasha blushed and looked away. She knew he didn't feel that way earlier on the mountain.

"I am worried about your safety here," he added. "It's going to get dangerous."

"I'm not leaving, if that's what you're suggesting," she replied defiantly and withdrew her hand from his.

"Not at all," he responded. "I do feel we'll need to work closely at all times."

The two stood together as if on cue. They embraced and kissed passionately. Lamar understood how strong her emotions were and considered that she felt guilt for not being with her friends in their time of need. If she was, though, she'd be dead as well or even worse – a mutant.

When their kiss ended, Lamar confessed, "I didn't trust you before, but I do now. I understand why this means so much to you and, I want you to know that we're in this together; however it turns out."

"Do you really mean that?"

"Of course, I do and I'll die, if necessary, to protect you."

"I have to ask you: What changed your attitude toward me from this morning?"

Lamar looked down, embarrassed. "It's the fact that you were always the one I wanted, Beanie. I never in my wildest dreams imagined it would come true. Oh, and a better understanding of the letter helps, too."

Tears streamed down her cheeks. "You've just made me so happy, Lamar. I was afraid you wouldn't want me around if you knew who I was."

"And why would you think that?" he asked curiously.

"I was afraid I was forcing myself on you. Maybe I'm trying too hard to be someone I'm not." They again kissed passionately. "Why don't we go upstairs since we're in a sharing mood?" she suggested.

Lamar was elated as he saw the desire in her eyes for him. He would do whatever it took to make their relationship work. After what he and Johnny survived during the last incursion, he didn't care anymore. Their happiness meant more to him than anything and he was tired of punishing himself over it.

Moonlight shone through the window and covered part of the bedroom. Sasha gently pushed him onto the bed and stood in front of him. She unbuttoned her blouse and tossed it on the floor.

He thought to himself, *I can't believe this is young Beanie. She's so beautiful and all grown up!*

Sasha unfastened her bra and tossed it to the floor. Lamar stared at her voluptuous breasts and grew more excited. She placed her hands around his head and pressed her breasts against him. He lapped at her nipples as she felt a rush of emotion take over.

Without missing a beat, Lamar unbuckled her jeans and slid them down to her ankles. She stepped out of them and crooned as he continued to pleasure her. When he slid his hand between her legs and gently massaged her, she was immediately overcome with ecstasy. Sasha gently grabbed his wrist.

"I've dreamed for so long about this moment," she said coyly. "Please don't be mad if I don't want to make love yet."

Lamar rolled onto his back and stared at the ceiling. Sasha turned on her side and rubbed his chest. She studied his expression in the faint moonlight. "Are you okay?" she asked, hoping that for now she was adequate.

He turned to her and smiled. "I'm better than okay."

"Soon, we'll consummate our relationship. I just need a little time," she whispered seductively in his ear and lapped at his nipples.

Lamar fondled her breasts as she grew more excited. They continued their game of foreplay, knowing that there was no satisfying end, only the anticipation of when they did make love for the first time.

"I hope I didn't disappoint you," she said apologetically.

"It was great, Sasha. It'll be great next time, too."

They kissed briefly and slept in each other's arms.

Now that his relationship with Sasha was back on track, Lamar was relieved that he could finally focus on the mutant creatures and help Johnny find a solution. Having Sasha there to support him already made a difference in his mental outlook.

# CHAPTER V

# AN ENEMY BORN

The short ride to the station was unusually quiet as Paula felt apprehensive about their situation. Johnny considered the various possibilities for her change of behavior and was worried about his partner/lover. Finally, when they parked in front of the station, he asked naively, "Are you pregnant?"

Paula stared at him briefly and then burst into laughter. "Why would you even think that?"

Johnny was baffled and replied, "I don't know. Mood swings, maybe."

Paula was amused but contemplated when she would have to reveal that she was infected. Feeling guilty about the concern she caused him, she explained, "It's nothing to do with you, I swear, and I don't want anything to come between us."

"And it won't," Johnny assured her, placing his arm around her shoulders.

She grew more unnerved by his unshaken confidence in her. He acted as though he already knew and understood what happened to her thus far.

"Are you okay?" she asked curiously. "You've been quiet as well."

"Never better," he answered cheerfully.

As they got out of their vehicles, they noticed shattered windows at the station and the front door was broken off its hinges.

"What the hell?" shouted Johnny. "This is bullshit!"

When they entered the station, they were devastated. Everything was a mess. Broken glass from three of the windows littered the floor. The desks were toppled. The cold weather jackets, which hung on a clothes tree, were shredded. Johnny and Paula stared in disbelief at the carnage.

"Now this is getting serious," grumbled Paula in frustration.

"I think it's time for someone to pay," Johnny added.

Paula picked up a broom off the floor in the kitchenette and swept.

"Put the broom down," instructed Johnny. "We're going up to the mountain to check on our miners. Then we're going hunting." Johnny flipped the desks upright and walked out.

Never considering that he might be able to read her thoughts, she wondered if he had some communication skills with the animals, too. She followed him out to the police SUV and decided that it was time for them to talk. The two paused when they reached the vehicle and stared at the trees.

"They're watching us," Johnny noted. "They're smarter than we thought."

"How do you know?" she asked.

"Just a feeling," he remarked and aimed his pistol at the trees as if he would fire. "Maybe even more than a feeling," he said in a somber tone.

"Don't do that," Paula responded and pushed the pistol down by Johnny's side.

"Why?" he asked with a puzzled expression.

"It's just that …" Paula was at a loss of words at that point. "It's a hunch. Let's leave it at that," she replied uneasily.

Paula glanced once more at the trees. She knew the coyotes were out there, watching them from the trees. She knew they weren't the culprits and, if she wanted to, she could easily locate them. Now wasn't the time. They entered the vehicle and considered what lay ahead of them.

The coyote's voice rang in her head: "Soon you will be one." Her head pounded as she fretted over the voice. Johnny noticed but said nothing yet.

As they drove away from the station, Johnny glanced at her repeatedly. Paula became concerned and inquired, "Something you want to talk about?"

"You said you wouldn't doubt me if I was honest with you. Well, I'm hearing voices."

Paula remained expressionless as she listened to him.

"I think the animals are talking to me," Johnny explained. "I know you think I'm nuts but I really do hear them."

Paula grew uneasy as she realized what she did to him. Her nip on his neck made him like her. She fought back the urge to panic and asked, "When did this start?"

"In the middle of the night. I woke up a few times but figured it had to be my imagination."

Paula placed a hand on his arm and revealed, "There is something telepathic with these creatures. They are mutated."

Johnny seemed relieved and asked, "So you hear them, too?"

"Yes, I do. It started yesterday," she confessed, "when I was outside the station."

After another moment of hesitation, Johnny asked, "What are we going to do about it?"

Paula stared out the window and wondered that herself. She again recalled the coyote telling her, "I will help you." Thoroughly perplexed, she considered what action they should take and how a coyote would be of any help to her. If only she could speak further with the coyote.

"We're going to figure out what they are up to – what their plans are," she said determinedly. "Then, we'll figure out how to stop them."

"I'm glad you're so confident," he remarked as he turned up the mountain road from the highway. "I know I'll always be able to count on you."

Paula again struggled over whether or not to tell him what happened to her and what she did to him. She feared how he would react. He might even turn violent and kill her. "What if something happens to me?" she asked uneasily.

"Like what?"

"What if I became infected and, well, turned into something different?"

"Would you still love me?" he asked kiddingly.

"Of course, I would, but would you still accept me?"

"So long as you don't eat me or try to get kinky on me. Oh, wait, we already did the kinky part," he joked.

"I'm serious," chided Paula. "If something happened to you, I'd give you every chance to be…human."

Johnny became suspicious of her and inquired, "Why do you bring this subject up?"

"When the wolf landed on me, I could have died. I could have been bit. Everything could have changed."

"Everything has changed," he countered.

Paula grew flustered with him. "What if it did? What if I already changed and you didn't know it?"

Johnny became annoyed. "I know you as well as you think you know me. We're gonna be just fine."

Paula was frustrated with his puzzling comments and struggled to find the right words to say to him.

Johnny sensed her displeasure with him and tried to lighten the mood. "So, let's say you became a mutant. Would that explain why our love-making is so great?"

Paula burst into laughter. "You are such a dick, Johnny!"

"I mean could it possibly make a difference?" he said innocently.

She broke into a broad grin, feeling more relaxed by his remarks. "We'll just have to find out, won't we?"

"If this *is* a consequence of getting infected, I'm liking it," he replied giddily and tweaked her nipple through her shirt.

That was all it took and Paula felt the urge to have Johnny there - in the vehicle on the side of the road. She suppressed it and wondered about his choice of words: *If this is a consequence…* He spoke as if he was already infected, too, and he knew it.

"Look, Paula, we have a lot to deal with and we're going to deal with it together," he explained. "It's going to be dangerous and we don't know if any of us will survive. You already know that I'm not normal after what happened last spring."

"I'll be all right," she assured him. "Just promise you'll stand by me, no matter what."

"Of course, I will, ET," he joked.

His comment struck her like a bucket of ice water. She was shocked that he called her ET. "Fuck you, Johnny!" she shouted and burst into tears. *I'm a human and I always will be*, she thought defensively.

Now Johnny was sure she was infected and knew he had to handle her much more delicately. He pulled her close to him and hugged her tightly. "All I'm saying is that maybe things aren't as bad as they seem," he continued compassionately. "I'm sorry if I upset you."

Paula looked like a frightened child as she stared at him and cried, "You wouldn't be saying that if you were infected."

Johnny pulled off to the shoulder where the mountain road intersected the highway. He stared at her until she made eye contact with him. "I am infected and I know you are, too," he confessed. "Now, what are we gonna do about it?"

Paula was speechless as he just admitted her worst fear. "I…, I don't know," she replied as tears streamed down her cheeks. "I tried to think of a way to talk to you about this but I was afraid you'd turn on me."

"We're both a bit nuts when it comes down to it," he responded. "Now that we've established that, we're still the same two people who fell in love and screwed each other's brains out on my desk."

Paula was stone-faced for a moment and then burst into laughter again. "You know, Johnny, I was right. You are a dick!"

He again hugged her tightly and kissed her. "We'd better get back to business before we do something lewd," he suggested, then put the SUV in 'drive' and continued up the mountain road.

Paula sat back in her seat, smiling over the pleasant turn of events in their relationship. Feeling a renewed sense of trust in Johnny, she asked, "So what do you know about the coyote?"

"What about it?"

"The animal voices: didn't you hear something about being one and that it would help us?"

Johnny thought hard about what he heard earlier. Ironically, he seemed to hear the coyote's message through Paula's mind but was reluctant to admit that yet.

"Yeah, I heard it all. That's why I came outside to check on you last night."

Paula was relieved that they were now on the same page. "And?" she pressured him.

"I know how you were frightened that you infected me."

Paula lowered her head and became teary-eyed again. Johnny placed his hand on her thigh and rubbed it affectionately.

"Relax, Honey. I'm not worried about it."

Paula looked up at him, perplexed by his congenial attitude over their condition.

Johnny continued, "Whatever is going on here, I think we needed this change to survive against the creatures up there. It also means that you and I are stuck with each other. Nobody else would have two whack jobs like us."

Paula wiped a tear from her cheek and breathed easier. "You know, Johnny, for a dick, you're all right."

"I hope that's not all you want me for," he kidded.

"Of course not. I do want to know your thoughts about what's happening up on the mountain, though."

Johnny considered everything that happened thus far and responded, "I think there are two sides at work here and we are being warned about one of them. I also seem to hear things only through you, as if I'm reading your thoughts, not theirs."

"Well, stop reading my mind," she warned and slapped his arm. "That's personal." She then calmed and suggested he get a magazine to occupy his mind. The two laughed and resumed a normal conversation.

• • ◆ • •

The Ardonean leader glided in a circle over the drill site and watched as Jo enter the trailer. When she stepped out carrying a laptop, the alien swooped in and knocked her down from behind. The laptop flew from her hands and landed a short distance away. Her forehead bounced off the bottom of the steel ramp, knocking her sunglasses off. The alien bit her arm and, before she realized what happened, the creature was gone.

Gino checked the fluids in the generator and returned to find Jo dazed on the ground. He immediately helped her to her feet and retrieved her laptop and glasses for her.

Jo dusted herself off, cursing the ramp as the cause of her fall. She inspected the laptop for damage and then connected it to the control panel of the drill assembly.

Gino questioned her about her fall and if she was okay, but she insisted everything was fine and placed her sunglasses up on her forehead for now.

After a few minutes of startup time for the laptop, she programmed the parameters for the drill assembly. Content with the results, she stowed the laptop and operated the controls for her drill assembly with a pendant attached to a long cable. Carefully, she maneuvered the assembly toward the target area on the mountainside.

The drill assembly was mounted on a four-wheeled crawler which maneuvered the drill wherever Jo targeted. Then she heard the voice in her head: Do not enter the mountain. Jo dismissed it as a hangover from the previous night and continued to operate the drill.

High above her in the trees was the winged alien. It watched her with keen interest and grew frustrated when she continued to operate the drill. The creature glided down toward her but then the police SUV arrived and parked next to her Escalade. Jo cast them a quick glance but continued to focus on her prized creation. The Ardonean reluctantly returned to the trees and monitored Jo's operation of the drill.

Johnny and Paula got out of their vehicle and observed for several minutes until Jo was satisfied with the drill's positioning. She turned off the power and set the pendant on the side of the crawler.

Johnny greeted her with a friendly wave. Paula, meanwhile, stood with her arms folded and studied Jo's reaction to them. She noticed something peculiar about Jo's eyes but couldn't tell what.

Jo approached them, sporting a devious grin. "Where's the Mayor? I thought he'd be anxious to speak with me about the other night." Johnny and Paula glanced at each other, both curious.

"He's taking care of some administrative issues," answered Johnny. "We'll be your liaison from here on out."

Jo and Johnny shook hands. When Johnny introduced Paula, Jo made a point that she wasn't interested in meeting her and placed her sunglasses down over her eyes.

Paula held her hand out purposely until Jo accepted it. When she shook Paula's hand she held on for an extended time, while staring into Paula's eyes. She saw Paula as someone weak and insignificant.

Paula still sensed something about Jo that wasn't right. She dismissed it for now and took it as a competitive thing between two women. Jo was trying to establish her female superiority over her and Paula couldn't let that interfere with the job. She noticed several odd cuts on Jo's arm and commented, "You have an accident or something, Ms. Fama?"

Jo glanced at her arm and chuckled. "Just a little fall on the ramp. It's nothing."

Then, to Paula's surprise, Jo led Johnny by his arm to the drill for a rundown of her operation and how it worked.

Paula didn't appreciate being ignored by her but refrained from responding. She walked around Jo's vehicles and peered inside the Escalade. Jo's pistol was on the passenger seat and caught her attention.

As she scanned the inside of the vehicle, Gino approached her from behind and touched her shoulder. "Good morning, Deputy. Do you have any questions I can answer for you?"

Startled, Paula pulled away and instinctively placed her hand on her pistol. Gino stepped back and held his hands up innocently. "Sorry, ma'am. I was just trying to help."

She breathed a sigh of relief and removed her hand from the pistol. "I'm sorry. You surprised me."

"I tend to do that to women," he said pleasantly and shook hands with her. "I'm Gino."

"Hello, Gino. I'm Deputy Paula Mason."

Their eyes locked for a second and Gino displayed an almost hypnotic smile that aroused her. She looked away, embarrassed by her emotions. Quickly, she regained her composure and inquired, "How long have you been with Ms. Fama?"

"About two months now. She hired me through the local college so I can do my internship with her."

"What do you think of her so far, Gino?"

Gino smiled coyly. She wondered what he was thinking as he seemed to delight in her inquisition. "That's personal, Deputy, but if it matters, I don't mind sharing."

Again, Paula felt aroused as she knew he was flirting with her. "Do you have a physical relationship as well as a business relationship with her?"

"Oh, yes. She handpicked Adam and me specifically to work with her in all aspects of the job… and other things."

Paula blushed as she realized what he meant. "So, you and Adam are intimately involved in the drilling operation?" she queried innocently.

Gino chuckled at her. "An interesting choice of words you've chosen, Deputy."

Paula was thoroughly embarrassed by what he perceived her intent to be. "I'm sorry, Gino. I meant that you and Adam are actively involved in the project, not Ms. Fama's personal life."

Gino folded his arms and grinned at her. "Ms. Fama offered to make us both partners in her company if we performed well."

"I see. And where is Adam?"

"He went to town for some parts. Apparently, he's been delayed a bit. Would you like to meet him when he returns?"

Again, Paula blushed as she knew what he alluded to. "No, that won't be necessary."

Jo took notice of Paula now that Gino was with her but continued her conversation with Johnny. Paula was pleased that she achieved some measure of revenge without actually trying. Perhaps now Jo would back off her close attraction to Johnny.

"What brings you and the sheriff up here?" Gino asked curiously.

Paula peered around the clearing at the trees. She sensed the coyote was near but couldn't place its location. There was something interfering with her ability to focus. Then, a noise in the trees caught her attention as if distracting her. She searched above them but saw nothing.

Gino noticed her vacant stare and interrupted her. "Deputy?"

"I'm sorry, Gino. Have you noticed anything unusual lately?"

Gino chuckled again. "Other than the mayor barging into our hotel room while Adam and I were entertaining Ms. Fama; no."

Paula was stunned by his response. "You're kidding, right?"

"Oh, no. I guess he mistook Ms. Fama's cries of passion for someone in trouble and kicked in the door. The three of us were in a very compromising position."

Paula was speechless and again Gino enjoyed her blushing reaction.

"Jo invited him to join us but he appeared out of his league and hurried off. He was nice enough to pay for the door, though."

Paula tried to forget Fama's sexual encounter with the two young men but she became aroused by the thought of open sex with them. She couldn't understand why, after a life of modesty, that she became so obsessed and driven by these urges. "How about the wild life up here?" she inquired. "Anything strange?"

"Oh, Deputy, we don't do things like that," he teased playfully.

"Damn it, Gino!" she exclaimed in frustration. "I'm serious."

"No, Deputy, nothing out of the ordinary. Ms. Fama did have a fall earlier today, though. I found her dazed behind the drill."

"Did she exhibit any strange wounds or sounds?"

"No, ma'am. She was upset by her clumsiness but that was all."

Something about the way he replied made her suspicious. She wasn't sure if it was the look in his eyes or the way he spoke that made her feel vulnerable. "Thanks, Gino," she said, unconvinced that he was being truthful and returned to the police SUV.

Jo stood next to Johnny with one hand on his shoulder and pointed to various sections of the drill assembly. She tilted her head against his as she meticulously directed his attention to several smaller components.

Paula bristled as she realized Jo wasn't backing down. She wanted to intercede but this was the part of a relationship in the work place that was difficult – maintaining professionalism under all conditions.

Without her mysterious telepathic ability, she couldn't tell what Johnny was thinking. It riled her that she grew jealous over Jo's behavior. It also bothered her that something could inhibit their new telepathic gift like this. Perhaps it was just one more clue to a complicated puzzle.

Jo held onto Johnny's arm and ushered him away from the drill toward the edge of the forest. Johnny became uncomfortable as he knew Paula watched. All he could think was *'She's a cougar and Paula doesn't like cougars.*

Jo explained to Johnny about her ex-husband and how he swore he'd get even with her over the drill assembly. She also revealed that he had ties to the mob and sending hit men after her was a reality that Johnny needed to be aware of. Noticing her distressed expression and teary eyes, Johnny instinctively hugged her.

As if on cue, Paula joined Johnny and Ms. Fama, curious as to how her contraption worked. Jo wiped her eyes and backed away from Johnny.

Paula glared at him, despite knowing what transpired. Innocently, Johnny assured her that they'd do all they could to protect her.

When Jo offered Johnny a personal invitation to come back tomorrow to see the drilling commence, Paula took the opportunity to question her on the drill's fundamental operation.

Jo was reluctant to give more than a few brief answers to her and Johnny, sensing that Paula was being slighted, pressed for the information based on Paula's questions.

"I see you two are a pair," Jo remarked. "Have you been together long?"

Johnny innocently replied, "No, Paula's new in town and she's very good at what she does."

Jo removed her sunglasses and ogled Paula from head to toe. "I'll bet she is," she remarked cynically.

"Excuse me," retorted Paula, becoming irked by the disrespect.

"Relax, dear. Perhaps you and I need to spend some time together, if you want to know more about my project. I just assumed this was over your head."

Paula didn't know what to make of her. *Was this a blonde joke or a challenge?* she thought. "Perhaps I'll take you up on that later," she replied curtly.

"Thanks for looking in on my well-being, Sheriff," Jo said coyly, "and please give the mayor my best."

Johnny shook hands with her and, feeling satisfied that everything was under control, he returned to his vehicle. Paula shook her hand but held onto it a bit longer, just as Jo did to her earlier. "Perhaps tomorrow afternoon, I'll stop up and we'll discuss your operation …if you have the time."

Jo was pleased by the challenge and suggested a four o'clock visit would be best. Paula forced a smile and returned to the SUV.

The winged alien took flight and circled high overhead. After three circles, it disappeared beyond the mountain.

When Paula climbed inside the SUV, Johnny eyed her and asked, "What's up with you and Fama?"

Paula was surprised by his question. "Nothing. Why?"

"I sense a little tension between the two of you."

"It's nothing," she replied. "I do have a weird feeling that something isn't right up here."

"With Fama?"

"Besides the fact that she's a slutty, old cougar; no. There's something in the air that bothers me about this part of the mountain in general."

"Like what?"

"I felt like someone or something was interfering with my thoughts. It wasn't you being a smart-ass, was it?"

"Of course not," Johnny lied. "I thought it was you blocking me from your conversation with your perverted little friend."

Paula stared at him in disbelief. "Gino's a nice guy. He was very polite to me."

"Whatever you say," he teased. "You had that look in your eye like you were feeling naughty."

"Once again, you can be such a dick!"

Johnny snickered and focused on the road.

Paula kept wondering about Fama and if she had ulterior motives. *Maybe she's just a pervert*, she thought. Then she recalled what Gino said about the mayor's intrusion.

When they parked in front of the police station, Paula hesitated with a sly grin.

"You have a fiendish look about you, Ms. Mason," Johnny remarked.

Paula asked, "Did Lamar say anything about a visit to Fama's hotel room the other night?"

"Only that I should definitely not go there. Why?"

"Just wondering," she replied giddily.

"I can call him when we get inside. Should I ask him about it?"

"Maybe."

Johnny inquired excitedly, "What did you hear?"

Paula returned a smile and shook her head in disbelief. "You wouldn't believe me if I told you. I'd rather you hear it from him."

"Did Lamar do her?" he asked giddily.

"No, but you're getting warm."

"Oh, man, this is good!" He peeked at her repeatedly and pleaded for her to reveal the details but Paula refused.

When they entered the station, Johnny put his arm around her and kissed her cheek.

"What was that for?" she asked.

"Don't worry. Jo's not my type."

Paula chuckled at him. "So now it's Jo, not Fama or Ms. Fama."

Johnny blushed. "Come on, Paula. I have my hands full with you."

"And I'll make sure it stays that way."

"You'd better," he kidded. "You aren't interested in her, are you?"

"You are a friggin' dick! I told you; I'm not into cougars, especially when I have you."

"You started this whole cougar thing, remember," he taunted.

"And I'm sure you'll never let me forget."

The two kissed and then set about straightening up the station.

---

Lamar and Sasha arrived an hour later at the station and were appalled by the state of disarray that still existed. Johnny installed wood planks over the broken windows while Paula swept up the broken glass.

"What the hell happened here?" exclaimed Lamar, shocked by the damage.

"Last night we had visitors again," Johnny answered and installed the wood over the planks on the broken window. "They must want something pretty bad to do this."

"Have there been any reports of animal attacks yet?"

"None so far," answered Paula.

"Strange. Very strange," uttered Lamar. "We need to take some defensive measures before they do."

"Where do you want to start?" inquired Johnny.

"First, we have to secure the town. How many people do we have here?"

Johnny explained that only about fifty people took residency and maybe a dozen contractors. They discussed creating a 'gated' or 'fenced' community for a first tier of protection for the townspeople.

"That's a little extreme, don't you think?" asked Paula.

The men stared at her somberly, knowing that she never experienced what they did during the first alien attack. Lamar informed her, "We're not taking any chances."

Next, they focused on the indigenous animals themselves. They discussed their behaviors and the coordination between them.

Paula pointed out moments of coordination she noticed between the bears and wolves and sensed that the coyotes were the passive creatures in all of this.

"Sounds like you've become our expert," Johnny kidded.

"I'm just observant," she replied defensively. "I'm sure that there's something controlling their behavior, though, and we have to find out what."

"And if we don't?" countered Lamar.

"Then their army will grow stronger and deadlier," she replied authoritatively.

Everyone agreed with her assessment. As bizarre as this sounded, no one wanted to underestimate the possibility of another alien invasion of their town.

Paula and Johnny wanted so badly to tell them about the coyote and the voices but they'd then have to explain how they knew. That would be another problem. Lamar might not like the idea of his sheriff and deputy being mutants.

Lamar requested a private conversation with Johnny outside the station. The two left, leaving Paula vexed.

Outside, they leaned against Lamar's truck.

"You alright?" asked Lamar.

"No," replied Johnny. "Things are so confusing right now. I don't know what to do."

"You mean the animals or Paula?"

Johnny was jittery that Lamar recognized his concern for her. "What makes you say that?"

Lamar smiled and remarked, "It's part of being a cop and a friend."

"Seriously, what makes you think Paula has anything to do with this and not the animals?" Johnny asked suspiciously.

Lamar looked insulted and frowned. "Come on, boy! It doesn't take a genius to see that you and she have a little fire burning for each other."

Johnny rubbed his eyes in frustration and leaned his head against the SUV's side window. "It's a little more than that, Lamar. She seems to understand what we went through and knows how to make me forget those horrors. I actually slept well last night without waking up in a panic attack."

Lamar grew silent and looked inside the station through the doorway. Paula and Sasha were engaged in a cheerful discussion.

"What? No response?" chided Johnny. "That's not like you."

"Maybe I'm in the same boat as you. I just don't know which way it's facing."

"Then it sounds like beer time," Johnny quipped. "I'll get with the contractors in the morning about fencing the west side of the town and installing gates."

"Where does the beer come in?" kidded Lamar.

"Six o'clock. We'll meet here at the station."

"Excellent. Sasha and I have some things to do in the meantime."

Johnny stared at him with a devious smile. Lamar grew flush with embarrassment.

"No, I don't mean that!"

"Whatever you say, Lamar," he teased.

They entered the station and joined the women in their discussion about animal behavior. When they finished, Lamar and Sasha said goodbye and stepped outside the station.

Johnny followed them out the door. He watched as Lamar's truck sped away.

Paula sat at the desk and sketched out a diagram of the animal attacks thus far: Lamar's crows; the deer carcass; the bears and wolves. *Maybe there's a pattern,* she thought to herself.

Johnny made a call to a contract supervisor and spoke briefly. When he finished the conversation, he sat on his desktop and eyed Paula. Something about her really got his attention. She was different than the other girls he dated. *I think I could handle her for the long haul in a relationship. Hell, I think I'd even marry her… someday,* he mused and picked up his files off the floor.

It excited him that she was so passionate when they made love. He felt possessed like a wild animal. It did cross his mind again that, whenever he imagined things with her, they seemed to occur. Right now, that was a problem he could live with. Then he thought back to Sally and recalled that she couldn't. Unfortunately, that thought brought his attention back to the animals on Graham's Mountain.

He considered how he and Paula became infected but are so different than the animals. Then he considered that being infected by another human versus one of the creatures could be the reason. Perhaps, the original contaminant mutates into something different before it is passed on. If only he could understand what the facts were, it would be so much easier.

Paula could read his thoughts again and grew curious as to why her telepathic ability returned away from the drill site. She was confident that the two of them could be a formidable team and have a lasting relationship so long as no other issues like Jo came along to ruin things. Regardless, she needed to understand her new 'assets' as well.

Johnny finished his review of the zoning code revisions that he and Lamar compiled. He gazed at Paula and inquired, "Why do I get the feeling that you want to tell me something?"

Paula grew uncomfortable as she was now aware he could read her thoughts at times, albeit at a much slower pace. "There is something but I'm not ready to talk about it yet. Give me a little time and I promise…"

The manager of a contract firm entered the station and interrupted their conversation. They shook hands and discussed the fencing project for half an hour.

"Excuse me, boys," interrupted Paula. "Johnny, I need a minute with you."

Johnny walked her to the door and asked, "We'll continue our discussion in a little while. I have to take care of this first."

Paula looked down sadly. Johnny feared that maybe there was something more serious that she needed to discuss with him. "What's wrong?" he asked.

"Nothing," she lied. "I'm going to pick us up something to eat. I'll be back in a little while."

"That'd be awesome, Paula." He opened his wallet and gave her a twenty. She forced a smile and left the station.

Johnny resumed his discussions with the contract supervisor. The man was curious as to why they needed a fence along the west side of the town. He was skeptical over Johnny's story about rabid animals but was anxious to take the contract just the same.

✦

As Paula got in her truck, she noticed two large flocks of birds flying south, away from the mountain. *That's strange*, she thought to herself.

Paula drove away from the station in her pickup to the south side of the town where the shops were located. As she cruised down the highway, she noticed more than a dozen deer racing east across the road toward Clearview. The deer showed no signs of mutation and she wasn't able to detect any telepathic communication. Everything seemed normal except that they were fleeing the mountain.

Further down the road, she noticed a bear and shortly after, two wolves. All seemed normal except for the migration south and east.

Paula considered that they knew something was wrong or something evil had entered their area and were smart enough to get out. She stopped at the deli and bought a couple of sandwiches and two cokes.

When she exited the deli, she sensed that something was watching her from overhead. Paula set the bag with the sandwiches and cokes inside the pickup truck. *Who are you?* she replied telepathically.

There was no response. She tried to identify the source but couldn't. *Answer me. Who are you?*

Paula grew frustrated and scanned the sky once more. She recalled the creature in the picture that Johnny took and feared it was tracking her. Content that there was nothing there, she got into her truck and returned to the station.

---

Lamar and Sasha sat on a bench in front of the municipal building. It was a beautiful day with moderate temperatures. Sasha pointed out that it was unusually quiet except for the occasional car that passed. There was no sign of the birds that usually filled the air with their chirping. Lamar listened and was miffed by the silence. He enjoyed the sounds of the birds as he walked back and forth to the municipal building.

Lamar stared at the mountain and looked disappointed.

"What's wrong?" asked Sasha.

"It's Johnny. He needs my help but it's not my job anymore. He has to show he deserves to be sheriff so he can't ask me for help, even if he needs it."

"Life still goes on around here, Lamar, and you are the mayor."

"Yeah, but what if he needs my help?"

Sasha nestled against him and assured him that Johnny would call if he needed him.

"We're getting together at the station around six tonight. Would you mind joining me?" he asked.

"I'd love to," replied Sasha. "I'll go anywhere with you."

As they cuddled, Lamar noticed a Crown Victoria parked across the street in front of the hotel.

"That's strange," he remarked.

Sasha pulled away and asked. "What is?" He nodded toward the vehicle and studied it closely.

"It's just a car," Sasha responded. "What's so strange about that?"

"I've never seen it before and it's in front of the hotel."

"Meaning?" she inquired, thoroughly confused by his concern.

"Let's take a walk." He took her hand and the two approached the hotel. Sasha hooked her arm in his and anxiously waited to see what he had in mind.

When they reached the front door, three men exited and drove off in the Crown Victoria. Lamar subtly took notice of their facial features and stowed them in his memory.

Inside the hotel, he approached the owner at the desk, Mr. Givens.

"Good morning, Mayor," Mr. Givens greeted Lamar. "Do you need a key?"

Lamar blushed. "No, thank you, sir. Can you tell me what those men wanted?"

"They are friends of Ms. Fama. Wanted to know where she could be found."

Lamar grew uneasy as he recalled what he learned on the internet about Jo's ex-husband and his company.

"Are they staying here?"

"No, but they did make a reservation for a friend - Leon Bartok, I believe," he said as he checked the computer screen in front of him. "Yes, Leon Bartok was the name. They paid in cash for the next two nights."

Lamar recalled that Leon Bartok was Jo's ex-husband and the CEO of Tri-Star Diamond Mining. He weighed the possible ramifications of the danger Jo could be in if these guys were thugs. "If you see or hear anything strange, please let me know right away."

Mr. Givens chuckled and replied, "You mean like the other night?"

"This is serious," Lamar chastised him. "I don't believe they are friends of hers and she could be in danger." He and Sasha left the hotel hurriedly.

Sasha was curious about Mr. Givens' reference to 'the other night'. "There's something you're not telling me, Lamar," she commented to him.

"I suspect they broke into the police station. They want the location of Fama's drilling operation."

"I sense there's something else," she mentioned suspiciously.

Lamar acted disinterested in her remark as they returned to the municipal building. When they sat on the bench, Sasha stared at him with a grim expression. "What happened at the hotel?" she asked in a persistent tone.

"Just business."

Sasha became frustrated and continued to press him for answers. "There's a little more to this than business. Why won't you tell me?"

Lamar finally lost it and shouted at her, "Because it was damn embarrassing! I heard noises and kicked the door in. Feel better now?"

Sasha was stunned by his outburst. "I'm sorry."

"Look, if it wasn't work related, I'd tell you."

She realized she pushed her limits with him and felt badly. "I'm sorry. I was afraid…"

Lamar knew what she thought. She suspected that he had an affair with someone, perhaps with Jo.

"I know what you thought." He tried to keep a stern expression but he burst into laughter.

"What's so funny?" she asked, red-faced with embarrassment.

"You had to be there. I thought someone was beating Fama up. That's why I kicked the door in."

"And?"

"She was in a threesome with her two interns."

Sasha's jaw dropped as she was stunned. "Wow! That really is embarrassing."

"No kidding. And she invited me to join in!"

"What did you do?"

"I went downstairs and paid the manager for the door. After that I ran back to my office and hid." They laughed over the incident.

"That was nice of you to pay for the door," she kidded.

"Yeah, well, I had to reclaim some of my dignity."

Lamar stood and glanced down the street where the Crown Victoria disappeared. "I've got to get to work. See you around five?"

Sasha stood and hugged him. "I'll be waiting, you big oaf. Just stay out of hotels before you get yourself into any more trouble."

Lamar kissed her and walked away. As he entered the municipal building, Sasha considered what to do with her free time. She wanted to focus on her story but she needed more details.

Lamar entered his office and was surprised to find a strange man waiting inside. "Excuse me, but do we have an appointment?" he asked defensively.

The man stood and approached him with a purposeful gait. After eying Lamar for a few seemingly long seconds, the man extended his hand. "Good day, Mr. Mayor. My name is Leon Bartok."

Leon was a tall, broad-shouldered man, balding and well-dressed in a three-piece suit.

Lamar cautiously shook hands with him. "I'm Mayor Whittington. What can I do for you?"

Leon approached the window behind Lamar's desk and stared out at the mountains. "I'm looking for a distant relative who, I understand took residence out here recently."

Lamar was annoyed that Leon took liberties with the space behind his desk. He folded his arms and stood next to Leon, attempting to make him uncomfortable by crowding him.

"I'm looking for a woman named BettyJo Fama. She is doing some excavating in the mountains around Parmissing Valley."

"And how can I help you with that?" asked Lamar, now convinced that his men were behind the break-ins at the station.

"I assume she has a permit for her little operation. I'd like to know where I can find her."

"I met with her earlier about the operation. She hasn't filed the paperwork yet for the permits."

Leon faced Lamar with a cold stare. "So, you have no idea where she plans to set up her project," he surmised menacingly.

Lamar refused to back down and stood nose-to-nose with Leon. "There are several locations she was considering. Until she submits the paperwork, I won't know for sure where she'll request to set up."

Leon smiled at him and walked toward the door. He paused with his hand on the knob and looked back at Lamar. "I can make it worth your while for cooperation. I can also make it painful if you resist." Leon tossed a card with a handwritten phone number. "I advise you to call me with her location very soon. My patience is limited."

"I can also advise you to keep your men out of the police station, Mr. Bartok."

Leon smiled at him with a distinct arrogance. "And why is that?

Lamar had no reply, which satisfied Bartok all the more. "Just as I thought. Have a nice day, Mayor."

Lamar bristled as Leon left his office and closed the door. "That son of a bitch!" he bellowed. "He's got a lot of fucking nerve coming in here and threatening me."

Lamar opened his desk drawer in search of his pistol but then remembered that it was under the seat in his truck. He couldn't do much with it anyway. He isn't the law anymore and Bartok would claim he never threatened him if he had Johnny arrest him. He had to catch him in a criminal act.

⋅⋅⋅✦✦✦⋅⋅⋅

Johnny and the contract manager continued their conversation until Paula returned. When she entered, the man shook hands with Johnny and left the station.

"Hi, Sweetie," Johnny said. He instinctively hugged Paula and kissed her cheek. "Everything all right?"

"I saw the strangest thing on the way to the deli," Paula announced. "Two wolves and a bear crossed the highway headed east."

"What's so odd about that?"

"Further up the road, I saw several deer also heading east."

"Okay, and that means what?"

"I saw birds flying away as if they were migrating to the south. They all looked normal compared to the animals on the mountain."

"Now I see where this is going," he said uneasily. Johnny leaned back in his chair and pondered. "We'll inform Lamar and Sasha later on. This is getting interesting." He picked up several files off the floor and attempted to organize them.

The station was restored to order and only the broken windows were left as a reminder of the damage the intruders did to their station.

Paula stepped around the desk and massaged Johnny's shoulders. "It's after five. Are we off the clock yet?"

Johnny glanced at his watch. "I believe we are. Lamar's coming by at six for a beer so …"

Paula sat on his lap and interrupted him with a wet kiss. Johnny responded instantly to her advance and pulled her close to him.

"So, what do we do now?" he asked between kisses.

Paula's heart raced as she unbuttoned his shirt. "Do you need an invitation?" she chided. "We only have forty-five minutes."

"I thought you were done with desktop pleasures?"

She smiled seductively at him. "I changed my mind." Paula stood up and slowly undressed in front of him. She tossed her shirt on the next desk over and unhooked her bra. Johnny was overcome with excitement as she slowly lowered it, revealing her supple nipples.

Johnny quickly unbuckled his pants and dropped them to the floor. Paula licked her lips seductively. "Want some of this?" she teased.

"You know it!" he bellowed.

She unbuckled her pants and dropped them to the floor. Johnny nearly fell over at the sight of her pink thong. Then Paula slid the thong down from her hips to her ankles. She kicked the thong away onto the vacant desk and spread her legs for him.

"I can't take anymore!" Amid a rising crescendo of moans and gasps, they reached their climax and lay depleted across the desk.

"Wow, what a rush!" exclaimed Johnny.

"You were so good, I could eat you alive," she remarked coyly and rolled on top of him. Again, without any conception of time, they were entwined in a series of passionate kisses.

Lamar's truck entered the small lot in front of the station and parked. He stepped out and walked around to the passenger door. Sasha was pleased when he opened the door and lifted her from the cab onto the ground.

"Why Lamar, you can be a gentleman," she commented cheerfully.

"There are a lot of things I can be, my dear. Just wait and see."

Inside the station, Johnny and Paula were startled by the sound of doors slamming. They scurried off the desk and frantically collected their clothes. Johnny pushed Paula into the restroom and quickly closed the door behind them.

Lamar and Sasha entered the station and peered about for their friends.

"Hello!" shouted Lamar. "You in here, Johnny?" He waited a moment and then called out, "Paula! Anybody!"

Inside the restroom, Johnny and Paula scrambled into their uniforms. Paula panicked when she realized her thong was missing.

Johnny instructed her to go out the window and get some beer and he'd take care of it.

Meanwhile, Lamar opened the refrigerator and was disappointed that it was empty. "I guess he got busy or something," he surmised aloud. "No beers to be had."

"I'll go get some," offered Sasha. "You stay here and wait for them."

Lamar tossed her the keys to his truck. "Don't hurt my baby," he pleaded.

Sasha put her hands on her hips and stared in disbelief. "How dare you treat your truck like a woman?" she challenged him defensively.

Lamar smiled at her, pleased to have riled her for a change.

Sasha exited the station and climbed inside his truck. As she inserted the key into the ignition, she noticed Paula climbing out the bathroom window.

Paula took out her keys and rushed to her Toyota truck. Sasha called out to her and startled her. "You need a ride, Paula?"

Paula was startled and dropped the keys. "No. I, um … I'm good."

"Beer run?" asked Sasha playfully and she pulled alongside her.

"Uh-huh," Paula replied innocently.

"Get in. I'll take you."

Paula reluctantly got in Lamar's truck and closed the door. She felt uncomfortable, wondering what Sasha thought about her at that moment.

"You always climb out bathroom windows?" asked Sasha, giggling.

Paula blushed and fumbled for words.

"Don't sweat it. Are you and Johnny that close?"

"We're getting there. Johnny's got a few issues to get over yet."

"Yeah, I know all about them. Lamar's got the same problem."

Feeling they had much in common, the women discussed their men enthusiastically. They developed a trusting relationship on the short ride to the store and back, becoming good friends.

<hr>

Lamar turned on the TV set and watched the evening news. Johnny emerged from the restroom while tucking his shirt in. His pants zipper was down and his shirt tail stuck out over his ass.

"Lamar, you're early!" he exclaimed. "I wasn't expecting you so soon. It's only…" He looked at the clock, still stunned with embarrassment, and continued, "…six o'clock."

"I see that," remarked Lamar. "Next time I'll call first." He was amused by Johnny's appearance and asked, "What the hell happened to you?" With a broad grin across his face, he taunted, "You look like the victim of a prison rape."

"No, I, uh … It's a long story."

"Where's the beer? I'm parched."

Johnny looked sheepishly at the refrigerator as he fixed his shirt. "It's …, um, it's on the way. Paula just left."

Lamar picked up the files off the floor and laid them on the desk. "What happened to the neatness freak? You two have a brawl or something?"

"Let's go with 'or something'. She'll be back shortly."

Lamar noticed the pink thong on the desk and chuckled. "Sasha just left in my truck to pick up some beer, too."

Johnny blushed as he picked up the thong and tucked it in one of the desk drawers. "It's just a dust rag. Paula's always cleaning something."

"I see," he remarked, amused.

Johnny straightened his pants and sat in his chair. "So how are things going with Sasha?" he asked, red-faced with embarrassment.

"We're doing fine. Actually, better than I expected," replied Lamar confidently.

"Anything new and interesting going on in your world today?"

"Funny you should ask. I met Leon Bartok - Jo's ex."

Johnny's eyes widened with surprise. "What's he doing here?"

Lamar frowned at him. "Now what do you think he'd be doing here?"

"What did you tell him?"

"Nothing yet. He won't go away; I promise you that."

"What did he say?"

"Well, I warned him to keep his thugs out of the police station. He laughed."

"That motherfucker!" shouted Johnny who then holstered his gun around his waist. "I'll take care of this."

"No, not yet," Lamar ordered and grabbed Johnny by the arm. "He's dangerous. We'll talk more about it when the women return."

"I'll get with Ms. Fama about it," decided Johnny. "You know there's going to be trouble."

"Yeah, there is. I'm worried about Sasha. I don't want her getting hurt."

"So, what about you and Sasha?" Johnny quizzed. "Is this getting serious?"

Lamar sat down across from Johnny. "This whole dating thing isn't easy for me. It's getting better, though."

"It's not easy for me either but, so long as none of those creatures eats Paula, I'll be fine."

Lamar was surprised by Johnny's choice of words and commented, "And Paula's your girl, now?"

Johnny realized that he trapped himself and quickly countered, "Nah, just a good friend."

"Sure, she is. And your fly is open," Lamar teased.

Johnny knew his alibi was blown. He groaned and fixed his zipper. "Okay, you got me. We're seeing each other but with the understanding that it can't interfere with the job."

Lamar grinned at him. He was pleased that Johnny and Paula found common ground for a relationship. They discussed going on a hunting expedition to eradicate the mutated creatures and, more importantly, they needed to find out how to diffuse their situation with the animals.

Paula and Sasha returned and entered the station with a case of beer and two bags of chips. Both were in exceptionally good spirits.

Lamar was amused to see the women return together and asked, "You run into Paula at the beer store, Sasha?"

Sasha gave Paula a playful look and replied, "No, she was having a little trouble getting into her truck. The lock was stuck so I gave her a ride."

Lamar knew there was more to the story and peered at Johnny, who looked away, again embarrassed.

Paula anxiously opened four cans of beer and gave one to each of them. "How about a toast to good friends?" she suggested.

"That's a wonderful idea," replied Sasha. They toasted their new friendships and discussed childhood events.

Johnny stood and announced on a more serious note. "Paula noticed something unusual today. I think you need to hear this."

Johnny nodded to Paula for her to explain what she saw. Lamar and Sasha listened attentively as she revealed the strange behavior by the wolves, birds and deer earlier and then questioned what it could mean.

Sasha interjected, "They were running from something. It's their instincts taking over."

"But from what?" inquired Johnny.

Paula knew the answer but kept silent. She listened as Sasha continued, "What if the animals sense a sickness or something worse?"

"And your proof is…?" questioned Johnny.

"After all, they sense danger when there's a fire, don't they?"

"You might have a point there," responded Lamar.

"Then we should focus our investigation on the animals still here," suggested Johnny. "And Fama's crew could be in danger on the mountain."

"They might also have information that could be helpful," added Lamar. "I can't believe someone as sharp as Fama wouldn't notice anything strange about mutating animals."

"Paula and I will go up there, first thing in the morning," Johnny announced. "I'm sure I can coerce her into revealing anything she might know."

"Speaking of Fama, there are some things you need to know," Lamar explained to the women. He related what he learned about Jo Fama's background and the arrival of the three men in the Crown Victoria. The women were surprised by Bartok's visit with Lamar.

"Where are they now?" Johnny asked anxiously.

"I'm not sure. They reserved a room at the hotel for Leon and drove off. Paid in cash."

"So we go to the hotel," Johnny concluded.

"Nope. No one's been there yet, including Fama and her interns."

Sasha added, "At least not since …"

Lamar cut her off. "That's enough, girl."

Sasha smiled and said no more.

"Let me and Paula handle things on the mountain," Johnny instructed him. "You keep an eye on Leon and company."

"And what about me?" asked Sasha anxiously.

Lamar looked to Johnny for help. Johnny smiled and remarked, "Why not? She might be, you know …"

"Johnny, zip it!" warned Lamar.

The women were amused by Lamar's defensiveness.

"Something you boys want to share?" asked Paula.

"And I might be what?" Sasha quickly added.

Both Lamar and Johnny replied behind nervous smiles in unison, "Nothing."

The women stared at them suspiciously with folded arms. They wanted an explanation.

"I think it's time we get going," Lamar finally announced. "We've kept you two out way past your bedtime." He took Sasha by the arm and escorted her out of the station.

Paula waited patiently with her arms still folded. Johnny burst into laughter but refrained from comment on Lamar's earlier remark about her auditioning to be his wife.

When Lamar and Sasha returned to his house, Sasha refused to get out of the truck.

Lamar leaned on the passenger door. "What's wrong now?" he asked as he suppressed a yawn.

With a straight face, Sasha replied, "I'm not going anywhere until you tell me what Johnny was going to say about me before you interrupted him."

Lamar gazed at her innocently. "It was nothing. Honest, Honey."

Sasha got out of the truck and walked to her Miata.

"Hey, where are you going?" he asked worriedly.

"I don't like secrets and I thought we were past this." She opened the door and slid inside her vehicle.

Lamar grew frustrated and approached her. "All right," he relented. "We'll talk inside. I don't know why it's such a big deal."

"I'm serious, Lamar. I don't like it when you keep things from me."

Lamar placed his hands on his hips and became annoyed. "Why do you have to overreact every time something comes up?"

"Tell me the truth and I won't overreact," she insisted.

*Damn it*, Lamar thought to himself. *She can be a real pain in the ass!*

"All right, I'll tell you! Now can we please go inside? I'm tired."

Sasha suppressed a smile, contented. The two entered his house and went upstairs to the bedroom.

Lamar quickly undressed and fell on the bed. Sasha stood over him impatiently. "I'm waiting."

He covered his eyes and reluctantly related the comment he made about Paula auditioning to be Johnny's wife.

"So, what does that have to do with me?" she asked, curious.

"I guess Johnny was insinuating that you're auditioning to be my wife. There, you feel better?"

Sasha undressed and lay on the bed next to him. "And what if I were?"

Lamar was caught off guard by her question and answered cautiously, "I don't know. I never thought of it that way."

"What if I told you Paula really was?"

Lamar sat up and asked, "Where are we going with this?"

Sasha told him about Paula climbing out the bathroom window and their conversation. Lamar laughed hysterically and related Johnny's appearance as he left the restroom in the station.

"So, Lamar, you didn't answer my question. What if I was auditioning to be your wife, not today, but for the future?"

Lamar fumbled for the right words, but was at a loss. Sasha grew concerned by his hesitation and questioned him further, "Is there something wrong with that?"

Finally, Lamar replied, "No, not at all. It's just ...," he pondered his words before he spoke and then spit out the truth. "I never expected to meet someone special like you out here and I sure never expected you to fall in love with me like this. I'm flattered."

"Are you okay with that?" she inquired.

Lamar leaned forward and kissed her. "Of course, I am. Just pinch me so I know it's real."

"So back to the original question," she pressed.

Lamar rolled on top of her and kissed her hungrily. "You don't have to audition. Just give me some time."

"That's all I needed to here," she said confidently. They kissed again briefly. Lamar laid on his back and slept soundly.

Sasha lay awake for a while and wondered if she pushed him too hard. She wanted this relationship to work and it seemed that he did, too. Perhaps she was being too tough on him and should let things happen naturally. *Maybe I will soften up on him*, she thought and then slept.

Johnny held Paula's hand and walked her to her truck. She was pleased by the attention he gave but pondered what was so secretive about his near slip of the tongue earlier. They reached the truck and kissed passionately.

"Maybe we should try for a night cap?" Johnny suggested.

"Maybe, you'll get a little more than a night cap if you tell me what's going on between you and Lamar," she suggested. "Sounded serious to me."

Johnny blushed with embarrassment and looked away sheepishly. "It was nothing," he assured her.

"*Nothing* doesn't make a grown man turn red like that," she commented bluntly. She nibbled at his neck and unbuttoned the top two buttons on his shirt. When Johnny succumbed to her advances, she licked his chin, neck and mouth to ensure she had aroused him.

Johnny felt a surge of emotion and attempted to kiss her but Paula backed away. "What are you doing?" he asked, looking dumb-founded. "I thought we were …"

"Tell me, Johnny, or I'm going home," she demanded.

"It's not that big a deal, Paula," he blurted, frustrated and reached for her. "Why do you care so much?"

She pushed his hands away and answered, "Because I'm your partner and hopefully more than that."

Johnny sighed and relented. When he finished explaining about her cleaning and' auditioning' to be his wife, Paula was amused. She smiled and slid her hand down his shirt and rubbed his chest affectionately. "What's wrong with that?" she asked coyly. "You feel guilty or something?"

"Maybe, just a little," Johnny responded. "So, are we cool?"

"I guess it depends," she teased. "You didn't realize that you were auditioning for me as well, did you?"

"How am I auditioning?" he asked defensively.

"I rated your performance both in bed and out," she teased. "I want to make sure I'm not getting a dud."

"That's just wrong, Paula!" complained Johnny. "I never thought you'd be so superficial."

"A woman needs to know her man is fully functional before she commits to anything," she reminded him.

Johnny threw his arms up and laughed. "And women say men are pigs."

"We're all pigs," she teased. "Women just hide it better."

"But they're evil, too."

As she leaned with her back against her truck, she looked past Johnny and noticed two glowing red eyes in the trees. They sent chills down her spine.

"Not necessarily the evilest, Johnny." She pointed toward the trees. "We have company."

Johnny turned and saw the eyes as well. "What the hell is that?"

"It's not the coyote," she replied.

He drew his pistol but Paula grabbed his arm and stopped him. "Get in the truck," she ordered. "I have an idea."

Johnny crept around the truck to the passenger side and glanced at Paula. She nodded and they both scurried inside. Paula started the truck but kept the headlights off. She placed the vehicle in first gear and inched toward the glowing eyes.

The adult Ardonean stepped out of the trees and stood brazenly ahead of them. It spread its wings and hissed at them. Its plume stood upright on its head as it shrieked.

"Holy, shit, Paula! What the hell is that?"

"I think that's the creature in the photo you took."

Johnny got out of the truck and aimed his pistol at the alien. Three wolves with the same glowing eyes then emerged from the trees and stood in front of the alien.

"What the hell are they doing?" Paula uttered aloud.

"The wolves are protecting it!" exclaimed Johnny.

"Get back in the truck, now!" Paula ordered and turned on the headlights. The animals squealed and darted away from the light. Two bears crept behind the truck without their knowledge.

"What do you make of this?" asked Paula.

"They have a damn hierarchy! They're organized like an army!"

The rear of the truck rose, lurched forward and dropped violently. Paula broke her nose on the steering wheel and Johnny smacked his head off the dash. He leaned back in the seat, stunned.

The truck jolted them again. Paula peered in the rear-view mirror and saw the bears behind them. "Oh, shit!" she cried. "Hold on, Johnny!"

She shifted from first to third, cut the wheel hard to her left, and jammed her foot down on the gas pedal.

The rear wheels fired out gravel from under the tread and forced the bears to retreat away from them. The truck spun around, facing the highway, and sped off.

Blood streamed from Paula's nose as she frantically raced down the highway. "Are you alright, Johnny?"

"Just fine," he answered and shook his head in disbelief.

"How the hell do you explain this?" she asked cynically.

"You don't."

Johnny removed his uniform and delicately wiped the blood from Paula's face while she drove. "Are you okay?"

Paula touched her nose and grimaced. "Yeah, I hope you have a good nose doctor in town. I think I'm going to need one."

They chuckled briefly and then stared ahead at the road. Neither spoke until they reached Paula's apartment and parked on the street.

Paula deduced, "That creature is the key to this whole mess!"

"Yes, it is and the next time we see it, we're taking it down," Johnny announced, determined.

"The other animals responded to it," she remarked. "And those eyes: they scare the crap out of me!"

"We'll handle it. I promise."

Paula uttered, "This is my damn fault! I should have left things alone."

"Let's get some rest," he suggested. "We'll figure this out in the morning."

Paula wiped tears from her eyes and regained her composure. She appreciated Johnny's sympathy but she knew she was responsible for what was happening. She knew she caused the coyote to mutate but had no idea where the winged creature, the Ardonean, came from.

They staggered out of her pickup and up the walkway. Paula opened the door and paused. She looked back at her truck. The rear was smashed and twisted upward, indicative of a bent frame.

"Something wrong?" asked Johnny.

"Yeah," Paula answered smartly. "Who's gonna pay for my truck?"

Johnny glanced at the damaged vehicle and then at Paula. "Send Lamar the bill. He'll take care of it." They chuckled and entered the house.

Johnny lay on the couch with an ice pack against his forehead. He considered calling Lamar but there was no point in waking him now. It could wait until morning.

Paula washed in the bathroom. Her nose was swollen and disjointed. She removed her blood-stained shirt and tossed it in a laundry basket.

"Are you alright in there?" Johnny called to her.

"Just fine," she grumbled as she stared into the mirror. Guilt haunted her as she realized what she unleashed. She clamped her nose with both hands and took a deep breath. As she exhaled, she yanked on her nose until it straightened. The pain was excruciating and she burst into tears.

Johnny rushed into the bathroom and saw what she did. He held her close to him and escorted her into the living room. They sat together on the couch, nestled in silence, until they both slept.

When daylight shone through the curtains, they gazed at each other through sore eyes and wondered if the previous night's events really happened or if it was a bad dream. Paula stood and groaned as she stretched. She considered that she had no sexual urges since the incident last night and thought it strange. It crossed her mind that the creatures were manipulating them to behave aggressively toward each other in what should have been conflict instead of sexual arousal.

Johnny admired her toughness and pulled her down onto the couch. They lay together, speechless, until Paula broke the silence. "You know, Johnny, there is such a thing called a bed. Maybe next time we should try it."

Johnny cracked a smile. "Nothing would make me happier."

The next day, Lamar and Sasha conversed next to his truck at home when Paula drove up with Johnny in her vehicle. They were shocked at its condition and, even more so, the bruised condition of their friends. Paula and Johnny stepped out.

"What the hell happened?" asked Lamar frantically.

"We were … We were attacked by … animals at the station," stuttered Johnny.

Lamar was speechless as he didn't know if he was joking or serious.

"Some new creature, possibly an alien with wings," explained Paula. "Like the one in Johnny's picture."

"Three wolves stood by the creature to protect it," added Johnny. "The bears attacked us from behind. We never saw them coming."

"They're organized," Lamar remarked. "This is really bad." He became stone-faced as he considered what this meant. The animals are mutants and are organized just like the human mutants were in their prior battle. After a moment of contemplation, he ordered them, "Get to the station. We have to do something before this gets any worse."

Sasha interrupted and asked, "Are the two of you okay?"

"We're fine," responded Paula.

"You don't look it." She turned to Lamar for his input.

"On second thought, we're going to the hospital," Lamar instructed them. "Get in my truck now." He drove them to Clearview Hospital in the next town. They discussed the animal attack and compared the details to the earlier attacks on Graham's Mountain.

Lamar paced the emergency room lobby until Sasha stopped him. "Johnny's gonna need help – your help. This is bigger than a sheriff and deputy," she suggested.

"I know. I can't let them risk their lives like this."

Sasha frowned at him and explained, "Paula and I spoke after I caught her climbing out the window at the station. They make a good team but so did you and Johnny. Work with him. He needs you."

"I have a duty to get these people out of here before it's too late," he replied somberly.

Sasha put a finger to Lamar's lips for silence. "It's a small town. It's not even populated yet."

"But people's lives are at stake!" he fretted.

"You don't need a panic and no one's been attacked other than us. It's as if the creature knows who you and Johnny are."

"But Paula's a part of this, too. She's been targeted as well."

"This thing's intelligent, Lamar. We have to be smarter. I'm sure it has its reasons and we have to figure out what they are."

He considered her words and reluctantly agreed. She squeezed his hand and gave him confidence that things would be alright.

The door to the first examination room opened and a young doctor appeared. "You may see your friends now, Mayor."

Lamar and Sasha passed the doctor and entered the room. Johnny lay on his back on a gurney and Paula sat on a chair with her arms folded. Neither looked very happy.

"Well?" asked Lamar anxiously.

"Johnny's got a mild concussion," answered Paula. "He's got to stay off his feet for a few days."

"And what about you?" Sasha inquired.

"Broken nose. Nothing to worry about."

Lamar and Sasha felt badly for the two of them. They looked exhausted. The doctor released them to Lamar and together they returned to Parmissing Valley.

Later that day, Lamar stopped by Johnny's house to check on him. Johnny laid on the couch and watched cartoons.

"How are you feeling, Johnny?"

Johnny frowned and complained, "I have a killer headache."

Lamar pulled up a chair and sat near him. He stared at him with a concerned expression.

"I'll be fine, honest," Johnny assured him. "Just a bad bump on the noggin."

Lamar stood and paced the floor. "It's not that. I know you're tough."

Johnny sat up, looking concerned. "Come on, Lamar. Don't leave me hanging like this."

Lamar sat down again and stared somberly at Johnny. "I brought Paula in here to keep you company. I wanted the two of you to be good friends but…"

"We are good friends," Johnny interrupted. "She understands what I'm going through."

"What happens if she gets hurt or worse?" Lamar challenged him. "How will you handle that?"

"Lamar, I mean no disrespect to you but don't you think we have bigger problems than my relationship with Paula."

"I don't want either of you to get hurt."

"That's the risk I'm willing to take," Johnny explained. "I think I'm in love with her and I'm going to see this through."

Lamar stood and went to the door. He hesitated and looked back. "Just be prepared. Don't let your heart control your mind." He left the house and drove off.

Johnny was frustrated by Lamar's lack of support for him. A few days earlier, he was all for Johnny's relationship with Paula.

The phone rang three times before Johnny answered it. He was surprised to hear from the contract supervisor. The work crews were chased from the area by sickly animals as they attempted to install the fencing along the west side of the town. Johnny slammed the phone and covered his eyes in disgust. "I've failed again," he grumbled. "Can't even get a stupid fence built in this suck hole town."

◆

Paula and Sasha conversed at the police station over the previous night's assault. Paula wore her deputy's uniform; tan shirt with dark brown pants and boots.

Sasha wore denim jeans and a red blouse with sneakers. With her overwhelming desire to know more about the creatures and Paula's determination to fix the mess she believed she created, the two decided to work together without the support of the men.

After a lengthy discussion, Paula invited Sasha to visit the drill site with her for company. Jo was expecting her around four o'clock anyway.

"What about the animals?" asked Sasha uneasily.

Paula took two pistols from the cabinet and two boxes of ammo in addition to the sidearm she already wore on her hip. "I'm ready this time," she declared confidently. "Now it's me they have to fear."

The two of them left in the police SUV and drove to Graham's Mountain.

---

Lamar left his house and drove to the municipal building. The sky was overcast and the air, warm and humid. As he pulled into the lot on the side of the building, he noticed Adam's truck.

Right away, he suspected something was wrong. He stepped out of his truck with his pistol drawn. Warily, he crept along the driver's side from the rear. No one peered in the mirror at him so he grabbed the handle and yanked the door open.

Adam lay across the seat with blood spattered across his swollen face. His arms hung awkwardly as if broken. Pinned to his blood-stained shirt was a note: I told you this could be painful if you resist. I expect you'll cooperate now, Mayor. See you soon."

Lamar quickly called 911 and waited for the ambulance to arrive from Clearfield. He checked Adam for a pulse on his wrist and neck but there was none.

"Motherfuckers!" cried Lamar. He punched the side of the truck and paced like a wild man. When he stopped, he noticed a bag from Radio Shack on the floor of the truck. For some odd reason, he took the bag and tucked it in his pocket.

# CHAPTER VI

## THE SITE

When the women arrived at the drill site, Jo sat on the cab atop the drill assembly, wearing dark glasses and a hardhat. She operated the controls and directed the drill tip into the mountainside.

The lasers surrounding the bore emitted an eerie glow as the drill cut deeper into the rocky strata. The ground vibrated faintly and the gear assembly churned like a freight train. Jo was in her glory as she operated the machinery like a maestro over her symphony.

Paula and Sasha watched the drilling evolution from their vehicle. Once Jo noticed them, she shut down the drill and hopped off. Paula and Sasha took that as a cue to meet with her.

Jo had a concerned expression on her face as she marched with a sense of purpose toward them. She was muscular for a woman while she still maintained her femininity, not at all like the feminine figures of Paula and Sasha.

The three women shook hands and, after brief introductions, Jo revealed that both her interns had gone missing. She also had a cynical comment for Paula about her two black eyes.

During the questioning, Jo admitted that Adam missed his friends at home and talked about returning when the project was over. Gino, on the other hand, had invested some of his own money in the operation. He left the site for the hotel the night before and never came back.

"Did you check their hotel rooms?" inquired Paula.

"Of course, I did," replied Jo. "We shared the same room."

"Any luggage?" asked Paula.

"That's the strange thing. Their belongings are still there."

Paula scribbled down notes on their conversation. She informed Jo that they'd do a thorough search of the area immediately.

Paula informed Jo of Leon's presence in town along with three of his thugs. Then she recalled the creatures with the red eyes and asked, "Ms. Fama, have you noticed anything strange out here with the wildlife?"

Jo took off her dark sun glasses and glared at Paula. "Strange doesn't begin to describe this place."

Paula and Sasha waited anxiously for clarification. Jo eyed the trees and explained, "Things are awfully quiet around here – too quiet."

"So, you haven't seen anything strange?" she inquired once more.

"There's a mangy looking coyote out here that looks like death warmed over. It drops by from time to time and watches me."

Paula grew nervous and Jo picked up on it immediately. "Something I should know about this animal, Deputy?"

Paula fumbled for an answer but had none. Sasha jumped into the conversation and explained, "The animal has a rare form of rabies. If you see it, you may want to steer clear of it."

"And what do you know about rabies, Ms. Bell?"

"I'm an animal psychologist," she lied. "I study their behaviors."

Jo folded her arms in disbelief and asked, "How do you explain the stillness out here?"

Sasha was now on the defensive. "What do you mean?"

Jo pointed to the trees around them. "Listen. Listen good. There are no birds chirping. There are no squirrels or other wildlife in the area."

"Perhaps the vibrations from the drill drove them off," suggested Paula.

"The coyote is the least of my concerns. It keeps its distance and just watches."

"And what is your main concern?"

"Something big flies by from time to time and scares it away. I hear it in the trees."

"Probably an eagle looking for prey," suggested Sasha.

Jo grew tired of their excuses and returned to the drill. She climbed up into the cab and peered back at them. "I know there's something you aren't telling me about this place," she challenged.

Paula replied sheepishly, "Only theories. We'll let you know when we have something substantial to go on. If you see the flying creature, put it down. It could be dangerous."

"I'll put it down alright. You just find out what happened to my interns. Oh, and keep Leon away from me. I can't guarantee his safety if I see him."

Paula nodded for Sasha to get in the SUV. Jo gave her the creeps as she eyeballed them while starting the drill.

As the girls drove off, Paula breathed a sigh of relief. "That woman scares me more than any of those damn animals," she complained.

"Fama's sharp," replied Sasha. "She's not gonna let this go for long."

Paula drove the police SUV along the mountain road and searched down the embankment for any sign of Adam or Gino's vehicles. Sasha scanned the rising mountainside on her right. Halfway down the mountain, Paula spotted a Toyota Celica wedged between two trees at the bottom of the mountain.

"I see something down there!" Paula exclaimed and parked the truck.

Sasha noticed something blue about twenty feet off the road on her side. "I see something, too. It could be a shred of clothing."

The women warily stepped out of the vehicle and stared down the mountainside at the car.

"Hey, you have three pistols," complained Sasha.

"Yeah, two are for backup since Johnny's not here."

Sasha folded her arms and stared at Paula. Finally, Paula relented and handed one to her.

"You know how to use one of these?" she asked.

"Of course, I do. I grew up with three brothers. One was a cop."

Paula thought that was interesting. "Did he, by chance, know Lamar?"

Sasha froze as she realized she just left herself open for speculation. "A lot of cops know each other from conventions and investigations," she replied unconvincingly. "They may have crossed paths."

Paula studied her eyes and knew she was lying. "So how did you meet Lamar - through your brother?"

Sasha grew frustrated and relented. "All right, I'll tell you. Lamar worked with my brother years ago. I always had a crush on him. This was my dream to find him one day and hope that we could get together."

Paula was amused and inquired, "So you never dated before?"

"No, just one beautiful kiss that left me wondering 'what if'."

"What stopped you?" Paula asked.

"My family. Lamar was close with them and didn't want to date little sister and risk upsetting them."

Paula smiled at her. "So little sister is on the prowl."

"Damn right, girl," replied Sasha proudly. "Just like you."

"It's okay, Sasha. I like that in you. We are both trying to get the man we want. It's kind of romantic knowing how you came all this way for him."

"Yeah, I guess it is," replied Sasha half-heartedly.

Her response made Paula wonder if there wasn't more to the story that saddened her. Then Paula asked her if she believed in the power of persuasion. Sasha was taken aback by it and questioned why she would ask that.

Paula revealed that she felt 'persuaded' to do things that she normally wouldn't do. She mentioned how aggressive she was in her pursuit of Johnny. It was so unlike her. Sasha suggested that it was just her release of pent-up emotions and nothing to worry about. Then she considered her behavior with Lamar and wondered if there was such a thing and if the men somehow had this power from their alien encounters in the past.

Paula turned her attention back to work and inspected the foliage at the side of the road. There were faint tire tracks - no skid marks, just tracks. She looked back at the road and saw brown liquid pooled in the middle of the road.

"If I didn't know better, I'd say this poor fellow hit something and drove off the road," Paula theorized. "He never applied his breaks so he must have been surprised."

"Maybe we should call Lamar for backup."

"Not yet. Come with me."

First, they inspected the shred of clothing up the slope. It was part of a man's t-shirt. There was no sign of blood on it although it had traces of brown oil on it.

"What is that stain - motor oil?" asked Sasha.

Paula sniffed it and winced at the odor. "Nope, not motor oil. Smells like rotten meat." Then she recalled the odor of rotten meat from the freezer at the police station. It quickly reminded her of what they could be dealing with – alien life forms.

"It looks like the same stuff in the road," Sasha commented.

The women carefully hiked down the mountainside to the wrecked vehicle. As they drew closer, they noticed that the driver's side door was missing.

The two women glanced nervously at each other as they approached the vehicle. Inside, the steering wheel and windshield were streaked with blood.

Branches snapped further down the mountainside and startled them. Sasha pressed Paula about returning to the truck but she refused.

Paula opened the glove compartment and removed a packet of forms. She scanned through the pages of a contract and found that Gino rented the car for a two-month term.

"This is one of Jo's vehicles, isn't it?" asked Sasha.

"Yeah. Gino was the driver."

Sasha discovered animal prints in the soft soil that lead to and from the car. The increased depth of the prints leading away indicated that it carried something or someone away, perhaps the driver. "See this, Paula," she whispered and pointed to the tracks.

Paula studied them and then searched the trees. "We have to get out of here now, Sasha," she announced, concerned. "Things have just gotten a whole lot worse."

"Finally," blurted Sasha.

The sound of snapping branches and breaking limbs was closer now. Chills ran down their spines as fear took over. The women climbed frantically up the mountainside, pushing through tree limbs in a mad dash to flee their invisible pursuers.

"We have another alien outbreak, don't we?" asked Sasha.

"This is much worse," replied Paula somberly.

They reached the vehicle and locked themselves inside. One of the Ardoneans settled on the road ahead of the SUV and stared at them with its glowing red eyes.

"Jesus!" exclaimed Sasha. "What is that, Paula?"

"Meet the alien. And now, I'm gonna kill that son of a bitch!" shouted Paula as she opened her door.

"No!" cried Sasha. "It's a trap!"

Suddenly three wolves darted from the trees near Paula. Sasha grabbed her by the shoulders and yanked her back inside the truck. Paula pulled her legs inside just as the first wolf crashed against the door and inadvertently forced it closed.

The wolves snarled through the glass at them and jumped all over the vehicle. Foam flew from their mouths onto the glass and smeared as their paws raked against the windshield and windows.

Paula broke into tears as she started the truck. Sasha trembled and slid to the middle of the seat away from her window. One of the wolves attempted to crawl in through the broken back window but Paula jerked the vehicle in reverse and the wolf fell off the back of the truck.

The truck sped forward, knocking the other wolves to the ground. They chased the SUV as it sped down the mountain road. At the intersection of the dirt trail and the stone road, an elderly homeless man stood motionless in front of them with vacant eyes like a zombie.

"Run it over, Paula! It's not human," shouted Sasha.

Paula closed her eyes and accelerated. When she struck him, his body deflected over the hood and bounced off the windshield. His head struck the glass and shattered it. She yanked the wheel left and right until the body fell to the side of the rode.

When they reached the main highway at the bottom of the mountain, Paula parked on the shoulder of the road and cried. Sasha put her arms around her. She trembled badly but fought back the tears.

Paula looked sadly at Sasha and revealed, "This is my fault. It started all over again." She and leaned on Sasha's shoulder and cried.

Soon after, they regained their composure and sat back in their seats in silence, contemplating all that just happened.

"Any idea how to stop this?" asked Sasha uneasily.

"It started with the alien tongue in the freezer. I tossed it in the trash and that friggin' coyote got to it."

"What if we kill the coyote?" questioned Sasha. "Will this end?"

"I don't know. There are still the other animals and that winged creature to deal with."

"Then we'd better have a plan for them."

"Johnny's gonna kill me for this. I was supposed to help him forget about this alien stuff, not rekindle it."

Sasha placed her hand on Paula's shoulder. "Let's be smart about this," she urged. "We'll meet with the men and figure something out."

"But now there are humans involved," Paula fretted. "That changes everything."

"Not necessarily," responded Sasha. "It still seems to me like the winged creature's in charge, not the coyote."

"And that's what complicates things. The coyote might be on our side."

"What?" exclaimed Sasha. "How would you know that?"

"Deductive reasoning," she lied. "It seems like the coyote and the alien don't like each other."

"That's really odd," Sasha remarked suspiciously.

Paula knew Sasha wasn't going to be fooled for long about her and Johnny and their peculiar knowledge of the creatures. "Yeah, it's real frigging odd. What else can I tell you?" she replied, baffled by the turn of events.

During the ride back to town, Sasha called Lamar and related the story. He instructed them to meet at Johnny's place as soon as possible.

Paula trembled as she drove down the highway. She hated knowing that she nearly became a victim because her emotions took over and clouded her judgment. "Thank you for saving my life," she said gratefully to Sasha. "I should have seen that coming."

"I couldn't lose my good friend like that," said Sasha, smiling. "Besides, I need someone to help me keep those two goof balls in line." The girls chuckled and the tension eased.

✦

Lamar arrived at Johnny's home and beat on the door repeatedly. Johnny opened the door and grumbled, "What the hell's wrong with you? I was asleep."

"You almost lost a deputy and I almost lost my girl," he replied and pushed his way inside. "And we have a murder on our hands."

Johnny was confused by his remarks and followed him into the kitchen. "You want to tell me what's going on. I don't have a crystal ball, you know."

"I found Jo's intern Adam in his truck … in my parking lot."

"What did he want?"

"Nothing. He was dead."

Johnny's eyes widened with surprise. "What the hell happened?"

"Bartok and his boys. They had a little message for me."

"Let me guess – play ball or else."

"Yeah, that about sums it up. They want Jo's location and are getting very impatient."

"Apparently, Jo hasn't returned to the hotel at night."

"She's a smart woman," remarked Lamar. "She knew they'd come."

Johnny paced the floor nervously and informed Lamar about the fencing supervisor's call. The two men were baffled about the situation.

Johnny surmised, "I'd better get over to the hospital and handle the arrangements." He attempted to pass Lamar and leave the kitchen but Lamar blocked his path.

"Relax," ordered Lamar. "I handled it."

"But we need to find them and arrest them for Adam's murder."

"Nope. They'll find us and I don't think we'll be arresting them."

Johnny sat down at the table. He knew what Lamar was insinuating. There would be no prisoners. "What happened to the girls?" he asked apprehensively.

"They're fine now. When they get here, they'll tell us all about it."

Johnny opened the cabinet over the sink and took out a bottle of scotch. He set it on the table along with four glasses.

"Good choice," remarked Lamar. "I think we're going to need it."

Johnny poured scotch into two of the glasses and sat across from Lamar. "You're sure they're okay?" he asked, concerned.

"Yes, by the grace of God," Lamar said somberly. "This thing has gotten too big already. We have to do something soon."

Johnny rubbed his forehead in frustration and drank from his glass. Lamar eyed his glass and did the same.

The SUV parked in the driveway and the doors slammed shut. A moment later, Paula and Sasha barged into Johnny's house. When they appeared in the kitchen doorway, Johnny rushed to Paula and hugged her.

Lamar stood and gazed at Sasha. She burst into tears and ran to him. The women related the details of the attack as they sat around the table.

"What about Jo?" inquired Paula. "Maybe she shouldn't be up there without protection."

"She's got to get out of there now," Johnny announced.

"I'll call her," Lamar replied with a sense of urgency. When he attempted to contact Jo on his phone, there was no answer. He lowered the phone and said somberly, "It may already be too late."

After much discussion, they determined that the vagrant was only a follower, much like the mutants. Gino was probably turned just like him.

The coyote's intelligence was limited by its brain size and that gave them the advantage, if there was one to be had. The alien was a new variable and they had no idea what to expect. Paula suspected that the creature had the ability to block their telepathy but she couldn't prove it yet.

They considered Jo's observation about the silence in the trees and Sasha's earlier comment about animals sensing fear and sickness.

"The animals fleeing the area means that there is a limited pool of creatures to deal with on the mountain and less likelihood of the creatures infecting many more."

"That could also explain the vagrant," added Sasha. "The problem is big but appears to be contained so far."

Paula expressed her frustration for not getting off a shot at the alien. They did learn from her experience that the animals were crafty and would work together as an army of sorts.

After each had a glass of scotch, they departed Johnny's place and returned to the police station.

They paused and inspected the door. There was no sign of forced entry through the new door jamb and lockset. Paula took the lead and entered first. She turned on the lights and did a quick search of the station. There was no sign of anyone or anything in the station. Half the windows had been replaced while the three front ones were still boarded up.

Quickly, she and Johnny gathered additional arms and ammo. Lamar and Sasha stood watch over the parking lot and their vehicles.

When she and Johnny returned to the parking lot, Paula suggested, "Suppose we return to the cabin. The creatures will likely come for us. When they do, we take them down."

"She's got a point," replied Lamar. "Or maybe even Leon and company will show up. Two for one."

"First, we find Jo," Johnny instructed them. "Then we'll go to the cabin." Everyone agreed with him.

Paula hosed the windshield of the SUV off, removing the dried foam and spittle from the wolves.

Johnny placed his arm around her waist and kidded, "Still the clean freak, I see."

Paula turned off the hose and dropped it to the ground. She turned to Johnny and nestled against his chest. "Now I understand what you went through. I am so sorry."

Johnny brushed her blond hair from her eyes and gazed at her confidently. "We beat them once. We'll do it again."

Paula burst into tears. "I hope you're right. This is nothing like I imagined."

Lamar and Sasha sat on the steps nearby, holding hands. "Sasha, I asked you once already not to go out there without me," he reminded her.

"I'm sorry. I couldn't let Paula go by herself."

"Well, from here on out, we stick together. Understand?"

"I don't think that will be a problem."

Lamar checked his watch and frowned. "It's six-thirty. I think we're going to need every minute of daylight to get prepared, so let's get going."

Everyone agreed and promptly climbed inside their respective vehicles.

The police SUV and Lamar's pickup truck raced down the highway and turned up the winding road to Graham's Mountain. After the first bend, Paula instructed Johnny to stop the vehicle. She got out with her pistol drawn and searched alongside the road. Johnny and Lamar joined her.

"This is where we hit the vagrant," Paula explained, baffled by the absence of a body. "He fell off the truck right here."

Lamar and Johnny did a quick inspection of the area and concluded either the guy left on his own, which was unlikely, or he was carried away by someone or something. They returned to their vehicles and continued to the cabin.

"There was a body on the road when we left," Sasha insisted. "I swear, Lamar. It was there."

"I don't doubt it. These things are smarter than the others we faced. They probably have a lair just like before and we'll have to find it."

"Like before?" questioned Sasha with mock surprise.

Lamar realized that he now admitted the alien story was real. "Okay, like before," he relented. "Now you know it was true. There. I said it. Are you happy?"

Sasha placed her hand on his thigh and smiled. "I always knew you were a hero, even if you wouldn't tell me."

Lamar was humbled by her high opinion of him. She didn't see him when he cowered inside the station in fear after his first encounter. It took a while before he gained the courage to fight against the creatures. Now, he'd have to do it again. He hoped that Johnny would be up to the task as well.

Both vehicles parked at the drill site. The Escalade and the U-Haul truck were both there. The drill assembly was idle and Jo was nowhere to be found. Lamar called out for her several times but there was no answer.

Johnny and Paula investigated the hole that Jo's machine bore into the mountain. It was twenty feet into the rock already.

Lamar and Sasha searched the area for any sign of a struggle or bloodshed. He again called Jo on his cell phone but there was still no answer. He scanned the mountainside around them and considered what escape route Jo would have used if she, in fact, escaped. Instinctively, he tossed the bag from Adam's truck inside the operator's cab on the drill assembly.

Johnny checked the inside of the Escalade and found only the file with the permits.

"Any sign of a gun in there?" inquired Lamar.

Johnny opened the glove compartment and replied, "None."

"That's good. She's armed."

They gathered at the edge of the clearing and looked down the mountainside.

"These things have a lair," Johnny commented. "We need to find it."

"I was thinking the same thing," responded Lamar. "What do you want to do, Sheriff? It's your game."

Johnny froze when he realized that Lamar ceded to him all responsibility to handle the situation.

"You can do this, Johnny," Paula encouraged him. "I believe in you."

Sasha clung to Lamar's arm, speechless over their situation.

"All right, let's find these bastards and kill them!" shouted Johnny. "Lamar, you and Sasha search the peak. Paula and I will move laterally around the mountain. I'm sure they'd want a good vantage point to see us coming."

Lamar agreed and cautioned them against potential traps by the creatures. Johnny instructed them to check in with him every ten minutes and established how far they would search before returning to the site.

Johnny and Paula set out to the west across the rocky slope. The two moved steadily toward a cliff on the far side of the mountain.

Lamar and Sasha followed a natural path diagonally up the side of the mountain toward the peak. They stopped randomly to check for any pursuers, but none came.

"I don't like this," complained Lamar.

"The silence is really disturbing," Sasha remarked.

"I mean having you out here with me," he clarified to her. "I don't want you getting hurt."

Sasha removed Paula's pistol from her jeans and displayed it to Lamar. "Don't worry about me. I've got your back."

Lamar rolled his eyes in disbelief and pressed on. Sasha enjoyed the adventure, although the earlier attacks by the animals left her edgy. She felt safe with Lamar by her side and a pistol in her hand.

After a half hour of steady ascent, they paused for a rest at the edge of a cliff, overlooking the entire valley. The view was beautiful from there and created a calming effect on the two of them. "It's so beautiful," commented Sasha.

Lamar put his arm around her waist and pulled her close to him. "Makes our problems seem so far away. Doesn't it?"

Sasha kissed his cheek and rested her head on his shoulder. When they sat down to rest, Lamar called Johnny to check in. Things were quiet at their end as well. They took in the fading rays of the sunset before heading back.

"I don't think the creatures strayed too far from the site," surmised Lamar. "And if they have a lair, they'll want to protect it."

"Do you think they could be tracking us?" Sasha questioned.

"It's really strange that we haven't seen any sign of them yet."

Lamar thought he heard something in the trees and tensed up. He motioned for Sasha to retreat behind a boulder with him and keep quiet. A wounded bear emerged from the trees and sniffed at the air.

"Oh, shit," muttered Lamar.

The bear turned toward them and growled. Then it stood upright and snarled. Lamar and Sasha were appalled at the mutated face on the bear and its glowing red eyes.

Lamar stepped into the open and aimed his pistol at the bear's head. The bear stalked him, still walking upright on two legs.

"Shoot it!" shouted Sasha.

"Not yet," he replied calmly and backed along the edge of the cliff. "I have one shot to kill it or else."

The bear stomped clumsily toward him. Lamar broke into a sweat as his finger pressed slightly on the trigger, ready to fire.

A shot rang out from the trees and startled them. Part of the bear's head exploded and it fell off the cliff. Lamar and Sasha trembled as Jo stepped out of the trees.

"You two alright?" she asked nonchalantly.

Lamar stowed his gun and breathed a sigh of relief. "You scared the living daylights out of me, Jo!"

"That bastard chewed through my power cable. It's the damned ugliest creature I ever saw."

Sasha stepped out from behind the boulder and stood by Lamar.

Jo was amused to see her with him. "Well, what does the animal behaviorist think about that?"

Lamar glanced at her and wondered what that was about. Sasha fumbled for an explanation but had none.

Jo wasn't surprised as she knew Sasha's story was bogus. She questioned Lamar about the creatures and what he thought was happening. Reluctantly, he revealed the incident with the alien tongue so long as she swore not to talk about it to anyone.

"Do we know how many creatures are involved?" Jo asked.

"Not really," answered Lamar. "It appears that most of the animals unaffected by this alien outbreak have fled the area. The affected ones appear to be organized into some kind of army."

"And the coyote is the leader I presume," she commented, glancing at Sasha.

Sasha looked sheepishly at the ground. "No, but it's involved somehow," she replied. "Everything started when it dug the tongue out of the trash."

"What do you mean everything?"

Lamar grew curious over Jo's questions to Sasha. He felt compelled to speak up as she was reluctant to say any more until he did so.

"There's a … um …flying alien," he mentioned. "It attacked me and Paula earlier but we escaped."

"A flying fuckin' alien! That's just great!" bellowed Jo. "And you were going to tell me when?"

"Easy," said Lamar calmly. "We still don't know what the hell we're dealing with."

"Obviously it's not human! And what about my ex and his thugs? Any idea what they're doing?"

"Probably on their way up here," he replied and then informed her that they killed Adam.

Jo fumed as she stood at the edge of the cliff and stared across the valley. Lamar and Sasha glanced at each other and wondered what she was thinking.

"I knew it was just a matter of time before they'd find me. I left false notes indicating six other locations on different mountains for my drilling operation. I assume they figured out that I was jerking them around."

"Well, it's a good thing you haven't been at the hotel. Leon's got a room there."

"I prefer the outdoors myself," she commented. "Besides, you all are the only ones who knew where to find me."

"Yeah, and he knows that. We've already met over this."

Johnny and Paula burst out of the trees. "We heard shooting!" exclaimed Johnny.

Jo stood with her hands on her hips and her pistol in hand. Lamar nodded toward her and responded, "Jo took out one of the bears."

Johnny and Paula were impressed and browsed over the edge of the cliff at the bear carcass far below.

"Those things die hard, don't they?" Johnny quipped.

"And it's time for a few more to go the same way," she declared. "I think it's time to go on the offensive. That cable's gonna set me back a few days and I just lost a good friend."

Johnny glanced at Lamar and then at Jo. Lamar returned a nod so Johnny understood to say no more about Adam's death.

"Why would the bear attack your cables?" asked Sasha curiously.

"Maybe they don't want us to have access to the cavern," Jo guessed.

"Then there's got to be another way in," Paula surmised. "All we have to do is find it and then we'll have them trapped."

Jo's eyes lit up excitedly. "And maybe I don't need to drill this stinking tunnel after all! Screw the cable, let's find the entrance."

"We don't know that for sure," cautioned Lamar. "Let's be methodical about this."

"Then we should go back to the cabin," Johnny decided. "Let them come to us."

"And we'll be ready," Lamar added.

"It's nearly dark. Are you sure it's a good idea staying up here for the night?" asked Sasha, nervous over the idea.

"We don't have much choice. The longer we wait, the more dangerous they become."

Everyone agreed and climbed into their vehicles. Jo followed Lamar's truck in her Escalade while Johnny and Paula drove in the battered police SUV.

Johnny vented on Paula for going up on the mountain with only Sasha for backup. She became upset with him and tried to make him understand that she had to fix this 'problem' that she caused. Johnny refused to listen and warned her about going anywhere without telling him. Tensions flared and they stopped talking to each other.

In Lamar's truck, he and Sasha argued about following orders and not venturing out on her own. Sasha was adamant about not being controlled, but agreed she would stay by his side in the future.

When they arrived at the cabin, darkness set in and the only light was from their headlights. Lamar and Sasha collected wood from the perimeter and started a fire in front of the cabin. Johnny and Paula searched the cabin for intruders and then boarded up the windows using wood pieces broken off of a bureau, with only a small slot for peering out. They turned on the gas and the generator, lighting up the inside of the cabin.

Jo retrieved a rope from Johnny's vehicle and tied it from post to post, across the porch about six inches off the ground. She then collected the empty beer bottles from inside the cabin and spaced them across the porch, just behind the rope. She then placed flares with white caps on them for easy targeting randomly around the outside of the cabin just off the porch.

Lamar admired her handy work and commented, "Looks like you've done this before."

"Spend a little time in Africa and you'll learn a lot of survival tricks."

"No kidding. What was your worst nemesis there?" he asked, curious.

"Someone killed a young lion. The mother was really pissed and wanted payback. Every night for a week, she got one of our people. It was us or her."

"How'd you get her?"

"Dug a hole at each entrance to the camp. It was a long shot that she'd fall into one of them."

"Did she?"

"Nope, but I was waiting when she circled around the unlit side of the camp. Put two holes in her head."

"And that stopped her?"

"Nope." Jo lifted her shirt and revealed an ugly set of scars in her side. "The bitch got to me before I put a bullet through her head with my .45."

"I guess I owe you a lot more respect than I had before."

"It's all business," she said stoically and then looked sadly into Lamar's eyes. "If you don't mind, Mayor, I need to know how Adam died."

Lamar placed his hands in his pockets and explained somberly, "He was beaten to death. I found him in his truck outside my building."

Jo drew close to him and inquired, "Why was his truck outside your building?"

Lamar felt somewhat responsible for Adam's death and floundered for the right words. "I, um … Leon came to see me. He wanted your location and I told him I didn't know yet. He warned me that this could be painful if I didn't cooperate."

Jo looked down at the ground sadly. "I see."

"I'm really sorry, Jo. I swear they'll pay for what they did to him."

"Oh, they'll pay all right. Now let's go kick some ass so I can get back to work."

"I'm glad to have you on our side," he complimented her. He was relieved that she understood the situation he was in. With that behind them, the two continued to toss wood on the fire and said nothing more on the matter.

Sasha watched from a distance and felt left out. Lamar was angry with her and didn't trust her to handle herself. Jo won him over with her scars and her lion story. Now, she needed to do something to earn his respect and trust as well.

Once they finished their tasks, they moved the vehicles onto the access road so the front of the cabin was unimpeded and then they retreated inside.

Paula and Sasha slid an old sofa in front of the door.

Lamar, Johnny and Jo each took a window on different sides of the cabin and peered out.

After a few hours, they grew weary and took turns napping. The fire out front was reduced to dying embers by midnight. Lamar and Johnny were asleep and the women had the watch.

Outside the cabin, three wolves approached. They sniffed at the ground suspiciously and eyed the cabin. Jo noticed and snapped her fingers. She indicated to Paula and Sasha that something was out there.

The vagrant's corpse appeared near Lamar's truck and deflated one of the front tires, without their knowledge.

Sasha woke Lamar and Johnny. Before they reached one of the windows, the sound of bottles rolling on the porch startled them.

Jo fired a shot at one of the flares near the fire. When it ignited, the wolves were in clear view. Jo fired three shots and killed one of them. The others fled into the trees.

Lamar and Johnny awoke. Lamar opened the door with his pistols drawn and stepped out on the porch. Jo fired a shot at another flare and ignited it. Lamar jumped and protested, "Don't do that without warning me!"

Jo smiled and suggested, "You might want to take a look by your truck."

Lamar noticed a man's silhouette and took aim at him. "Come out with your hands up," he shouted.

"You're kidding me, Mayor!" groaned Jo. "He's a frickin' zombie." She fired two shots at the vagrant but he disappeared behind the truck.

Sasha felt a degree of satisfaction that Lamar didn't know everything. She and Paula inspected the dead wolf on the porch while the others searched for the vagrant near the vehicles. Frustration set in when they failed to find him.

"I know I got him twice in the chest!" Jo complained.

"Perhaps we have to aim for the head like before," Johnny suggested.

Lamar cringed as he recalled their previous encounters with mutants. It took a head shot, usually pretty messy, to put them down permanently. "Then, I guess it's time for heads to roll," Lamar responded cynically.

Suddenly, the sky was filled with the sound of hundreds of crows. Just as they retreated to the porch, the shattering of wood from the rear window alerted them that something breached the rear window of the cabin.

The crows circled above in growing numbers.

"Get to the trucks, fast!" ordered Lamar.

They raced to the vehicles and piled in. One of the bears emerged from the cabin entrance and charged at them.

Jo leaned out the window of her Escalade and fired at one of the flares. It ignited and frightened the bear. She fired a second shot at another flare near the bear's rear leg. The heat from the flare singed its fur and it staggered sideways. She leaped out of the truck and approached the bear with her .45 aimed at its head.

"Get back here!" ordered Lamar from his truck.

"I got this," Jo replied confidently as the bear stalked her.

"Damn her!" groaned Lamar. Fearful, Sasha gripped his arm and watched out the rear window.

Johnny and Paula watched out the back window of the SUV in horror. "What the hell is she doing?" Johnny fretted.

"We have to do something," Paula blurted, nearly in a panic.

"No kidding!" he yelled frustratedly.

Jo stopped and calmly aimed at the bear's head. It snarled and fled into the forest.

"Come on, you big puss!" she taunted. When she lowered the gun, two wolves darted from the trees and lunged at her. Jo shoved the gun in the first wolf's mouth but before she could fire, the second wolf pounced on her.

Paula hurried out of the SUV with a flashlight and pistol. She used the light to target the wolves and fired.

"Get back in the truck!" ordered Johnny, horrified.

The bear returned from the trees and charged at Paula from behind.

"Jesus! Look out Paula!" Johnny shouted.

The bear knocked her down and latched onto her leg with its powerful jaws.

Johnny got out and fired three shots at the bear. He pulled the trigger twice more but nothing happened. "Damn it!" he shouted and replaced the empty magazine in his pistol, while the bear dragged Paula screaming into the woods.

Lamar leaped from his truck and fired at the wolves. He wounded them but they escaped, dragging Jo off into the forest. She desperately held the gun in the wolf's mouth but the wolf's fangs blocked her from pulling the trigger.

"Stay here," Lamar warned Sasha.

"Be careful," she pleaded.

Despite its wounds, the bear dragged Paula away from the cabin. She cried frantically, "Help me, Johnny!"

Lamar grabbed Johnny and struggled to hold onto him. When Johnny elbowed him, Lamar tackled him and punched him in the mouth. "It's a trap, Johnny! If you go after her, they'll have you, too."

Johnny burst into tears. "We have to save her."

The coyote stood by the side of the cabin and stared at them with pity in its eyes. Lamar fired a shot at it but missed.

"All right, genius," Johnny shouted cynically. "Now what do we do?"

"We get the hell out of here until daylight."

Johnny stared at the trees where Paula vanished and reluctantly retreated to his vehicle. Tears streamed down his cheeks as he feared what was happening to her.

As Lamar reached his truck, the crows swarmed around the vehicles and blocked their visibility. The noise was deafening.

Sasha sat quietly with tears streaming down her cheeks. Lamar bit his lip and thoughts raced through his head. *How does this relate to what happened during the first incursion? Why did they take them alive?* Somewhere there had to be a clue and he was determined to find it. The sound of the crows was maddening and distracted him from focusing on details.

"Please, Lamar, make them stop," begged Sasha. "I can't take it."

"Just hold on," he urged her.

————— ·•✦••· —————

Paula tried frantically to aim her pistol at the bear as her body bounced off rocks and tree limbs. The bear shook her by the leg like a ragdoll as it retreated through the trees toward their cave. She gave up hope when her head struck a rock and she lost her pistol.

Three coyotes darted from the trees and leaped on the bear's back. They gnawed ravenously at the thick fur on the bear's neck until red blotches appeared. The bear released its hold on Paula and stood erect, howling in anger.

Paula heard the bear's howls and realized that she was free from its grip. She turned her head sideways and pointed the flashlight. Her pistol was just a short distance away.

The bear rammed its shoulder into a tree and threw the coyotes off. Paula crawled to her pistol and retrieved it. She turned in time to see the bear maul two of the coyotes and pin the third, the sickly one, with one of its paws. Before it could strike, Paula heard a voice in her head. "Please, help me!"

She struggled to her knees and fired three shots into the bear's head. The bear staggered backwards and fell to the ground, mortally wounded.

Two wolves dragged Jo from the trees toward the cave. One released its hold on her arm and charged at Paula. She fired two shots into the wolf's chest and killed it.

With her arm now free, Jo fired her pistol and killed the remaining wolf. The two women stared at each other in shock. They lay still for several moments, frightened.

Finally, Paula turned her attention to the injured coyote and tried to communicate with it. She sensed it was in severe pain and it couldn't reply to her thoughts. Confused as to whether she should shoot it or help it, she watched helplessly. Jo understood her thoughts and instructed her not to do anything.

Branches snapped in the trees behind the coyote. Paula instinctively shined her light in that direction. Gino's body appeared from the trees and picked up the coyote in his arms. His face was ashen and he appeared in a zombie-like state. He looked at them sadly and carried the wounded creature away.

"Well, there goes my other fucking intern!" complained Jo.

"What the hell is going on?" blurted Paula as she stared in disbelief at the trees where Gino vanished.

"We're caught in the middle of a war, Missy," replied Jo. After three attempts, she stood and hobbled toward the cave.

"Don't go in there," warned Paula.

Jo looked back at her and reconsidered her warning. She backed away and waited for Paula to get up.

"I'd help you if I could but I don't think I have the strength," Jo uttered feebly.

Paula frowned and struggled to her feet. "I wouldn't have expected you to, regardless."

Jo sneered and hobbled back toward the cabin. Paula took note of the location of the cave and followed her.

The sound of flapping wings from above caught their attention. The women searched above but saw nothing. A few moments later, Paula spotted the flying alien creature swooping in from behind. "Run, Jo!" she shouted.

Jo looked back and saw the creature. "Holy shit!"

The two women staggered toward the cabin. Paula looked over her shoulder repeatedly, ready to fire but the creature would disappear briefly and reappear as if toying with them.

Paula tripped and fell face-first to the ground. She frantically turned and waited as the alien glided toward her.

Jo looked over her shoulder and saw the alien approach Paula. She hid behind a tree and took aim, patiently waiting for it to draw near.

· · ◆ ◆ ◆ · ·

Sasha became panicked over the deafening sound of the crows and honked the horn repeatedly. Lamar grabbed her wrist and stopped her. For an instant, the crows cleared the windshield. Sasha pulled her hand back and apologized.

Lamar leaned on the horn and held it. The blaring sound drove the crows away from the vehicles. "That's it, Sasha! It worked!"

Lamar gestured for Johnny to lead the way. Johnny sped down the dirt access road. Lamar followed unaware of the flattened front tire.

As soon as they reached the first curve, Lamar's truck veered to the left and rolled down the embankment about forty feet until it struck a tree and lay on its passenger side. Sasha lay against the passenger side door with Lamar on top of her. They were both dazed and bloody from the impact.

Johnny looked in the rear-view mirror and panicked when he saw only darkness. He stopped the vehicle and. pounded the steering wheel. "I've lost everyone!" he moaned distraughtly. When he regained control of his emotions, he uttered aloud, "All right, you bastards! Now you're gonna get a piece of me."

He reloaded his pistol and retrieved a Browning 30-06 from the back seat. After loading it, he backed his vehicle up the mountain until he spotted the headlights from Lamar's truck down the side of the mountain. "Jesus!" he blurted and parked with his headlights aimed off the road.

The crows disappeared and the mountain was eerily quiet. Johnny left the vehicle, armed with a floodlight and his guns. He carefully descended the side of the mountain until he reached Lamar's truck. After a quick search of the area with the light, he noticed the front tire was flat with no sign of a cut or blowout. He climbed onto the side of the truck and peered inside.

He was relieved when Lamar and Sasha shielded their eyes from his light. After several tries, he yanked the mangled door open and climbed down inside the truck. With the rifle and floodlight outside the truck, Johnny fretted that the creatures would attack again while they were defenseless.

Lamar pulled himself off of Sasha and, with Johnny's help, climbed out of the truck. Johnny lifted Sasha and slid her up through the open door and onto the driver side of the truck. Both Lamar and Sasha lay across the truck's side in a dazed state.

"Lamar, you have to help me," urged Johnny. "You both need medical attention."

Lamar slid off the truck and fell to his knees. Johnny got down and slid Sasha off the truck and held her.

Lamar looked up passively and groaned, "I can't make it, Johnny."

Sasha reached for Lamar and took his hand. "You can do it," she uttered softly. "I know you can."

Lamar pulled himself to his feet and took a deep breath. "Let's do this," he said, struggling to stand.

"You take the guns and the floodlight," Johnny instructed him. "I'll carry Sasha."

"No," he replied with renewed determination in his voice. "She's my woman. I'll carry her."

Johnny reluctantly passed Sasha to him. Lamar looked up the mountainside and took one step at a time. Johnny followed him, armed with the rifle and floodlight.

It was only forty feet up the slope to the road but it seemed like miles. Johnny scanned the trees around them but saw no sign of the creatures.

Suddenly the silence of the night was broken by gunshots. At first, he recognized the sound of Jo's .45, but then more shots ensued that sounded like Paula's 9 mm. Johnny grew hopeful and hurried ahead of them to the police SUV.

There was still no sign of the creatures on the road. Johnny helped Sasha into the back seat along with Lamar.

"Are you two all right?" asked Johnny.

"That's a stupid question?" uttered Lamar. "We'll live, if that's what you're asking."

"You heard the shots. Paula and Jo could be alive."

"It's your call, Johnny."

"I was afraid you'd say that."

Johnny started the SUV and drove back up the dirt road. As the cabin came into view, Jo and Paula emerged from the trees. They staggered onto the porch and collapsed. The two women were covered in blood and their clothes were tattered.

"Be careful, Johnny," Lamar warned. "We don't know if they've been infected."

"I understand," answered Johnny uneasily. He feared that Lamar would learn that Paula and Jo were turned by the alien creatures. Soon after, he'd figure out that Johnny was as well.

Lamar cradled Sasha in his arms and held her close to him. He needed to help Johnny but could barely move. His head still spun from the impact and he felt nauseous.

Sasha's right shoulder was injured and she also had a head trauma, fading in and out of consciousness.

Johnny drove the vehicle to the cabin porch and parked it. Immediately, he rushed to Paula's aid. When he lifted Paula to her feet, a wolf charged out of the trees at him. Johnny drew his pistol and fired a shot into its head. The wolf tumbled face first into the ground and lay dead in front of him.

Paula didn't respond, only staring. Johnny carried her and placed her in the front passenger seat. Jo staggered toward the truck without assistance until Johnny helped her into the back seat with Lamar and Sasha.

When he sat in the driver's seat, he heard the flapping of wings. He took his floodlight and scanned the sky. Then he noticed not one, but three flying aliens circling above them. Johnny took the Browning rifle off the dash and targeted the creatures. He took the first shot and struck one of the aliens. The creature shrieked and fell headfirst into the trees. Before he could fire again, the others disappeared from his view.

To his left, he saw one of the wolves. He fired a shot and caught its flank. The wolf howled and raced off.

"How's that feel, bitch!" he shouted at the ailing wolf. He closed the SUV door and sped away from the cabin.

Johnny reached for Paula's hand and held it tightly as he turned onto the highway.

Paula muttered weakly to him, "We know where the creatures are hiding."

"Not now, Paula. I have to get you to Clearview."

"Johnny, that's why they chewed the cable," added Jo. "The creatures are hiding inside the cavern and I'm drilling right into their lair."

"We'll talk about this later. Just be quiet and rest, all of you."

# CHAPTER VII

# ON THE RUN

Johnny's head was filled with crazy thoughts now. If the creatures were using the cavern, their secret is out. *Did they purposely let Paula and Jo escape?* he wondered. *Perhaps this is another trap to lure us inside.*

Twenty minutes later, he pulled into the parking lot of Clearview Hospital. An intern sat on a bench outside the emergency room and smoked a cigarette.

"I have four injured people here!" Johnny shouted.

The intern threw the cigarette away and rushed inside for help. He quickly returned with two nurses and a doctor. They each pushed a gurney. "What happened?" the doctor questioned him.

Johnny pointed at the gurneys with Jo and Paula on them. "Those two were attacked by animals, possibly rabid animals. The man and woman were injured in a crash."

The medical staff moved their new patients into the ER and immediately examined them. Lamar bellowed at the doctors and emerged from the examining room. He glared at Johnny in the waiting area and appeared ready to explode on him.

Johnny looked up at him and grew frightened. "Okay, say it, Lamar. I deserve a chewing out."

"It's not just you, Johnny. Neither of these friggin' women will listen. What if Paula and Jo are infected?"

"I know what that means. I know you warned me about my relationship with Paula."

"It's not just that. We need to get all of them out of here unless..."

"Unless what?"

"If Paula and Jo were infected, we can't risk ..."

"Don't think about that, right now, Lamar," Johnny said sternly. "Let's deal with the problem at hand first."

They stared each other down as Lamar wasn't used to Johnny challenging him like that.

Johnny knew it was just a matter of time before Lamar found out. He'd also deduce that Johnny was infected, too, based on his relations with Paula.

Lamar paced with a limp. His chin was cut and his eye swollen. "The women have become a distraction and we can't afford it anymore."

"What do you propose?" Johnny asked sheepishly.

"You're the sheriff. I shouldn't be telling you how to do your job."

Lamar stormed back into the examining room and slammed the door. Johnny feared that Paula and Jo would need to be put down if Lamar believed they were infected. How could he stop him?

Johnny covered his eyes and sobbed. This was never supposed to happen again. He worried that if word got out about a new alien presence, they could face quarantine and possibly extermination unless they control the situation fast. Panic set in and he desperately tried to develop a plan of attack.

He noticed the night was cool and the smell of rain was in the air. It had a calming effect on him as he tried to rationalize everything that just happened. There had to be a way to trap and kill the creatures before things got worse.

Fatigue overtook him and he fell asleep on the bench. He found himself looking in at the back seat of a police car. There, he saw Pam feeding on one of his fellow officers. Then she grabbed him and that tongue – that horrible tongue – tried to push its way into his mouth. Lamar arrived and shot her before she could infect him. Then he realized that the moisture from her tongue across his lips was alien DNA. It was a small dose but it would change him subtly.

He then dreamed of having Paula in his bed. Everything was so beautiful. She slid herself on top of him and made love to him. They kissed hungrily and then she bit his lip.

"Oops. Sorry, Johnny," she said innocently.

"No big deal," he replied and they kissed again. Suddenly her tongue grew and pushed down his throat. He gagged and panicked as he knew she was one of them, an alien like Suzie Beauchamp. He wrestled with her elongated tongue and shuddered when her eyes glowed red. He heard her voice ring out in his head, "We're not done with you."

Then he recognized the mass inside the tongue sliding toward his mouth. He struggled frantically to get free but couldn't. Then he heard a scream and awoke. It was his scream.

Lamar ambled out of the ER and stood over him. "Are you finished?" he asked condescendingly. "You scream like a friggin' woman."

Johnny was soaked in sweat and trembled. "Jesus, Lamar! I just had the worst dream."

"Yeah, well it's not that bad if it's just a dream."

Johnny stood up and pushed his damp hair away from his eyes. "You're pissed at me, aren't you?"

"I'm pissed about a lot of things right now."

"How are the women?" Johnny asked humbly. "Are they okay?"

"Paula and Jo have superficial cuts and bruises from being dragged through the woods. The doctor wants them here for observation for possible concussions."

"What, no bites?"

"Jo was dragged by her jacket and boot. Her shoulder is clean. Fortunately, the bear dragged Paula by the ankle and its teeth never penetrated her boots."

"Are you sure?" Johnny asked eagerly.

"Yeah, the doctor did a thorough exam on them."

Johnny was relieved.

Lamar continued, "They each had scabs from previous wounds so it's not likely they were bitten and healed that quickly."

"Lucky for us," Johnny commented sarcastically. "And Sasha?"

"She's got a concussion and a fractured cheek bone."

"I guess she's lucky that's all she's got," Johnny quipped.

"Nope," replied Lamar stoically. "She's got a piss poor attitude to go with it." The two of them burst into laughter.

"They're staying here for a while, aren't they?" Johnny asked, hoping to keep them safe.

"Yeah, now let's go take care of these bastards."

The two men shook hands and got into the SUV. During the ride back to the station, Johnny shared his thoughts about the cavern and being targeted with Lamar. Then Johnny mentioned, "What if there is a revenge factor in this somehow for what we did to the other aliens?"

Lamar pondered his idea and asked, "How would that work?"

"Maybe there was something in the alien DNA in the tongue we froze that sensed we killed the aliens."

"Sounds a little farfetched but maybe."

"Look, the animals could have bitten or killed Paula and Jo but they didn't. It's like they wanted hostages to bait us into a trap."

"That does make me wonder," Lamar replied with a faraway gaze in his eyes. "Maybe they want us for something else, perhaps for what we know. These things are much smarter than the aliens we fought before."

"But I don't understand how."

"What if there are two sides to these creatures?"

"Like they're having a war between them?" suggested Johnny.

"Exactly. That business with Gino seemed to suggest the coyote was on one side and the flying freaks are on the other."

"So why would the coyote help us?"

"Maybe we're the only hope the coyote has to survive," he surmised. "But then maybe, this is bigger than us and Parmissing Valley. Maybe the winged things are superior to the coyote's alien and that's why it needs our help."

"That's freaking scary, you know."

"It's more than scary," replied Lamar somberly. "What if these things are in other parts of the world?"

Johnny grew more frustrated over the thought that this could be a waste of time and they would die anyway. They turned their focus on the road ahead.

When they reached the station, they were shocked to see the front door smashed in and all the windows broken. Johnny and Lamar approached the building cautiously with pistols drawn and flashlights.

Johnny stood on the patio beside the entrance ready to fire while Lamar peered in through the broken window. There wasn't any movement inside. He nodded to Johnny and joined him at the doorway. They turned their flashlights on and stepped inside the building.

Johnny scanned the left side of the office and Lamar, the right. The desks were overturned and papers littered the floor. The TV lay on the floor in the corner, smashed to pieces.

"Those sons of bitches!" muttered Johnny. "They broke my damned TV."

In the kitchenette, the refrigerator lay on its side and the stove was pulled away from the wall. Johnny turned on the lights. A message was scrawled in blood across the wall: TIMES UP. Johnny and Lamar stared at the message uneasily.

"Leon's screwing with us, Lamar!" Johnny shouted and punched the wall.

"Yeah, and I think we're next on his hit list. Let's get out of here."

The two men were immediately met by a mutated bear with several bullet wounds in its hide at the door. "Jesus H Christ!" hollered Lamar.

The bear had missing patches of fur, replaced by rough, reptilian skin. Two small horns grew from its head and its face resembled that of a dragon. It snarled at them and poised to attack.

Johnny and Lamar both aimed at its head and fired. Part of the head splattered across the wall. The bear wailed an unmerciful howl.

Johnny and Lamar fled to the kitchenette and leaped out the window. They ran to the battered police SUV and sped away from the station.

"Now what?" complained Johnny angrily.

"Go to the municipal building. We'll be safe there."

Johnny looked in the mirror and remarked sarcastically, "We have company, Lamar."

Lamar looked back and saw a pack of wolves chasing the truck. "Step on it, Johnny!"

As Johnny sped away from the animals, he inquired cynically, "And go where?"

Lamar thought for a moment. "Turn around and head toward them."

"Huh?"

"You heard me."

Johnny spun the vehicle around and raced toward the wolves. The pack split apart as the SUV darted between them. Two wolves leaped on the truck and bounced off the glass. The windshield shattered and Johnny had limited visibility through the glass.

The two wolves each had the same patches of skin that the bear had. Their faces were contorted and reptilian as well. Lamar noticed that both had flesh wounds as well.

"Those are the same wolves we killed earlier!" exclaimed Lamar. "They aren't dead anymore!"

"Ah, shit!" fretted Johnny. "We've got big troubles." He turned the vehicle around and raced toward Clearview. When they left the city limits, the wolves disappeared off the road.

"I think we lost them," Johnny uttered shakily.

"It might be safer for the townspeople if we weren't in town tonight," suggested Lamar. "Let's go back to the hospital."

---

Inside one of the hospital rooms, Paula and Jo lay awake in their beds. Neither spoke but each knew what the other was thinking. Finally, Paula broke the ice.

"You were flirting with the sheriff up on the mountain, weren't you?"

Jo grinned and responded, "Now we're getting somewhere."

"You knew he and I were involved. Why would you do that?"

"There is so much going on here that you don't understand," Jo chastised her.

"I'm only concerned about Johnny right now. What was that all about?"

"I learned the hard way to take what's mine, even if I have to fight dirty to get it. I also learned that it's a dog-eat-dog world and I'll take what isn't mine if I want to."

Paula sat up and glared at her. "You can take whatever you want but if you go near him again, you'll deal with me. I will fight for what's mine and you'll be surprised what I'll do."

Jo chuckled at her. "That's cute. Keep that attitude for me."

Paula was about to unload a verbal barrage on her when Lamar and Johnny entered the room.

"The caped crusaders have arrived just in the nick of time, Paula," kidded Jo. Paula bit her lip and ignored her comment.

Johnny pulled up a chair and sat next to Paula's bed. "Well, ladies, things are getting weirder," he announced.

"What happened?" asked Paula. "You look you've seen a ghost."

"Actually several. Those animals we killed… well, they're alive."

Paula and Jo were stunned.

"How can that be?" Jo asked, still in awe.

"Also, Leon's men trashed the station again and there was a nice message on the wall for us," explained Lamar. "Then a bear attacked and the wolves chased us down the road for quite a distance before we lost them."

"By the way, it was the same bear that you killed, Jo," Johnny remarked. "And the wolves were the same ones that we killed, Paula."

"Wow, this is getting really fucking weird," quipped Jo. She seemed more amused than concerned, which bothered the men.

"What happened when the bear dragged you away, Paula?" inquired Lamar in a somber tone.

"What the hell do you think happened?" she barked at him. "I got my gun and shot the SOB!"

"Nothing strange occurred?" he probed curiously.

"Yeah," she cried, "neither of you tried to rescue me. Anything else you want to know."

Johnny lowered his head dejectedly. He knew she was right.

Lamar interceded and explained, "You have to understand, Paula, it could have been a trap to lure the rest of us into the trees."

"Paula, we had no choice," Johnny responded, now teary-eyed.

"Sometimes love comes before self-preservation," Paula countered stubbornly. "That's all I'm saying."

Johnny stormed out of the room, upset with himself that he let her down. He sat on the floor in the hallway and cried.

Lamar grew more frustrated with the situation as he considered what he would have done if it were Sasha in that situation.

Jo remarked, "I might have something to say if anybody gives a shit."

"I'm sorry," replied Lamar. "Did you see anything unusual?"

"Hell, yeah!" she blurted. "There's a war going on up there and we're in the middle of it."

"And you know this how?"

"The coyotes saved our lives. The bear and the wolves took us to the entrance of a cave. When the coyotes attacked the bear, Paula had the chance to draw her pistol. She put down the bear and then one wolf. That gave me the chance to fire my pistol at the other wolf and finish it off. At least we thought they were finished."

Lamar stared at Paula suspiciously. She glared at him and replied, baffled by the turn of events, "So much happened so fast, I'm not sure what I saw or heard anymore."

"What do you mean 'heard'?" he asked with increased interest.

"I thought I heard a voice speak to me. I don't remember what it said but I distinctly heard it."

"I see," Lamar responded, now more confused than ever.

Sasha awoke in the next room and heard their voices. She stepped into the hall and stood by Johnny. "Are you okay?"

Johnny looked up and sobbed. "No, not at all. I let Paula down."

She knelt by him and explained compassionately, "No you didn't. You did the logical thing and really the only choice you had available to you."

"But what about Paula? She could have died today."

"She didn't. You realized how much she means to you. Now you have to build on that." She extended her hand to him. "Let's go talk to them. We're all in this together."

Johnny wiped the tears from his eyes and followed her into the examination room.

Lamar was surprised to see Sasha up and about. He took her by the hand and they left for a walk.

Paula got out of bed and took her bag of clothes into the bathroom.

Johnny knew what she was doing and shuddered over the grief to come. Jo eyed him curiously until he noticed and complained, "What are you staring at?"

Jo smiled coyly and suggested, "You should let her go. She's too immature for you, Sheriff."

"And what's that supposed to mean," he countered.

"You and I have a better chance of taming these creatures than she does and I think I know just what to do to kill these bastards."

Johnny grew suspicious of her motives and inquired, "So what do you want in return?"

"Since I'm out of interns, my boy toys, I need someone to satisfy me. You look like you'd do just fine."

Johnny was about to respond when Paula emerged from the bathroom, dressed in her torn and dirty uniform.

"Take me home, now," she ordered Johnny.

"You can't just leave, Paula."

"You know, Johnny, go fuck yourself." Paula stormed out of the room and left the hospital.

"Paula!" Johnny called frantically and chased after her.

As he hurried down the hallway in pursuit of Paula, Lamar and Sasha appeared from around the corner. His arm was around her shoulders and they seemed happy. "Whoa, Johnny! Where you rushing off to?" he asked.

"Paula just split. She's pretty upset."

"I'll go get her," he offered.

"No, this is my problem and she's my deputy," Johnny replied. "I'll handle it."

"But…"

With a somber expression, Johnny put his hand up for silence and left the hospital.

Outside, Paula walked across the parking lot toward the road as Johnny hurried after her. Almost immediately the two got into a heated argument. Johnny tried repeatedly to make his case about not rescuing her.

Inside the hospital, Lamar grew concerned and frowned at Sasha. "This isn't working out real well."

"Relax," she urged calmly. "Give them a chance."

Lamar smiled and hugged her. "You know, Sasha, I think…" Two men he recognized from the hotel earlier walked down the hall and turned into Jo's room. Each wore a suit with a vest and appeared to be armed, based on the bulge underneath the suits at waist level.

"Hold that thought, Sasha," Lamar continued and approached the room.

Sasha crept toward the room behind him. She recognized the men from the hotel as well and was worried that Lamar would get hurt.

The men stood next to Jo's bed with arms folded. Jo seemed irritated by their presence. "Well, hello, Harry. Hello, Roy. You boys lost or something?"

"It was only a matter of time before we'd find you, Jo. You cost us a lot of money."

"Kiss my ass!" she bellowed at them. "That drill was my idea, funded by my sources and built in my own facility. You thieves think you can bully me around and take it, well you got another thing coming."

Harry yanked the pillow from underneath her head. "You'd better tell us where the drill is or else."

Jo held up both hands and gave them the middle finger. "Take that back with you."

Harry smiled and replied, "I think I'll just finish you off now. Leon will be thankful, either way."

"You tell that scumbag Leon…" Before she could finish, Harry placed the pillow over her face and pressed down on it.

Lamar peered in and was horrified. He rushed in and punched Roy in the back of the head, flooring him.

Sasha watched nervously from the doorway. She wanted to help but had no weapon to use. In desperation, she hurried outside, hoping to stop Johnny before he left.

Harry let go of the pillow and drew his pistol. Before he could fire, Lamar grabbed his wrist and twisted it until the pistol fell to the ground.

Jo gasped for air and was red-faced with tears in her eyes. She searched frantically for something to use as a weapon. In a panic, she pulled her IV out of her arm and stabbed Harry in the neck with it. Harry panicked and gave Lamar the opportunity to grab his other arm and twist it behind his back.

As Roy tried to stand, Lamar lifted Harry from behind by his arms, nearly yanking them off, and threw him down on top of Roy. The two men remained down on the ground, both injured badly.

"Not bad, sheriff," Jo kidded.

"I'm just getting started," he replied in an angry tone.

"Thanks for the help, by the way."

"My pleasure," he responded sarcastically.

A nurse rushed into the room and was stunned. "How did they get in here, Mayor?"

"I don't know, but I know how they're going out."

The nurse dressed the wound on Harry's neck. Johnny rushed in with Paula and Sasha. "I leave you for five minutes, Lamar, and look what happens."

"Get Clearview's boys to take care of these clowns. Charge them with murder – Adam's murder."

Paula went to the nurses' station and summoned the police by phone to the hospital.

Jo got up and grabbed her bag of clothes. She pushed past them and went into the bathroom.

Johnny handcuffed Harry and Roy until the Clearview police arrived. He attempted to question them but they refused to talk. When Jo came out, she was more than happy to reveal their identities and the crimes they were part of in her ex-husband's company.

When the local police came and took control of the men, Harry warned Jo, Leon's going to get both you and that drill, no matter what."

Jo got in his face and replied sarcastically, "I'm gonna put a drill so far up his ass, he'll need dental work when I'm done."

The two local cops chuckled and took them away.

"And where are you going, Ms. Fama?" questioned Lamar.

"I'm getting the hell out of here. It's safer out there with the animals."

Sasha put her hands on her hips and complained, "Well, I'm not staying here all by myself."

The nurse was annoyed with all the commotion and suggested, "I can make a call and get you all discharged but only if you promise to never come back here again. This used to be a quiet place until you showed up."

They laughed and agreed to avoid Clearview in the future.

# CHAPTER VIII

# SUSPICIONS

After dropping everyone off but Paula, Johnny parked in front of her apartment and stared ahead at the building in a daze. Paula eyed him, curiously and finally broke the silence, "If there's nothing you want to talk about, then I'd like to go inside. I'm tired."

Johnny banged his head against the steering wheel in frustration. "Look at the mess I've made here, Paula," he replied dejectedly. "I've ruined everything. We're no closer to stopping these creatures than when we started. My own station has been trashed twice and, worst of all, I've ruined our relationship. I'm so sorry."

Paula felt sympathy for him and asked, "What do you want from me?"

Johnny answered sadly, "Forgiveness."

Paula considered his request and recalled that Lamar restrained him from aiding her. She remembered Lamar's rebuke of Johnny's attempt to follow her. Perhaps, she thought, she was being too hard on him. "All right, you win," she said stoically.

Johnny peered at her, somewhat confused by her change in attitude. "I don't want to win. I want you."

Paula smiled and slid toward him. She decided it was time to reveal what she knew.

"First," she began, "I understand what happened back there. I know you tried to come after me and Lamar stopped you."

Johnny was elated to hear that. "I swear; it killed me to see you dragged off like that," he confessed to her. "I couldn't live without you."

"I know. I would have felt the same. That being said, you don't need my forgiveness."

Johnny hugged her tightly. "Thank you so much. That means a lot to me."

"Easy, Johnny. Before you get too excited, there are some things I need to explain. I believe we do have something to go on with these creatures." Johnny grew concerned about what she might have kept from him.

Paula was still embarrassed by what she did to him, leaving bite marks on him, thus her apprehension. "Let's start with the obvious. Jo was right. There are two sides to these creatures, like a war between the animals."

"I agree."

"The coyotes were responsible for saving Jo and me."

"And you're sure about this?" he asked, surprised by her revelation.

"Yes. I sense that we ought to be helping the coyote's side."

"And the other side?"

"It's controlled by a new alien life form - a very hostile life form."

"So, you're thinking that we can work with one side against the other."

"Maybe. I think they need us after this latest attack."

"And what happens afterward if we succeed?" Johnny inquired, curious. "We can't have alien creatures running around here."

"That's where it gets complicated." Johnny waited patiently for her to continue.

Paula's eyes welled up with tears. "The voices we hear: the animals have a weak form of telepathy. Ours is much stronger."

Johnny asked uneasily, "Do you think that you infected me?"

"I'm pretty sure I did," she muttered, trembling. "You heard the voices. That's one of the symptoms."

Johnny pulled away and leaned against the door. He covered his face with his hands.

"Johnny, I'm so sorry. I didn't know."

"The bites on my lip and neck – did you do it on purpose to make me like you?"

"No, not at all. I was really in love with you and my passion for you was out of control."

Johnny got out of the vehicle and paced back and forth. He considered everything Paula just told him and was bothered about what he should tell her. Cautiously hiding his thoughts from her, he realized that he was likely already infected before he met her and maybe he was the one who infected her.

Paula got out and approached him. "Please, say something, Johnny. I hate when you hide your thoughts from me."

Johnny embraced her and explained, "We're in this together but this stays between us. Lamar can't know."

"I get it," she replied gratefully. "Thanks for understanding."

"What do you think this infection will do to us long-term?"

Paula looked at him with pleading eyes. "I promise, I'll tell you as soon as I know."

"That's good enough for me," he replied and kissed her. "Oh, and one more question. What about Jo?"

"Yeah, that bitch is infected too. I don't trust her one bit, either."

"Well, we'll deal with her in the morning."

The two of them entered Paula's apartment and slept peacefully throughout the night. In the morning, Paula realized again that there were no sexual urges and wondered.

---

Lamar and Sasha were nestled together in his bed, pondering the day's events. Lamar was torn between helping Johnny and handling Jo's ex-husband and his thugs.

When morning came, Lamar suggested they go out to breakfast. Sasha was pleased by the idea and looked forward to a relaxed day of recovery from the accident. They drove beyond the east end of town and parked in front of a little brick building.

Flying over them was the adult Ardonean. It spotted the store owner taking out a trash bag and swooped down upon him. Before the man knew what happened, the creature clamped its jaws on his neck and hauled him onto the roof. It savagely devoured his flesh like a machine, gnawing at each limb until only bone could be seen.

Lamar opened the front door for Sasha and escorted her inside the café.

There were small tables and chairs in front of the store and baskets of flowers decorated the inside of the store window.

Lamar selected a table by the window and, like a gentleman, slid a chair out for Sasha to sit on. He eyed the shop but saw no one. The smell of fresh bacon and toast filled the air.

"Hello!" Lamar called out but no one responded. He approached the counter and called again, "Anyone here?" Still there was no answer.

"Stay here," he ordered Sasha. She sensed his concern.

Lamar stepped behind the counter and went into the back room. "Hello," he called out again but still no answer.

The stainless-steel counter had freshly sliced vegetables on it and the coffee urn was filled with hot coffee.

The squeak of the rear door caught his attention. Lamar picked up a knife from the counter and approached the back door. As he nudged the door open with his foot, he searched the parking lot. There was only the owner's mini-van. As he stepped away from the building, the remains of the corpse dropped down from the roof in front of the door.

"Holy shit!" Lamar blurted out.

The sound of shattering glass and Sasha's scream sent him into a panic. He hurried back inside and leaped over the counter.

The winged alien with the plumage gripped Sasha's shoulders with its talons and dragged her outside through the broken window. Lamar charged through the broken window and leaped onto the creature's back. He attempted to stab the creature but lost the knife in his effort to hold on to it.

Sasha's cries renewed his strength. "Hold on, Sasha!" he repeated to her.

Lamar wrapped his arms tightly around the Ardonean's neck but it still took flight with Sasha dangling from its claws. The creature shrieked as it flapped its wings erratically, overburdened by the additional weight.

Tears streamed down his eyes as he realized he was helpless and could only hang on until they reached the creature's destination. Sasha's continued cries for help broke his heart.

---

Johnny and Paula finished breakfast and donned their holsters. Each checked the magazines and loaded their pistols.

"I gotta' say, Paula: you cook a mean breakfast. That was awesome."

"Only the best for my man," she said with a coy smile. "Thank you again for understanding what happened to us."

Johnny studied the pistol for a moment and stowed it in his holster. "It is what it is. I don't want to lose you and if we have to learn alien sex then I'm good with that."

"You sick bastard," she joked.

"Seriously, we have to figure out what the repercussions are with this."

"And we will."

They left the apartment and got into the damaged police SUV. Johnny drove with Paula riding shotgun.

"I have an idea, regarding repercussions," Paula announced. "We're gonna try and communicate with the coyote next time we see it."

"Maybe, if we're lucky, this telepathy thing works both ways," Johnny suggested.

They pulled up in front of Jo's hotel. "Should I go get her?" asked Johnny.

Paula replied sarcastically, "You'll do no such thing. I'm coming with you." Johnny chuckled, knowing she felt threatened by Jo's advances toward him. The two of them entered the hotel together.

Mr. Givens read the newspaper at the counter as they walked past. "Looking for Ms. Fama, Sheriff?" he inquired, without looking up.

Johnny and Paula hesitated by the stairs.

"Yes, we are," Johnny replied. "Why do you ask?"

"She hasn't been back in a few days. Neither have her friends."

Johnny frowned and complained, "She's up on the mountain alone - again." Paula wondered if that could be a good thing. They hurried out to the police SUV.

Mr. Givens was amused by the attention that Jo received from the police department and recalled the night Lamar kicked in the door. He resumed reading his newspaper.

As the SUV raced down the highway toward the mountain, Johnny called Lamar several times on his cell phone but received no answer. "That's strange," he commented.

"Maybe he's sleeping," suggested Paula.

"No, not Lamar. Something's wrong."

"You don't think they went up on the mountain with Jo, do you?" asked Paula.

"I have no idea. He still should have answered."

They turned onto the mountain road and slowed up. Paula searched down the embankment until she saw Lamar's truck. As she looked closer, she saw someone next to it.

"Stop, Johnny! Someone's down there."

Johnny slammed on the brakes and the vehicle skidded to a stop. The two of them rushed to the edge of the slope and observed the figure.

"It looks like Gino," Paula whispered. "What's he doing at Lamar's truck?"

Johnny looked perplexed. "He's gotta' be turned. This could be a trap."

"I'm going down. You cover me," she instructed him.

"Bullshit. We stay together," Johnny ordered.

Paula was pleased by his response. They crept down the mountain slope together toward Lamar's truck, which was now turned back on its wheels. Johnny and Paula were wary as to what the animals or aliens would want with the truck.

Gino saw them but wasn't concerned. There was something inside the truck that had his attention.

When they got close to the truck, Johnny warned, "Stay where you are or we'll shoot!"

Gino backed away from the truck and held his hands up for them to see. They both heard a voice in their head, *He won't hurt you, nor will I.*

Johnny glanced at Paula and asked, "Did you just hear that?"

"I sure did. He's a 'friendly'."

Johnny approached Gino with his pistol trained at his head. "What's in there?" he inquired in a firm tone.

"The coyote, it's … dying," responded Gino.

"So much for that lead," he complained.

Paula peered inside the truck. On the seat was the coyote. Its stomach was ripped open and it panted heavily. Before she could look away, the coyote hacked up a clot of blood and died.

Paula felt sad for the creature but maintained her focus on their situation.

Gino looked at them with a vacant expression in his eyes. He seemed lost.

"You got something to say?" Johnny challenged him callously.

Gino struggled to put his thoughts together and finally replied, "Yes, I do. I need your help … and you need mine."

Johnny and Paula glanced at each other, wondering where this was going.

"Are you Gino?" Paula questioned him.

"I left that creature," he explained pointing toward the dead coyote, "and moved into this body."

"So, you killed Gino?"

"No, he exists but only in his subconscious right now."

Johnny was unconvinced and inquired, "If you leave his body, will he live?"

"Yes, but I do not know if he will be the same."

Johnny was angered by the response and pressed the barrel of his pistol against Gino's head. "You see, that's where I have a problem."

Paula restrained him and pushed the gun away from Gino's head. "Why did you change bodies?" she asked.

"I needed to communicate with you. The forest creatures have limited mental capacity."

Growing impatient, Johnny was determined to get facts from Gino. "What do you want from us?" he asked impatiently.

"Your friends are in danger," Gino replied. "Aliens arrived here a few days ago. Ardoneans they are called. Their race has been at war with us as long as we have existed."

Johnny folded his arms and waited impatiently for him to continue. Paula probed Gino's mind using her telepathy in search of clues that would validate his information. He made no attempt to hide facts.

"They saw what happened here before and how your people could be mutated into a formidable army. They also believed they could learn from our mistakes and be more subtle about taking over your world."

"And how do they plan to do this?"

"The first stage of its plan is to turn the forest creatures into an army that no one would suspect. In stage two, it will spread their DNA at a frightening pace until humans are turned as well. The third stage will see their mother ship arrive and herd this army of mutants for battle in another sector of the universe."

"I'm not liking this at all," complained Johnny. "Why are you willing to stop them on our behalf?"

"Those who came before us were criminals from my world. We do not believe in mutating other races. It is better to forge alliances than to invade and mutate."

"Let's say, we believe you," Johnny countered. "What can we do about it?"

Gino became distracted and searched the sky. "Our nemesis is nearby and he has someone of yours."

"And this flying alien is what's infecting the forest creatures," surmised Paula.

"Yes, and it is much more dangerous than what you have previously seen of my race," Gino warned. He backed away from them toward the cover of the forest trees. "We will meet at your station tonight. I must leave you now." He turned and rushed into the trees.

Johnny aimed his pistol but couldn't shoot. He grew frustrated and holstered the gun.

Paula put her arm around him and pondered what to do next. The two left Lamar's vehicle and ascended the slope back to the road. Once inside the police SUV, Paula inquired, "Any ideas?"

"Yeah, we take out the creatures in groups until we get to ET."

"And how do you propose to do that?"

"Let's see if we can draw the crows to the cabin."

"You're kidding!" she exclaimed.

"Nope. That'll eliminate one part of its force." Paula was unconvinced but didn't argue.

They drove up the dirt road to the cabin and parked. There was no sign of any of the creatures and neither of them sensed a presence in the trees.

Johnny approached the propane tank on the side of the cabin and checked the gauge. It was half full. Satisfied, he entered the cabin, followed by Paula. They secured the windows.

Johnny searched the closet and kitchen until he found a screwdriver and hammer. He pried on several boards in the bedroom closet until he could see the crawlspace under the cabin. He peered underneath and could see daylight at the rear.

Paula finally asked, "Is this our escape route?"

"Fuckin' A it is." Johnny then pointed to the gas stove and explained, "We're going to cook those bastards once they get inside."

Paula became receptive to his plan. She cuddled against him. Johnny grinned and glanced at the bedroom. She smiled and took him by the hand.

"I'll be pissed if we're interrupted," he quipped.

"We'll know when they're coming," she assured him and removed her boots.

Johnny unbuttoned her uniform and removed it. She kissed him hungrily as he unfastened her belt. The two of them fell against the wall as Johnny slid her pants down to her ankles. Paula eagerly unbuckled his pants and promptly pulled them down as well. The urge was back and she briefly considered her persuasion theory. Perhaps Johnny was using the power of persuasion on her to get her aroused. Then she had an idea. *What if I try to use persuasion on Johnny?* She wondered if she could manipulate him.

Johnny slid one hand under her bra and another into her panties. Paula crooned with delight as she kicked off her pants. "What are you waiting for?" she taunted seductively, as she projected sexual images to him.

Sliding on top of her and, without any foreplay, he promptly thrust himself inside of her, pounding away with an unquenchable desire. Then she imagined him slowing down and then speeding up, like a sports car quickly changing gears on a mountain road.

Paula's moans grew louder as she felt her insides quiver. Then she saw it and froze. Johnny's eyes turned red, just like hers.

"Don't worry about it," he whispered as he continued sliding in and out of her – first quickly, then slower – quickly, then slower. "I love you so much," he said softly.

"I love you, too," she replied. With renewed vigor, she placed her hands on his hips and urged him on until she cried out loudly and climaxed. Now she had some control over him and it felt good.

Johnny exploded inside of her and seconds later, they both sighed aloud with delight. He rubbed himself against her and kissed her passionately. Paula let out another long sigh.

"I've never met anyone who came like you, Paula," Johnny remarked.

"You know, Johnny, I never did this before. It's a bit embarrassing."

"I think it's a turn on. At least I know I satisfied you."

"That you did." Paula rolled over on top of him and grew giddy. "Geez, Johnny. I think we scared the animals away."

"Yeah, that was… That was… I have no words for it," he said as he breathed deeply.

Then Paula wondered if Johnny was infected prior to meeting her. Perhaps he started this sex-crazed path the two of them were on.

Paula rolled onto her side and stared at him, pleased by the outcome of things. Johnny turned onto his side and faced her. "Yes, dear," he remarked coolly.

"How long have you been infected?" she asked, curious.

Johnny thought for a moment. "I don't really know," he replied as he considered that he was likely already infected. Paula found his answer to be a bit strange.

Johnny brushed her cheek with his fingers and smiled. "I would never hurt you and I know you would never hurt me. I also know that if you became something else, I would become that, too, just to be with you."

Paula became teary-eyed and blurted, "I love you so much, Johnny."

"And I love you, too. We're gonna win this war together. I promise."

They kissed again and, as they became aroused, both sensed the crows coming. Johnny complained, "I knew it wouldn't last."

"So, you can feel the creatures, too?" she inquired with a keen interest.

"Yeah, I can. It took a while but when I finally understood what was going on, it sorted itself out."

The two dressed and hurried into the kitchen. Johnny unscrewed the gas line behind the stove and motioned for Paula to stand by the closet in the bedroom. He paused by the front door and waited.

The caws from the crows filled the air as they approached the cabin. Johnny opened the front door and stood on the porch where they could see him. He hurried back inside the house and into the bedroom.

He and Paula waited until the crows burst through the open door. Paula pulled Johnny inside with her and slammed the door shut behind her. The sound of the crows grew deafening and the cabin vibrated.

"Holy shit!" remarked Johnny. "It's like the Wizard of fucking Oz out there."

"I hope you're right about this," Paula uttered nervously. "They sound really pissed."

The crows attacked the door with unbelievable force. The wood splintered as they pecked relentlessly at the door.

"It's time," said Johnny. "Let's get out of here."

Paula slid down through the gap in the floor boards and crawled underneath the cabin to the rear. Johnny dropped down behind her and slid the boards back in place.

When the two of them emerged from the back of the cabin, all of the crows were inside. Johnny and Paula crept around front and peered across the porch.

The walls rumbled as the crows seemed determined to decimate the cabin into a pile of sawdust. About twenty crows were still perched on the railing as if on guard.

Johnny took a pack of matches from his pocket and handed them to Paula. As he searched the area around them, he removed his shirt and created a make-shift torch. Paula held the branch while he tied the sleeves and shirt tightly around it.

"The shirt's not going to burn very well," she informed him.

Johnny smiled at her and scooped up a pile of dried leaves off the ground. He tucked them inside the shirt and took the home-made torch from Paula. "It doesn't have to," he explained confidently. "Go ahead and light it."

Paula struck a match and lit the leaves in three places. When the flame was visible, she tucked the matches inside for added insurance that the shirt would burn, too.

Johnny rushed across the porch and tossed the torch inside. The crows took flight off the railing and attacked him. As he slammed the front door closed, the crows clawed and pecked at his back and shoulders.

Before Paula could help him, the cabin exploded. She was knocked backwards away from the side of the cabin and lay dazed on the ground.

Johnny was thrown away from the cabin by the blast and was motionless in front of the police SUV.

The cabin burned furiously and the crows lay dead or dying across the front porch.

Paula staggered to her feet and went to Johnny's aid. Realizing he was unconscious, she dragged him inside their vehicle and cried as she watched him lie motionless. "Please be okay, Johnny," she said between sobs. "I need you."

When he still didn't respond, she pounded the steering wheel and cried. She waited for hours as the flames in the cabin dwindled and turned to smoke. When fatigue overwhelmed her, she fell fast asleep.

Gino's voice startled her in a dream. "You and your partner have adapted well to the genetic changes. You have maintained control of your thought processes and sustained minimal physical mutation."

In her dream, Paula lay next to a stream in a dense forest, searching for the source of the voice. "What about long-term effects from the mutation?" she asked.

Gino's voice sounded fainter as if it moved away. "You and your partner will discover them together," he assured her. "It will be fine."

"What happens after we defeat this alien? Is that the end of it?" she inquired before the voice was gone.

"It is just the beginning," he replied almost in a whisper.

Paula panicked. "What do you mean the beginning? The beginning of what?" she begged him to tell her. There was no reply as she shouted out the question again. Suddenly she felt smothered and gasped for air. When she opened her eyes, Johnny was awake and embraced her.

"Johnny!" she exclaimed cheerfully. "I was so worried about you."

"I'm good. How about you?"

"Yeah, I'm fine. I just had this terrible dream though."

Johnny kissed her forehead and asked jokingly, "Are you sure it was a dream?"

"You had it too?" she responded excitedly.

"If this is just the beginning then yeah, I had it too."

The sun was nearly down and the sky darkened. Paula wore a concerned expression as she took in everything that happened from the gas explosion in the cabin to her cryptic dream.

Johnny was much more relaxed about the situation and got out of the truck. He entered the smoldering remains of the cabin and was pleased by the sight of all the dead crows. When he returned, he was confident that the first phase of their operation was successful. He climbed in the driver side as Paula scooted over.

"You think this was all of the crows?" she asked eagerly.

"It sure was. Unfortunately, this was the easy part."

Johnny started the SUV and drove back to the station. Paula rubbed his thigh and tilted her head back against the seat's headrest. She breathed a sigh of relief as she weighed the consequences of losing Johnny.

"I'm not going anywhere," he assured her with a comforting smile.

Paula was still surprised by the development of Johnny's telepathy from the mutation. Her guilt still weighed on her as she fretted that he would eventually resent the fact that she infected him during one of their sexual encounters.

"I know what you're thinking," he commented. "It doesn't matter, Paula. I still love you and it was an unintended consequence for both of us. We'll live with it."

Paula appreciated his loyalty and honesty but she feared that would one day change. "I'm still getting used to this link between us, Johnny. I never meant… I mean I'm sorry for all this."

Johnny reached his right arm around her and nestled against her. They had been together for almost a week and yet he would die for her. *Love is a funny thing*, he thought to himself.

Paula stroked his cheek affectionately and then rested while he drove.

•••◆•••

Later that evening, Johnny and Paula sat inside the station and sipped hot coffee. The front door creaked open and in walked Gino. Johnny instinctively grabbed his pistol and stood, ready to fire. Paula stepped in front of him to deter his shot.

"I have important information for you," announced Gino, unfazed by Johnny's aggressive move.

Paula pushed Johnny's gun down and nodded for him to sit. Johnny reluctantly complied.

"What's wrong?" Paula asked Gino uneasily.

Gino approached them and sat next to Paula's desk. He knew better than to get too close to Johnny. "Your dark-skinned friends have been captured by the alien."

"Bullshit!" shouted Johnny. He quickly took out his cell phone and called Lamar.

"How do you know this?" inquired Paula.

"My creatures saw them taken into a cave on the mountain."

"Damn!" shouted Johnny as he stowed the phone. "There's no answer."

"We need to get them out of there and fast!" Paula exclaimed frantically.

"In the morning," replied Gino. "It's too dangerous at night."

"Are they okay?"

"So far. The alien is awaiting reinforcements so tomorrow is critical for our success. It needs the two of you as well."

As they spoke, Jo arrived at the station and peered inside the doorway. She was stunned to see Gino with them. Perhaps he hadn't been turned into the undead creature that they believed.

Her first thoughts were that Paula swayed Gino away from her. She recalled the day Paula and Johnny visited the drill site. While she attempted to capture Johnny's attention, Paula went for her young sex toy, Gino. *That bitch is more conniving than I imagined,* Jo thought to herself. Then she recalled that Paula would do whatever it took to protect Johnny.

"Will you take us to the cave?" Johnny requested, still suspicious of Gino.

"Yes, I will. Meet me at the cabin tomorrow."

"Where will you stay tonight?" asked Paula, somewhat concerned about their new ally.

"The woods have many hiding places," answered Gino.

"You can stay here if you like."

Outside the door, Jo heard enough. She would exact her revenge on Paula at a later time. Without another thought, she hurried off toward her Escalade, full of anger and vindictiveness.

"It's not safe here," Johnny responded somberly. He wasn't anxious to have an alien sleeping in his station. "After all, the station was attacked twice by thugs already."

"We observed but chose not to interfere. It was necessary to determine your reactions and responses to your other enemies."

"What the hell for?" demanded Johnny.

"To evaluate all threats to our group."

"Our group, huh? What if we were killed by those men?" continued Johnny.

"Then I would call in some of my own race to neutralize the problems."

"Great. An alien war on our own planet," grumbled Johnny.

"We will do everything possible to avert such a war," assured Gino. "The Ardoneans have to be stopped here or the consequences will be catastrophic for both humans and Geols alike."

"The coyote's host was a Geol?" asked Paula.

"I am a Geol. Now I inhabit your friend as a host."

"Do you have a name?"

"Safa. I am the leader of my people. I was chosen to take the life form of the egg you freed to save your people. Shurek had no knowledge that the eggs were destined to be his demise."

"So, you did come from the tongue," Paula remarked uneasily.

"Yes. There were others but, unfortunately, you terminated them."

"We're really sorry about that," she said apologetically. "We didn't know."

"And I realize that. Our communication was limited while I used the animal as a host."

Johnny sneered as he found this hard to believe. "How does a race, whether it be alien or any other, determine who inhabits an egg?"

Gino laughed at him. "You are a silly man," he taunted. "The eggs were our means of stopping Shurek if you failed. Unfortunately, the evil woman (Suzie) modified one of the churlis with a sporatin and ruined our plans."

"I ain't buying this crap for a second," blurted Johnny.

"You don't realize what powers you have at your disposal."

"And what are those powers?" asked Johnny.

"You will find out in time. Have faith in me."

Johnny fumed. The last things he needed were riddles. "Fuck you, Safa. We don't need you to defeat those assholes!"

"You will recant those words when you see what awaits you," Safa warned him.

With nothing more to discuss, Johnny and Paula left the station. Gino slept on the floor, oblivious to the discomfort.

--------

Jo fumed as she drove off to her drill site despite the darkness. Not only did she lose her two interns, but now she faced the possibility of being alone in Parmissing Valley. For years her husband neglected her for younger women at the company. She was purposely kept away from his headquarters because he felt threatened by her technical knowledge and to protect his little harem from her.

After twelve years of being the company laughing stock, she decided the best way to get even was to beat him at his own game. When she developed the new drill after filing for divorce, he immediately knew the impact it could have for his competitors against him. Even worse, he had to face the board and explain why his soon to be ex-wife could possibly ruin their stock and put them out of business. Suddenly his 'harem' was a detriment to his job and not a status. The board could vote him out.

Jo became accustomed to having two young men at her beckon. They never argued and always kept her satisfied. She realized that having lots of money does breed the desire for control.

Now that Paula was threatening her stability, she had to do something. It bothered her that Gino would desert her and take up with Paula at the station. Perhaps Paula needed to be taught a lesson – one she'd never forget. Jo knew what she had to do to protect her property. Paula would have to pay and pay in a way she'd never forget.

# CHAPTER IX

# HEROES AND HOSTAGES

The adult Ardonean descended through a hole in the lofty ceiling to the rough terrain along the floor and dropped Sasha onto the rocks. Lamar released his hold on the creature's neck and fell next to her.

Exhausted from dragging two humans to the cave, the creature settled down on a ledge across from them and rested.

Further along the ledge were two smaller Ardoneans, resting as well from their arduous trip to Earth. On the floor were the carcasses of the alien Johnny shot down and another that died entering the Earth's atmosphere.

Two bears entered through the tunnel in the side of the cavern and sat beneath the ledge as if guarding them.

Already inside the cavern were two wolves. One perched next to the alien on the ledge and the other remained at the side entrance.

Sasha sobbed as Lamar attempted to console her. It was difficult to see in the darkness so their vision was limited. Only a narrow ray of light from the hole in the cavern ceiling and another from the side tunnel beneath the sleeping alien could be seen.

"We have to find a place to hide until help comes," Lamar insisted. "We can't stay here."

Sasha looked up at him and said sadly, "We're going to die here, aren't we?"

Lamar hugged her tightly. "No way. I'll kill every one of those creatures with my bare hands to protect you. I'll make sure we get out of here and that's a promise."

Sasha appreciated his confidence but knew they were in a dire situation. She sat back against the rocky wall of the cavern and tried to fight back her tears.

Lamar felt along the walls and, as his vision adjusted to the darkness, he could make out the shape of the cavern wall. On the far side was the faint glow of minerals and possibly diamonds. He considered crossing the cavern floor but the wolves and the bears watched his every move.

Sasha wondered what it was that gave him the heart of a lion to survive the horrors of the last alien incursion and how he fearlessly acted in this one. He was much more of a hero than she imagined him to be.

Lamar climbed up onto a small ledge and discovered a shallow depression that could provide some protection at least from the sides and above. "Sasha, hurry," he called.

Sasha reached up for his hand and held it tightly. He lifted her onto the ledge and ushered her inside the shallow opening. They sat together inside, not more than four feet from the ledge. Lamar knew that it would be difficult but possible to fight them from there. This was their only chance to survive.

"Do you think Johnny and Paula will find us?" asked Sasha.

"I don't know. They're pretty smart so we have to believe that they will."

"I promise, Lamar, if we get out of this, I'll never mention another thing about aliens again."

"I'll hold you to that." He held his pistol in his left hand and kept his arm around Sasha's shoulders with his right.

"Now what do we do?" she asked, hoping for something to build on.

"There are the bears, wolves and the alien creatures out there. Each one I kill will increase our odds of survival."

"And how many bullets do you have?"

Lamar frowned and answered unconvincingly, "Enough, if I make a perfect shot each time."

Overcome with exhaustion, Sasha nestled against him and slept.

Lamar considered moving onto the ledge and drawing the animals toward him, one at a time, by throwing rocks at them. He needed to fire from close range at their heads to have any chance of killing each with a single shot. But then, the other creatures they killed didn't stay dead so he had no idea what to expect.

As he contemplated his odds, one of the smaller Ardoneans dropped onto the ledge and shrieked, scaring the daylights out of both of them. Sasha screamed as the creature grabbed her legs in its jaws and pulled at her.

Lamar held onto her and fired a shot into the alien's chest. It shrieked again and retreated away from them. When the alien attempted to fly off the ledge, it tumbled and fell to the ground below, badly injured.

Lamar peered down and saw his opportunity. He picked up a large rock and leaped down on the creature, crushing its head with the rock. After a sickening thud, the creature became motionless. Lamar scurried back onto the ledge, concerned over Sasha's injury.

Sasha sobbed and clutched at her wounded leg. He pulled her back inside the nook. "How bad is it?" he asked, concerned.

"I don't know. It's my ankle and shin."

"This plan isn't going to work. Time for Plan B," he announced determinedly.

---

Just after sunrise the next morning, Johnny and Paula returned to the station. Gino sat outside and waited for them.

"Get in, Gino," ordered Johnny. "We're going after Lamar and Sasha."

Gino climbed into the back seat and said nothing. As they drove up the mountain trail toward the cabin, Gino ordered, "Go to the drill site. Forget the cabin."

Paula urged Johnny to comply with his instructions. Johnny steered to the right and followed the dirt road away from the cabin. "I hope you're right or there's going to be some…"

Paula interrupted him and asked Gino, "So what are we looking for?"

There are two entrances to the cavern. We need to seal off one of them and then secure the other."

"What about Lamar and Sasha?" asked Johnny.

"They are still alive," replied Gino unemotionally. "I am sure of this."

Johnny glanced suspiciously at Paula but she nodded to him that he should trust Gino.

"Can we kill this creature with our weapons?" asked Johnny.

"There are four creatures," Gino informed them. "They are mortal but they won't die easily."

"Four! When the hell did this happen?" Johnny grumbled.

"During yesterday's sunrise," he answered. "Their arrival was masked by the sun's light."

"Shit! So now we have four flying monkeys and the friggin' animal kingdom to worry about."

"The animals aren't our concern anymore; only the Ardoneans."

"The what?" asked Paula with a baffled expression.

"Ardoneans," repeated Gino.

"Fucking Ardoneans," Johnny complained. "So much for immigration control." He parked the SUV near the drill assembly and banged his head against the steering wheel in frustration. Paula rubbed the back of his neck and projected confidence to him, another test for her curiosity.

"Come on, Honey," she urged him. "We can do this."

Johnny peered at her and felt a surge of confidence. "All right. Let's kick some alien ass." Now convinced, she marveled at the possibilities.

The three of them stepped out and scanned the area. Jo's Escalade was parked nearby but there was no sign of her. They expanded their search around the other vehicles and the drill assembly.

Johnny noticed that the power cable to the drill and the connector for the remote cable were repaired. "She's been here recently," he informed Paula. "She can't be far."

━━━━━ ✦✦✦ ━━━━━

Lamar stood on the ledge and scanned the cavern. The bears snarled at him from time to time, forcing him to retreat. He threw stones at them until they came at him. As he reached for another rock, he bumped his knee into a boulder the size of a small child. He eyed its position on the ledge with the path that the bears ascended to reach them. He leaned into the boulder and attempted to roll it down the path. At first it wouldn't budge but when he leaned his back against the cavern wall and shoved with all the strength in his legs, the boulder budged.

Sasha was amazed at his perseverance and stepped onto the ledge. She understood what he was doing and threw rocks at the bears to distract them.

As the bears lumbered up the path toward them, Lamar gave one more push and shoved the boulder down the path. It gained speed and, before the bears could react, the boulder struck both animals. The two tumbled to the ground below, both injured badly. The boulder rolled across the rear legs of one bear and rested against the side of the other. Their wails filled the cavern as they lay in agony. The two wolves immediately rushed at Lamar in their defense.

"I hope you're a damn good shot, Lamar," Sasha uttered. "Here they come!"

"I guess we'll find out," he replied and took aim. As soon as he saw the outline of the first wolf approach, he fired a round into its side. The wolf yelped and fell to the ground. It writhed in agony and then lay still, breathing slower until it died.

The second wolf disappeared. Lamar could hear the echo of its paws on the rocks but couldn't tell where it was. "Get back inside," he instructed Sasha.

Just as he looked up, the wolf leaped down upon him. He lost his grip on the pistol and held onto the wolf's jaws with both hands. Overcome by both fear and anger, he desperately fought the wolf.

Sasha saw his pistol and reached for it. She wanted to fire but feared hitting Lamar. As she watched fearfully, Lamar punched the wolf in the side of the head with one hand and dazed it. He tried to twist its jaw and break its neck but the wolf was too strong.

The wolf clawed at Lamar's chest and struggled to break free from his hold. Lamar groaned in pain as the wolf inflicted several gashes in his chest.

In desperation, Sasha approached them and fired a shot into the wolf's head. It struggled and then died. Lamar threw the carcass off the ledge and lay still.

"Are you all right, Lamar?" Sasha asked, trembling in fear.

Lamar felt the blood on his hands and knew he was likely infected. Then he realized that so was Sasha. Anger flared inside him as he realized what the consequences would be.

"I'm just fucking fine!" he blurted. Then he regained his composure. "Thanks for saving my life. I think I was losing that battle."

"Can we get out of here now?"

Lamar took the pistol from her and checked the magazine. "I have four left. I'd hate to leave without using them."

"Can't we just leave? We can come back later when we have help."

Lamar stared at the pistol and then up at the alien creatures' perch. "You're right. Let's get the hell out of here."

The two of them hobbled around the perimeter of the cavern to the side entrance. They heard one of the aliens descend onto the ground behind them. Lamar knew it was telepathic and would soon warn the others.

Suddenly, five bright balls of light passed through the opening in the ceiling and dropped onto the cavern floor. They glowed for several moments before fading. Lamar and Sasha were stunned.

"Oh, shit! Run, Sasha!"

The two of them limped around the perimeter of the cavern to the side entrance.

"What are they?" asked Sasha as she entered the small cave leading to the outside world.

"I think our alien friends just got reinforcements," he answered, fearing the growing threat. "We have to get help fast."

Sasha stopped and looked back. The faint glow produced an eerie image of the aliens as each of the five new cylinders on the ground opened.

Small aliens emerged from the pods and huddled together.

"Will you look at that?" uttered Lamar, pausing briefly to see them. "They're infants."

Sasha looked back, too. "Why infants?" she asked.

Lamar pulled her by the arm and replied, "Remember, that big one you called the leader hasn't been here very long. I think those others are gonna grow real fast." He took aim at one of them and waited for a sure shot.

"Don't Lamar. Let's get out of here!"

"Lamar reluctantly stowed his gun and they hurried toward daylight at the cave's entrance.

---

"You have a plan, Gino, or is this one on me?" chided Johnny.

"I need an explosive device to seal the opening in the top of the mountain."

"We have some dynamite for clearing landslide debris," offered Paula. She went to the rear of the SUV and retrieved it for Gino.

"Paula, you search for the second entrance," ordered Gino. "I'll search for the entrance to the top of the cavern."

"And let me guess, you want me to stay here," replied Johnny sarcastically.

"Yes. If your friends return or if we need help, you will need to respond."

Johnny folded his arms, looking irate. If it wasn't for Paula's insistence, he'd never listen to Gino in the first place.

"Don't enter the cavern, Sheriff, until after you hear the explosion," Gino warned and then he hurried off into the trees.

"Be careful, Paula," warned Johnny. "I don't like this at all."

Paula nodded in acknowledgement and headed west, the opposite direction as Gino.

Johnny checked the area around Jo's drill assembly and her vehicle. He wondered what could have happened to her. She knew how to defend herself and wouldn't be easy prey for these creatures. There would at least be a carcass or two if she was attacked.

---

Paula crept through the foliage as she searched for the cave. When she climbed over a fallen tree and emerged from the bushes, she found herself face to face with Jo.

"Holy shit! You scared the hell out of me," she exclaimed.

Jo was unfazed by her reaction. "There's a cave not far from here. I tracked one of the bears to it."

"Any other creatures near this cave?"

"No, but since the bear is dead, I propose we find out."

"Very well."

Jo led her through a dense portion of forest. The mouth of the cave was well hidden by bushes, although a path had been worn with a variety of animal tracks leading in and out. The mouth was somewhat narrow but high enough for a person to enter in a stooped position.

Jo heard a voice that told her to attack Paula and take her prisoner. She tried to shrug it off but it was overwhelming. The recollection of Paula and Gino filled her mind with thoughts of revenge and punishment. Then she wondered if being infected by the bear was intended to drive her into conflict with her peers. "How friggin' ridiculous," she complained to herself.

Paula approached the cave with her pistol and a flashlight drawn, unaware of Jo's dilemma.

"Why don't you wait for Johnny to back us up?" suggested Jo.

"He's back at the drill site," she replied. "It's just me and you."

Jo smirked as Paula turned away from her and peered inside the cave. She took advantage of the opportunity and struck Paula in the back of the head with the butt of her pistol. Paula slumped to the ground unconscious.

"I have obeyed your command," muttered Jo in response to the voice. She lifted Paula over her shoulder and carried her in the direction of the cabin.

The alien leader's voice repeatedly told her to kill Paula and that she wasn't necessary for the plan. Jo responded that she would take care of it in due time.

⋅⋅✦✦✦⋅⋅

Johnny heard the explosion and was relieved that one of the cavern's entrances was sealed. His thoughts were interrupted by the sound of a vehicle approaching. As he hid behind the Escalade, a dark Crown Victoria parked next to the Escalade and Leon stepped out with a large man in a suit. They approached the drill assembly and inspected it.

Johnny emerged from behind the vehicle and asked, "Who are you gentleman and what do you want?"

"Where's Jo?" Leon asked.

"Don't know," answered Johnny. "We're looking for her."

"Bullshit!" shouted Leon. He held the camera up and explained, "Your pictures gave away the location. You knew all along she was here."

"I'm the law here and you'll answer to me," warned Johnny.

"Not anymore," Leon replied and drew his pistol. Before Johnny could respond, he fired two shots into his shoulder and chest.

Johnny staggered backward and fell to the ground. Numbness quickly took over his body as the fear of dying sent him into a brief panic. Laying helpless and waiting for his last moments to pass from him, he felt sadness for not saying goodbye to Paula. He recalled how much fun they had together. As his strength faded, he could see Jo carrying Paula. He heard the alien creature's instructions to Jo as well.

In desperation, he tried to block Jo's mind from the Ardonean's voice. He remembered Jo and her invite at the hospital to be her boy toy. Lewd images filled his head as he attempted to distract Jo from the voice. Then he wondered what it would be like to see Paula and Jo make love to each other. As he faded from consciousness, the visions of the two women in bed together seemed almost real. Then he saw Sasha join them. The last thing Johnny remembered was the women inviting him to join them. Blackness enveloped his mind as he slipped away.

Leon instructed the other man to get the drill assembly into the U-Haul truck. He lit a cigar and smiled at his good fortune.

⋯◆◆◆⋯

Lamar and Sasha tumbled to the ground from the explosion. Rocks fell around them and forced them away from the entrance.

"So fucking close!" he shouted angrily.

Once inside the cavern again, rocks continued to fall from above. Lamar pulled Sasha back to the depression in the wall. One rock struck him in the shoulder and staggered him.

The aliens shrieked and took flight. Three were crushed on the floor as they attempted to flee. The others flocked to the cavern exit and crept through the partially obstructed cave in a desperate attempt to escape. Clawing voraciously at the rocks, they continued frantically until they cleared enough space to exit the cavern.

Lamar lay on the ground, clutching at his injured shoulder. Sasha panicked as she saw their opportunity to escape vanish before them. "Come on, Lamar," she pleaded. "We have to get out of here."

Lamar rolled onto his side and tried to get up. The excruciating pain forced him to the ground. "Give me a moment, Sasha," he muttered.

Sasha reluctantly stuck by him. She knew if the aliens could get out, so could they.

Outside, the aliens took flight and circled high overhead. Leon and his partner, oblivious to the alien threat, disconnected the wiring to the drill assembly and coiled it on top of the generator.

The adult Ardonean with the colorful plume on its head descended in front of the drill assembly and folded its wings. It stared at Leon with black empty eyes.

"What the hell are you?" he shouted and fired three shots from his pistol into the creature's chest. The thick skin limited the bullets' penetration and only irritated the creature further. A dozen tendrils shot from its chest and wrapped tightly around Leon's head. The sharp ends drove into his skull and lodged in his brain.

His partner, Tommy, rushed to his aid, but before he could fire, the remaining three aliens leaped upon him from behind and fed off his body.

Leon was paralyzed and left in a trance by the Ardonean leader. It released its hold on him and ejected a long tongue from its mouth into Leon's. A slithering sound ensued as alien eggs were deposited inside Leon's digestive tract. He would serve them as a host for their offspring and then be fed upon like his peers. The aliens took flight and returned to the cavern. Once inside, they settled on an upper ledge and slept. Leon wandered into the forest with his commands embedded in his brain.

Lamar and Sasha again tried to leave the cavern. They climbed through the rocky debris to the cave and were excited by the sight of daylight. Once they exited the cave, the two of them hurried through the forest until they found a secluded area by a stream to rest and ascertain the extent of their injuries.

"What's going to happen to us?" Sasha asked sadly as Lamar tended to her injured leg.

Lamar removed his shirt and soaked it in water. His chest was covered in deep gashes from the wolf's claws. The bleeding stopped but the wounds were deep. He wiped the blood off Sasha's leg and sighed. "I guess time will tell."

Lamar lay on his back and stared at the sky. He knew what their injuries meant. They would mutate into something other than human, but into what? He was ashamed to face Johnny and Paula with the news that they might have to put the two of them down like rabid animals.

Sasha watched his expression change as he pondered the few options they had. "It's all right, Lamar. Whatever is gonna be, will be."

"But nothing good can come of this, Sasha."

"Let's wait and see. Sometimes fate has a strange plan for all of us."

"I wish I could believe that," he said tearfully.

• • • ✦ ✦ ✦ • • •

Jo entered the abandoned cabin. Inside the bedroom, she tossed Paula's prone body on the bed. Her first course of action was to tie Paula to the bedposts securely and then find something to drink.

The voice rang out in her head and brought her to her knees. "You will obey my command. Kill her now!"

Jo tried to fight the voice. It created immense pain in her head until tears streamed down her cheeks. She rummaged through the cabinets and refrigerator until she found a bottle of Jack Daniels and a six pack of Yuengling. "I guess this will have to do," she muttered and opened the bottle of liquor.

"Fuck you, you flying pig!" she shouted. "No one tells me what to do!" After several healthy swigs, she turned her attention to Paula. She was still unconscious and blood stained the pillow behind her head. Jo recalled watching Gino with Paula inside the police station and felt her rage return.

Paula had the sheriff to satisfy her needs but she had to have Gino, too. Now, Jo was going to have all of them. She could read Paula's thoughts as Paula searched through the darkness in her mind for Johnny. Jo's eyes glowed red as she acknowledged her new powers and basked in the knowledge that she would rule them all and then some. She would defy the alien and kill it when the time came.

Then thoughts of her making love to Paula confused her. She tried to clear her mind but then images of her, Paula, Sasha and Johnny in their own little orgy aroused her.

*Oh, the possibilities*, she considered, but then asked herself, *Why now?* Then the voice flushed away those thoughts and pressured her to kill Paula.

After another healthy swig of whiskey, she unbuttoned Paula's shirt. After having young men at her whim, she always wondered what it would be like to have a young slut like Paula to herself. *Screw the torture*, she decided. *I'm getting some action.*

The sexual images continued in her mind and tuned out the alien voice. As she slid Paula's open shirt aside, she admired her shapely breasts under her bra and became envious. Jo's breasts were a bit larger but hung low compared to Paula's. She slid one hand under Paula's bra and another under her own. Feeling naughty beyond her expectations, she undressed Paula and then removed her own clothing. One more swig of whiskey and she was ready for her first girl-on-girl experience.

Paula groaned as she awakened and panicked when she realized she was a prisoner and naked. "What the hell's wrong with you, Jo?" she blurted with teary eyes.

Jo knelt with her head between Paula's thighs and declared proudly, "I'm gonna give you a night you'll never forget."

Paula squirmed to get loose but once Jo's face vanished from her sight and she felt her tongue press inside of her, Paula was soon overcome with passion.

Jo enjoyed controlling Paula's emotions with just her tongue and fingers. She manipulated Paula further, probing her at will, while lapping hungrily. Paula moaned with pleasure as Jo brought her to an uncontrollable orgasm. Soon, Paula climaxed in the midst of a long and whining moan.

"Your turn," Jo remarked sarcastically and mounted Paula in a sixty-nine position. Paula couldn't help becoming a willing participant and the two women pleasured each other until both were exhausted.

Jo moved her face to Paula's and kissed her lustily, "How does it feel to be my whore?"

"Please let me go," Paula begged. "You didn't have to do this."

"You took Gino from me. Wasn't the sheriff enough?"

Paula looked at her with a confused expression. "Gino?" she replied with surprise. "I didn't take Gino from you. The alien left the coyote's dying carcass and took up inside of him. He gave us information about the flying creatures."

Jo was embarrassed by her revelation. "You mean that really isn't Gino?"

"No, it's not. Now, please untie me."

"Sorry, deputy, but I'm not finished with you yet." She kissed her again, while massaging Paula between her legs. "You see, I think I like this arrangement," she commented between kisses.

Paula tried to rebuff her but the more she struggled, the more Jo forced herself upon her. As Jo descended between her legs once more, the front door opened and startled her.

Jo stood up and retrieved her pistol from the bureau nearby. "Don't move, honey. I'll be back for you," she said confidently.

The bedroom door swung open and Leon stood there, eying her with a pale complexion. He hid his right arm behind his back.

Jo looked pleased to see him. She aimed the pistol at his head ready to fire. "I've waited a long time for this, Leon."

Leon stared with vacant eyes at her and then revealed an ax in his right hand. "It's time to die, Jo. You cannot access this mountain with your device."

Jo became disappointed and complained, "I wanted to kill the real Leon, not an imposter inside him." She fired three shots into his chest. He looked down at the wounds with a lost expression and then continued toward her.

Jo lunged at him and tried desperately to pull the ax from his hand. The two wrestled on the ground while Paula tried frantically to free her wrists from the rags that bound her.

When Jo managed to point the pistol at Leon's head, he head-butted her and she lost her leverage on him. He punched her in the face and knocked her senseless.

Paula freed her wrists and desperately untied the rags around her ankles. She searched for something to use as a weapon but there was nothing available.

Leon raised the ax to strike Jo in the face with a twisted smile. Paula saw her opportunity and wrested the ax from him.  He looked up at her, wide-eyed with surprise.

Paula questioned Jo before striking Leon, "Now, who's the whore, Jo?"

Jo refused to answer. Leon turned his attention back to Jo and strangled her. When Jo's eyes rolled back, Paula struck him in the head with the blunt side of the axe. Leon released his hold and was momentarily stunned.

"Once more, Jo: who's the whore?"

Jo replied hoarsely, "All right. I'm your whore. Now kill this son of a bitch!"

Paula struck Leon in the back of the neck with the sharp end of the ax. His head drooped forward and brown blood spurted over Jo, pooling across the floor.

As Leon's arms dropped to his side, Jo delivered a strong punch to the side of his head and knocked it off his shoulders. The headless corpse fell on its side.

Jo broke into tears and sobbed. Paula wanted to hit her with the ax as well but couldn't bring herself to do it. She tossed the ax on the couch in the living room and locked the front door.

Standing over Jo, Paula pondered Jo's assault on her. She felt sympathy and helped her to her feet. "Why don't you shower off?" she suggested to Jo. "That blood stinks."

"I don't want to be alone," she sobbed. "Come with me, please."

Paula relented and nudged her into the bathroom. Feeling violated by Jo, she also questioned her reaction to Jo's advances. Part of her enjoyed having a woman go down on her, but still, her heart was with Johnny. She feared that she betrayed him but wondered if he'd understand, given their physiological changes.

As Jo waited for the water to warm, Paula was excited by the sight of her nude body from behind. She never thought of Jo as attractive before but then, she never thought about Jo.

When the air became warm from the heated water and the mirror steamed up, Jo stepped in behind the shower curtain. Paula became aroused and followed her in. Jo was pleased when she appeared behind her. Paula brushed her wet hair out of her eyes and kissed her gently. She picked up a bar of soap from the soap rack and lathered Jo's body.

When she finished, Jo took the soap from her and did the same. The women fondled each other and kissed until the hot water turned cool. They left the shower and went back to the bedroom.

⋅⋅◆◆◆⋅⋅

Lamar and Sasha staggered to the drill site and noticed the police SUV next to the Escalade.

"Johnny and Paula must be here somewhere," he noted as he looked around. "I hope they're okay." Sasha held his arm tightly and nodded, hoping for their safety.

Next to the drill assembly was a large patch of blood in the grass and a few shreds of a blood-stained suit. They glanced at each other uneasily and searched beyond the drill.

When they looked behind the Escalade, they were horrified to find Johnny, lying motionless with two bullet wounds. Lamar checked for a pulse but it was faint.

"We've got to get him to a hospital fast!" he exclaimed with tear-streaked cheeks.

Gino emerged from the forest and approached them. He saw their grief and sensed that Johnny was near death.

Lamar and Sasha were apprehensive when Gino urgently knelt down and placed his hand on Johnny's chest.

"What are you doing?" questioned Lamar.

"I can help him."

Lamar glanced at Sasha. Both refused to believe that Gino's alien presence had that kind of power.

"How can you help him?" he inquired as he wiped the tears from his eyes. A faint glimmer of hope showed in his facial expression.

"Your friend's physiology has been altered. He has, as you would say, mutated. I sense that both of you have begun to mutate as well."

Lamar and Sasha became edgy at his remark. In a sordid way, Lamar and Sasha were relieved that they weren't alone in dealing with the mutation.

"Just save him, already!" urged Lamar. "Skip the physiological babble."

Gino leaned his face close to Johnny's and opened his mouth wide. A small tentacle extended from Gino into Johnny through his mouth. His eyes turned white as his body took on a frozen state while inserting an alien substance into Johnny.

Sasha was mortified and turned away. Lamar tried but couldn't take his eyes off of them. He had to know more about these alien powers.

When Gino finished, he retracted the tentacle back inside his own body. After several seconds, his eyes became normal, although he still wore a pale complexion.

"Well?" asked Lamar anxiously.

"He will heal," replied Gino. "It will take time, though."

"Can we move him?"

"Yes. The internal wounds have already clotted. His blood needs to regenerate and that will be a slow process. His head injury, although serious, has begun to heal as well."

Lamar looked confused by the last part of his statement until Sasha explained, "He means Johnny's concussion."

Lamar attempted to lift Johnny but couldn't with his injured shoulder. Gino stepped in and picked Johnny up. He carried him effortlessly to the police SUV and set him in the back.

"Thank you," said Lamar appreciatively, still amazed at what just transpired.

"I'll drive him to the hospital," offered Sasha.

"No," answered Gino sternly. "He must remain here."

Lamar nodded to her, urging her to comply.

"Your people cannot know what any of you have become."

Sasha backed away with her hands up defensively. "Whatever," she remarked suspiciously. "You guys know more about this alien voodoo crap than I do."

"What now?" Lamar asked Gino.

"We wait for your deputy to return."

"Do you know where she is?"

"No, but I sense she'll know where to find us."

Sasha approached Gino and inquired bravely, "Why are the aliens hunting us?"

Gino stared at her, curious, and placed his hand on her shoulder. "It's not all of you," he explained. "This man (Johnny) and the dark-skinned man (Lamar) defeated our renegades and destroyed one of our spaceships in space. This concerns the Ardoneans greatly."

"So, they want to kill Lamar and Johnny?" she asked.

Gino responded, "No, not at all. They fear them and their methods. They wish use their tact by controlling them to build a new army here on Earth. The rest of you are expendable for their war."

"Shit," she uttered and turned away.

Lamar leaned against the tailgate of the SUV and observed Johnny with concern. Sasha tried to console him with her hands on his shoulders.

Gino sat on a log and seemed frozen in time. His eyes turned white and he appeared like a statue.

Lamar then tried to reach Paula by phone but there was no response. He fretted that she was in trouble and considered searching for her. Sasha understood his dilemma and offered to help. She felt helpless when Lamar requested that she sit quietly.

••••◆••••

Paula dried Jo with a towel and studied her body with envy. Jo was shapely with a well-defined ass to compliment her beautiful breasts. She was everything a man wants in a woman compared to her petite body.

Sensing Paula's attraction to her, Jo turned and took the towel from Paula. She kissed her passionately and then dried her body as well. She was surprised at how Paula perceived her. Perhaps, despite her fear of aging, she really was a beautiful woman. She pointed out the irony of their views of each other to Paula and, as the two of them stood by the bed still nude, they again admired each other's physical characteristics.

"We ought to get back to the drill site," suggested Paula, feeling guilty about their affair.

"Yeah, I know what you mean," replied Jo. She gazed into Paula's eyes and confessed, "I need to have you one more time."

"I know. I feel that way, too." Paula wrapped her arms around Jo and nestled up to her. "We really should go."

Once you return to Johnny, we won't be together again," Jo reminded her.

Paula suggested that they get together once in a while to rekindle their relationship. Jo was encouraged by her offer but knew that her duties and her commitment to Johnny would prevent that from happening.

"What about him?" asked Paula, pointing to Leon's corpse.

"Screw him. Let the animals have him." Jo grabbed the headless body and dragged it out the door to the side of the cabin.

Paula picked up Leon's head and looked away in disgust. She stepped outside and handed it to Jo. "Here. You do the honors," she said.

Jo took the head and walked over to a PVC plate next to the porch. She unlatched it and opened it. Her face grew contorted from the gross smell that arose from inside the septic tank. "Well Leon, you were always a piece of shit. Consider this a family reunion," she mocked him and dropped his head into the tank, followed by his headless body. Relieved, she closed the cover and latched it. The two women left the cabin, eager to arrive at the cave before sunset.

Jo retrieved Paula's holster, gun and phone from the bushes and mentioned humbly, "I'm sure you'll want these back. I… um… I'm sorry for what I did to you."

"Thanks," replied Paula as she appreciated Jo's trust in her. She fastened the holster and belt to her waist and checked the gun's magazine. It held seven rounds. Content with her inspection, she inserted the magazine into the pistol and holstered it.

"I really am sorry about hitting you, Paula. The alien got into my head and ordered me to kill you. Then I remembered when you were with Gino at the station. I was sure you took him from me."

Paula pondered her experience and asked, "What made you want to …make love to me …instead of killing me?"

"I don't know," answered Jo, somewhat skeptical. "It's like someone wanted us to do it."

Paula became more suspicious. "I think I know what you mean, Jo."

"I'll make it up to you; I swear, Paula. I really didn't want to hit you like that."

"Let's pretend that part of our day didn't happen," Paula suggested. She checked her cell phone and noted several missed calls from Lamar. She called Lamar's number and waited.

Lamar was relieved to see her number come up on his phone. "Paula, are you alright?" he asked excitedly.

Paula explained that she lost her phone as they explored the higher elevation of the mountain. She informed him about their altercation with Leon and that Jo was with her.

Lamar instructed her to return to the drill site immediately. When she asked about Johnny, Lamar hesitated and then repeated that she should return promptly.

Paula knew something bad happened and relayed Lamar's instructions to Jo. They hurried back to the drill site as darkness descended over the west side of the mountain.

When she saw Johnny in the back of the truck, she rushed to him in a panic. "What happened?"

"We found him with two gunshot wounds," explained Lamar. "Gino did some alien ritual to him and says he'll be all right."

Paula broke into tears. She felt guilty as though this was her fault for staying away so long.

Jo knelt in front of Gino and gazed at him. She was relieved to know that he hadn't left her for Paula. He was all she had left and she couldn't do the drilling operation alone. Then she realized that he may not be the Gino she once knew. Knowing that they all inherited an ability to read thoughts to some degree, she tried to open up to him and communicate.

After several attempts, Gino responded but in a vague manner. He was frightened and wanted to be held. Someone else inside him assured him that he would be himself soon.

Paula noticed Jo's anxiety but couldn't leave Johnny. Her relationship with Jo was going to be more complicated than she thought.

Gino finally became alert and approached them. He stood before them with a crazed look in his eyes. As he looked up to the sky, he opened his mouth and quivered. Tentacles appeared from inside his mouth and latched onto his shoulders. Then the alien, a small, gray, pulsing mass, appeared in his mouth.

Everyone stared in awe at the alien creature. After a moment of nerve-wracking tension, the alien let loose a high-pitched wail. Each of them felt pain shoot through their brains. When the pain subsided, they stared at each other, baffled by the incident. The alien retreated inside Gino's mouth and slithered down his throat.

"What the hell just happened?" asked Sasha tearfully.

Gino announced that their mental capacities were enhanced to place them in synch with each other. This would be a critical weapon that would help them defeat the alien creatures.

There were so many questions about their mutation that needed to be answered but no time to understand. Gino urged patience and then informed them that their defining moment would soon be at hand.

Sasha regretted that she ever sought out the details of the alien incursion and wanted to flee Parmissing Valley as fast as she could. Lamar's firm hand on her shoulder and gave her confidence that things would be all right.

Johnny stirred and opened his eyes. "I'm alive! Holy shit!"

Paula wrapped her arms around him and hugged him tightly. "I'll never leave you alone again," she swore.

"I thought I was dead," Johnny continued. "But here I am – alive and with you."

"Of course, you are," she replied. "I'm so sorry I wasn't here to watch your back."

"Did you see the men who did this to me?"

Paula glanced up at Lamar for his response.

"We didn't see anyone," he replied. "Who were they?"

"Jo's ex-husband and one of his thugs," Johnny answered,

"Leon did this to you?" Jo blurted to Johnny with a mortified expression. She felt both embarrassed and responsible for what happened to Paula first and now Johnny. Johnny related what happened.

"Leon won't be a problem anymore," Jo assured him. "Paula and I took care of him."

"What about his sidekick, the big guy?"

"We think the Ardoneans got him. All that was left were shreds of his suit," Paula related.

"A fitful ending for what they did to me, those bastards," grumbled Johnny.

"Ardoneans, huh?" commented Lamar.

"That's what they are," replied Paula. "Gino told us."

Lamar wondered if they were further along with their mutation than he was led to believe. *Maybe Sasha's right*, he thought to himself. *Maybe it doesn't matter what we are.*

Johnny felt an itching sensation, then scratched underneath his shirt and retrieved a mushroomed bullet. While he examined it, the itching sensation returned. He scratched the skin around his shoulder and retrieved another bullet. "What the hell is happening to me?" he asked frantically.

"Don't worry about it," Lamar told him. He placed his hand on Johnny's shoulder and assured him that he'd be fine. Johnny was more concerned that Lamar knew he was infected and had mutated somewhat.

Gino explained that the healing Johnny had was the same process that brought the wolves and bears back to life, although they suffered the same limitation as Johnny – blood loss.

The sound of flapping wings caught their attention. Gino advised, "The Ardoneans are coming. We must find shelter."

"Everyone inside the vehicle," ordered Lamar. He closed the tailgate and hurried in the driver's side.

Gino reluctantly entered the vehicle and warned, "This will not be enough to stop them."

"Then you suggest something," replied Lamar impatiently.

Gino stared at Paula and commented, "You and Jo know where to go."

The two women were stunned by his comment. Both were uncomfortable over his request and wondered how and what he knew of their time at the cabin.

"To the cabin," Paula instructed Lamar.

Lamar gunned the motor and raced down the mountain road toward the intersection and then the road to the cabin.

Johnny inquired from the back of the SUV in a weakened voice, "The cabin was quite an experience, huh?"

Paula and Jo glared at him from the back seat. Johnny had a sly grin on his face.

"What do you mean by that?" Paula asked defensively.

"I'm sure the two of you did a real number on Leon."

The women glanced suspiciously at each other, not sure if Johnny knew of their relationship.

"Seeing the state that he was in was sure enlightening," explained Jo. "He became a mutant - like some kind of zombie."

"Killing him was … shocking," replied Paula uneasily. "It felt like murder except that he wasn't human."

Lamar understood the emotional conflict she felt. "You did what you had to do," he said compassionately. "Leave it at that."

"So, what made you go to the cabin," inquired Sasha curiously.

Paula was at a loss to explain what Jo did to her and how things changed between them. Jo felt her unease and interceded, "I knew Leon was close by. I had to lead him away from the rest of you for your own safety. Paula suspected something else and followed me."

"Thank goodness we're all in one piece," responded Sasha.

Lamar turned the crowded SUV up the trail toward the cabin. The Ardoneans circled overhead and followed them. One of the creatures landed on the roof of the SUV and rocked it wildly. Lamar struggled to keep the vehicle moving without going off the road.

Paula drew her pistol and aimed upward. She calculated where the creature was positioned on the roof and fired twice. Two rounds ripped through the vehicle's roof and struck the creature in the chest. It released its hold on the SUV and tumbled across the road.

As the vehicle drew near the cabin, two of the aliens landed on the roof and yanked repeatedly on it. Jo and Paula fired at them but the wounds were not lethal.

The creatures rocked the SUV until it veered off the dirt road, bouncing crazily over the rough terrain and then flipping over on its roof. Soon, the smell of gas leaking from the tank filled the air.

Lamar kicked out the front windshield and helped Sasha out of the front seat. Paula and Jo climbed out of the side door and assisted Johnny.

Gino was dazed but crawled out the side door behind the women and then collapsed on the ground.

Everyone, get to the cabin!" ordered Lamar.

Sasha rushed ahead and opened the door while Lamar and Paula helped Johnny. Jo ushered Gino close behind them.

The four Ardoneans swooped in from behind. One of them knocked Gino to the ground. Jo turned and attempted to aim her pistol at the creature but it collided with her, knocking her to the ground as well.

Before she could recover, it latched its talons firmly into her shoulders and lifted her off the ground. As the creature reached the edge of the cliff, Jo managed to pry its talons open with her hands. She tumbled near the edge and clung desperately to a handful of vines. The ground crumbled around her and she slid over the edge, screaming frantically for help. Her body jerked as the vines held her weight a short distance from the edge. She strained to pull herself up but the creature hovered next to her and raked her back with its talons.

Gino's inner self took over when he saw Jo fall over the side of the cliff. He rushed at the creature, full of rage, and dove off the cliff onto its back. The weight was too much and the creature plummeted to the bottom of the mountain with Gino on top of it. They lay sprawled across the rocks below, the alien body contorted and broken. Jo screamed out in agony as she peered down at Gino.

The remaining creatures swarmed on Lamar, Paula and Johnny. They were determined to capture Johnny as he was the weakest of the group. Lamar fired a shot and blasted a hole through the back of one creature's head.

Lamar and Paula fired several rounds into the creatures, killing a second and wounding a third. The nearly crippled creature dropped to the ground near Paula and, with short, painful leaps, it attempted to assault her. As she retreated, she fired three shots into its head and finally killed the relentless creature.

Johnny staggered to his feet and stumbled toward the cabin. Sasha shouted frantically for him to hurry but he was still in a weakened state from his wounds.

The adult Ardonean with the plume on its head knocked Lamar down and ripped the pistol from his hand. Before he could recover, the creature grabbed Johnny by his arms and flew off with him.

"No!" shouted Paula as she aimed her pistol at the fleeing creature. She cried as she lowered her weapon. A desperate shot could hit Johnny and kill him.

Lamar's arm bled from the Ardonean's talons as he recovered his pistol. "We're going after them, Paula," he announced. "Sasha, stay here at the cabin."

After what she just witnessed, Sasha replied adamantly, "No friggin' way."

"We're gonna finish this once and for all," he uttered gruffly.

Unaware that Jo was alive, they loaded extra ammo into a backpack from the toppled SUV and left for the cavern entrance.

Climbing up the vines, Jo pulled herself up on solid ground, sobbing as she looked down at Gino's body. She searched the area around the cabin and was shocked that her friends were gone. Rage took over as she was determined to get revenge for the loss of her young lovers and possibly Paula as well.

# Chapter X

# The Power of Interaction

Lamar's arm bled badly and caught Sasha's attention. She stopped him and inspected the wound. "Let me tie this off. You're losing too much blood."

"It's fine," he grumbled.

Paula stepped in front of him and blocked his path. "Let her fix your arm. We need you if we're going to get Johnny back."

Lamar relented and let Sasha tend to the wound. She removed her shirt and tore it into shreds. Paula was distracted as she eyed Sasha's body. She turned away and tried to focus on Johnny's rescue but her urges took over again. She paced frantically as she tried to control herself.

Lamar noticed and remarked, "We have a big problem, don't we, Paula?"

She glanced back at him, unsure of what he referred to.

Lamar turned to Sasha, looking very concerned. He defaulted to her to say the right thing.

"We're all infected," Sasha revealed. "I can feel us changing."

"What do you mean?" Paula asked defensively.

Sasha finished wrapping Lamar's arm and stared at her. "We feel each other," she explained. "We know what we think. We're mutants."

Lamar added, "The urges you feel aren't just happening to you. This thing that is happening to us; it magnifies our emotions. We'll have to learn to control it."

Paula was ashamed as she realized Sasha and Lamar could read her thoughts of lust.

"We also know that Johnny's alive," he added. "The creature is using him as bait."

"I'm so sorry. I can't help what I feel," she replied with tears in her eyes. "I'm obsessed with desire just like Jo was."

"Don't worry about it," Sasha said compassionately. "We'll figure out what and who we are when this is over. Right now, we have to rescue Johnny and kill those bitches."

"You know, Sasha, I can't help feeling that Johnny has something to do with these urges of lust." Sasha patted her arm and assured her that things would work out.

Lamar was impressed by her confidence and pleased that she was stepping up. Paula felt reassured by Sasha's words of encouragement and hugged her. Paula then turned to Lamar and confessed, "I thought you'd want to kill Johnny and me when you found out that we were infected."

"No, not unless you lost control and became monsters. Actually, I feared you'd have to put us down first."

They chuckled and then resumed their march to the cavern. When they reached the cave, Paula and Sasha remained outside and guarded the entrance to prevent an attack on Lamar from behind.

Lamar crept through the darkness, carrying the backpack with only the flashlight to guide him to the cavern. The cave stretched back into the mountain for almost a hundred feet and was filled with debris from the earlier explosion.

Outside the cave, Sasha fretted for fear that Lamar would be hurt or killed.

"He means that much to you, huh?" Paula asked.

"Yeah, he does."

"Go to him. I got this covered."

Sasha thanked her and hastily entered the cave. She felt her way along the walls as she approached the cavern.

A muffled sound caught Lamar's attention as he exited the cave into a large cavern. When he directed the flashlight across the walls of the cavern, he noticed the twinkling of crystals embedded in the walls. He was amazed by the beauty as he realized these were the diamonds Jo wanted to drill for so badly.

There were other strange minerals as well. *If only Jo was here to see this,* he thought to himself. Then he wondered if she could have somehow survived the fall. He regretted that they couldn't search for her and Gino but Johnny's safety and the death of the Ardoneans was paramount.

He heard something move across the stones at the base of the cavern and stepped quietly onto a ledge to the right of the cave to see.

On a flat rock near the center of the cavern, Johnny lay motionless. Long tendrils emerged from the Ardonean leader's chest and reached toward Johnny's head.

Lamar aimed his pistol and was about to pull the trigger when the creature spoke to him telepathically. *If you kill me, more will come.*

Lamar was amazed at how clearly he could understand the alien. *And we'll kill them just like you,* he responded.

*If you pledge your allegiance to me, I'll spare your friend. If not, I will deposit enough eggs inside of him to spawn an entire army of my kind.*

Lamar hesitated as the tendrils hovered over Johnny's head. Then Lamar understood what the alien's goal was. The tendrils would extract all the information from their minds, including how to defeat their opponents in space. Then it would implant a living transmitter in each one's brain to control them. They would be controlled just like the animals were.

The alien again became upset when it realized what Lamar learned from it. It placed the tendrils on Johnny's head and prepared to penetrate his skull.

Lamar thought quickly and knew he would have to kill the creature with a perfect shot. Even worse, the light was dim and the distance was too great to guarantee he could make that shot.

*How about a truce?* he suggested desperately. *You spare him. I'll spare you. We both live to fight another day.*

*You foolish creature,* the Ardonean responded. *We both know that won't work.*

Lamar broke a sweat as he aimed again and considered taking the shot.

Sasha entered the cavern and she, too, was stunned by the beautiful glow from the minerals. She heard only traces of the communication between Lamar and the creature. The development of her telepathy was still too immature to be effective.

Lamar crept forward and shined his light on the creature but it was oblivious to him. He was horrified when he saw the tendrils already resting on Johnny's head. Flashbacks of the past nightmare ran through his mind as he contemplated what to do. If he didn't act now, Johnny would suffer a horrible fate. Then he made his decision.

"No, you don't, you son of a bitch!" He rushed at the creature and grabbed the tendrils, preventing them from harming Johnny. His momentum toppled the alien to the ground. The creature scrambled to its feet and grabbed Lamar by the throat. Its tendrils coiled and reached for his head.

"Lamar!" Sasha screamed. In a panic, she fired several rounds at the creature.

The cavern rumbled from the sharp echoes. Rocks rained down from the ceiling. One of them struck the creature in the head and knocked it to the ground. Lamar crawled to his feet and tried to move Johnny.

"Come on, Johnny!" he urged frantically. "We've got to get out of here!"

As he lifted Johnny to his feet, Johnny awoke.

"Jesus, Lamar, what the hell happened?" he exclaimed weakly.

"Let's move before we get crushed!"

The falling rocks forced them against the cavern wall for safety.

Two wolves appeared from a ledge above and pursued Sasha. Lamar warned her to escape while she could. She fled the cavern and rushed through the cave. As the wolves drew closer, she turned and fired her last three rounds at them. One squealed from its injury and tumbled to the ground.

The cavern shuddered again and the ceiling fractured from the ringing of gunfire. Rocks broke away from the wall and blocked their access to the cave.

Lamar and Johnny huddled against the cavern wall, waiting anxiously for the danger to pass.

Paula was startled by the tremors and retreated away from the cave's entrance. She grew frantic as she feared for her friends inside.

A gray cloud of dust and dirt filled the air around the cave's mouth. Sasha staggered through the rubble and emerged from the dusty cloud as the walls of the cave collapsed, blocking any access to the cavern.

◆ ● ● ●

Suddenly, one of the wolves appeared from out of the dust and tackled Sasha from behind. She screamed frantically for help.

Paula instinctively rushed at the wolf and leaped on its back. She beat on its head with the butt of her pistol until it threw her aside.

Paula crawled to her feet and remembered what Gino told them about their powers. She focused on the wolf and attempted to get inside its mind. When she did, she was stunned by the images she saw. The wolf's mind was the mind of the alien from afar. She could see memories and thoughts of not just one, but many of the Ardoneans as if she was part of them and they were all one being.

The wolf froze when it realized she had influence over its thoughts. Paula took advantage of the intrusion and created thoughts of her own, showing her friends traveling to the creature's world and destroying its inhabitants with a variety of weapons.

Inside the cavern, the alien leader suddenly became panicked and retreated to the far end of the cavern. She then projected an image of her dissecting the alien in a laboratory. When the alien became enraged, its wolf poised to attack her. She generated an image of her dissecting its brain. The now frantic creature charged at her. Paula fired three shots into the wolf's head and killed it. Without the alien's influence in its mind and body, it died quickly.

Paula helped Sasha to her feet and ushered her away from the cave. Sasha hugged Paula and thanked her repeatedly. Then she again broke down into tears as she blamed herself for trapping the men inside the cavern.

The two women used their flashlights to inspect the entrance to the cave but confirmed what they feared most: there was no way in.

"We need to find shelter for the night," Paula explained sadly. "Maybe we can figure out a way in by the morning."

"But they could be dead by then!" cried Sasha.

"You have to believe in them. Lamar and Johnny survived the first invasion. They'll know how to survive this one."

Sasha realized that she was right and relented. The two women hiked back to the cabin in search of rest and safety. As they walked, Sasha inquired, "Did you recently have thoughts about making love to me?"

Paula wasn't sure what to say and asked, "Can you be a little more specific?"

"I had these urges or fantasies that I was involved in an encounter with you and Jo. Am I cracking up or is this something that you experienced as well?"

Paula was shocked by her revelation. This was becoming too frequent to be a coincidence. "I did have that same dream when I fell and was unconscious."

"I've never done that kind of thing and I don't know if I could," Sasha explained sheepishly.

"Don't worry, Sasha," Paula assured her. "It was just an illusion. I still have this sneaking suspicion that Johnny has something to do with this." Sasha was pleased that Paula had no expectations for her to involve herself with them. "Perhaps we should have a discussion with Sheriff Watkins," she suggested.

"Oh, we will," Paula promised. "When I'm finished with him, he'll never try his persuasions on us again. Sasha was pleased that it likely wasn't her desire for the women.

⸻ ✦✦✦ ⸻

Lamar and Johnny sat with their backs to the cavern wall and contemplated their situation.

"Are you okay?" asked Lamar shakily.

"Yeah. That son-of-a-bitch dropped me on my head so don't laugh at me if I'm a little stupid right now."

"We're in one hell of a predicament," he remarked.

"Any sign of our alien friend?" Johnny asked cynically.

"No. If we're lucky it was killed by the rocks."

"Gino said something about mental hocus-pocus before and how we could use it to defeat the aliens."

"Yeah, he did."

"Any idea how it works?"

"Beats me. How about we get some rest and then we'll work on that later?"

"I'll take first watch," volunteered Johnny.

Lamar was exhausted and gratefully accepted his offer. He nestled against the rocks and slept. Johnny chuckled as Lamar's snoring echoed softly around the cavern. Only falling stones occasionally interrupted the sound of his snores.

Johnny thought about Paula and what it would be like to share her with other women. He considered Jo and Sasha for a moment and then laughed it off.

<hr>

When the women reached the cabin, they were surprised to find Jo sitting on the porch. She stared blankly at the trees until she saw the women and then perked up.

"Jo, you're alive!" Paula shouted. She rushed to her and hugged her. "I was so afraid you were dead."

Sasha watched the two women and felt disappointed as she was a third wheel in the group. Paula and Jo found time to develop a friendship that seemed to mean more than her.

"If it wasn't for Gino, I would be," replied Jo sadly. "The poor kid gave his life for me."

"Was it Gino or the alien that saved you?"

"The alien tried to stop him. His emotions were too strong and his will took over."

"So, the alien and Gino are both gone," commented Sasha sympathetically.

"I'm afraid so. Let's get inside where it's safe. I've seen enough of those creatures for one day."

The three women entered the cabin and closed the door. Jo had already straightened up the cabin a bit and scrubbed the blood off the floor.

Sasha sat on the couch and pondered how to save Lamar. She was exhausted and slept.

"The place looks much better than last time," quipped Paula.

"Well, I was thinking of calling it home. I have nothing else to live for and no place else to go. I could stick to my project here on the mountain and mine diamonds."

Paula hugged her and promised that she'd always be her friend. Jo glanced toward the bedroom and gazed at Paula with hopeful eyes.

Paula felt her emotions swirl again as she recalled their previous encounter. "You're feeling it, too," she commented.

"It's strange how it happens at certain times," Jo remarked.

"I have noticed that," Paula responded. "We'll discuss my theory about this later."

◆ ·‧◆◆‧· ◆

Lamar and Johnny were now both awake.  Being trapped in the cavern left each feeling desperate to find a way out.

"Seen any sign of our winged friends?" asked Johnny.

"None at all. I'm sure they haven't forgotten about us either."

"So, what are we gonna do about our conditions?"

"You mean the fact that we're mutants, just like the ones we killed before?" kidded Lamar.

"Yeah, that's exactly what I mean," Johnny replied bitterly.

"Well, we're not quite like the ones we killed. We're still human, just a little more screwed up than before."

The two of them discussed what changes they noticed and how they might use them against the alien. The sound of flapping wings interrupted them for a moment and then the cavern was quiet again.

"You know, Johnny, I always thought of you as the son I never had."

"That'd go over real well at a family reunion," he kidded. "The Honorable Lamar Whittington with a white son." They both chuckled at the thought.

"It's funny how things worked out," Lamar remarked pleasantly.

"You know, Lamar, I do think of you as a father, too. But then, sometimes you're just a big pain in the ass."

The two men again chuckled over the comment. Lamar reached over and hugged Johnny.

"In case we don't get out of this, I want you to know that you're like family," Lamar said somberly. "If we somehow manage to get out of this, things will be different between us."

"I'd like that. Things are happening between me and Paula, I mean serious things, and I'd like to have someone to share that with."

"So, you and Deputy Hot Lips are in love," he joked.

"We sure are," he affirmed. "How about you and the mystery writer from the big city?"

"She's more of a science-fiction writer actually. She says she came here for a story on the aliens. Then, we kind of fell in love. At least I think we did."

Johnny reminded him about the note that he presumed was a breakup message. "She really likes you, Lamar. I can tell."

"I guess she does. It's a shame my lady gunslinger got us trapped in here."

"I'm sure they're working on something to get us out of here," Johnny assured him.

"It's a shame Jo got killed," lamented Lamar. "She could have driven that drill of hers right through the cavern wall and rescued us."

"Are you sure she's dead?" asked Johnny.

"I don't see how she could have survived the fall off the side of the mountain."

"How about we try out that alien mind crap that Gino told us about?"

"It's worth a shot."

The two men focused on communicating with the women but their thoughts were clouded as if a curtain of interference stood between them.

"Maybe it's those damn minerals blocking our thoughts from reaching the women."

"Then focus on what's in here," Johnny instructed him.

As they concentrated, they saw the alien's thoughts and memories.

"Holy shit!" uttered Johnny. "We're inside its mind!"

"Concentrate," urged Lamar. "This is important stuff."

They could feel the hatred that the alien had for them. Then they sensed the desperation and fright the alien felt over being trapped in the cavern. It wanted, no, it needed to contact its spaceship to request reinforcements. For some reason, it could not project its thoughts out of the cavern.

Suddenly, the alien realized they were invading its mind and it became enraged. The Ardonean darted to the ledge and clawed at the two men, shrieking madly.

Lamar and Johnny fought the alien off and fired several shots into its chest. They could feel the alien's pain from the wounds, but it was relentless in its attack.

Lamar crawled frantically down the pathway a short distance. He slid into a niche in the wall to avoid the creature's talons. The alien pursued him and resumed its assault on him.

Johnny searched frantically for a more effective weapon but only found a rock with a blunt edge. As he struggled to lift it, Lamar's painful screams drove him to try harder. Finally, he lifted the rock and staggered awkwardly toward the sloped path. Once he started down the path, he lost his balance and trod wildly toward the creature.

The alien clutched Lamar by his shoulder and dragged him out in the open. As Johnny tumbled forward, he lunged at the creature and drove the edge of the rock into the back of the Ardonean's neck. The alien creature fell to the ground, motionless with a broken neck.

Johnny lay face down on the rocky ground, aching from the fall and his earlier wounds. He struggled to get up.

Lamar groaned as he tried to stand. His shoulder and arm were a series of gashes with blood streaming from the wounds and dripping off his hand.

"I'm not gonna make it, Johnny. That bitch got me good."

Johnny helped him back to the ledge and tried to comfort him. When Johnny gave him a reassuring hug, Lamar burst into tears. Soon Johnny sobbed with him.

"Jesus, look at us," moaned Lamar. "We're worse than a couple of schoolgirls."

"It doesn't matter. We're in this together. We're going to make it."

The two of them sat on the ledge, patiently waiting for death to come for them.

———————— ·+·◆·+·· ————————

When morning came, Paula was surprised to find Sasha and Jo on either side of her. In a way, they felt like sisters but their sexual desires were something else.

Suddenly, the women went wild. Sasha went to her knees and straddled Paula's face. Instinctively Paula thrust her tongue inside Sasha and held her ass firmly with both hands. Then Jo descended between her legs and lapped hungrily. Paula felt a powerful rush that created intense spasms.

She gasped and pushed Sasha away from her face. She then clenched her thighs around Jo's head and begged her to stop.

A loud thunderous sound filled the room and startled them. The planks flew off the boarded-up windows, allowing the sunlight to enter the bedroom. The furniture launched against the walls away from the bed. Paula cried out as a surge of power and emotion erupted within her. At first, Jo and Sasha were concerned but then they understood how her emotion fueled her powers.

Paula sat up, wide-eyed. "Who's next, ladies?" she asked coyly. "Let's see what your special powers are.

Paula instructed Sasha to close her eyes and let her imagination run wild. Sasha eagerly lay on her back and allowed her friends to ravage her.

Panting heavily, she began to climax. She gripped the bedpost so tightly that it snapped. The sounds of various creatures outside filled the room. Birds chirped and flapped their wings wildly. Bears and wolves could be heard howling in the distance, their calls magnified from miles away. It was as if nature had been turned upside down. Once the power stabilized inside her, she knew she transcended to something more. "I'm so embarrassed. I didn't mean to …"

Paula and Jo hugged her and praised her for having the courage to embrace her power.

Now it was Jo's turn to escalate or activate her real power. Jo had no trouble imagining herself with both women and all the men as well. The thought of Paula and Sasha watching her arousing herself enhanced her fantasy even more.

The surge of power nearly killed Jo as she arched her back repeatedly, while gasping for air. Finally, she gave a loud sigh and her body relaxed.

"Fucking A! That was awesome!" she blurted drunkenly.

Paula and Sasha helped her to her feet but she could barely stand. The three women hugged each other.

Paula announced, "I hope you both realize that we now have something very special and very powerful."

Sasha crooned with delight and was quite pleased by the outcome. Jo tried to speak but her voice was hoarse and she was still weak.

"Save your strength, Jo. We're going to take care of business today."

They left the cabin, anxious to use their new-found powers.

"Something is bothering me," Jo remarked. "Your power, Paula, moved the furniture and blew out the planks on the windows, kind of like projecting real energy. Sasha, your power seemed to affect the animals or nature, if you will. What is my power?"

"I'm not sure," replied Paula. "It seems that it hasn't revealed itself yet."

"Perhaps, it did and we just don't know it yet," suggested Sasha.

Jo looked down despondently as they approached the drill site. Paula sensed her disappointment and assured her that she received something. They all felt the surge of emotion when Jo climaxed. There had to be something that she received.

"So why is it that these powers manifested themselves when they did?" asked Sasha curiously.

"I think when either Gino or our alien friend enhanced our telepathic powers, we also developed certain others," explained Paula. "When we reached emotional peaks, I think it triggered these new powers."

"You mean like an energy level to stimulate our powers?"

"I sure do, plus we did it together."

"I think you got some bad-ass kinetic control power," Jo remarked to Paula. "I never saw anything like that before."

"If that's what it is, I need to refine it and control it."

Sasha paused and focused on the trees for a moment. "I can understand the small creatures hiding out there," she announced excitedly. "They fear the aliens and their mutants."

"So that's why the larger animals fled," surmised Paula. "They knew that the aliens didn't belong here and were a threat to them."

"I don't know what to add to that," said Jo sadly. "I got nothing."

"Whatever it is, I'm sure we'll know soon enough."

Jo pondered as they drew closer to the drill site. Paula and Sasha each held her hand to cheer her up.

"Will the two of you get Gino's body and bring it back to me while I get the drill ready?" Jo requested and tossed them the keys to her Escalade. "I want to give him a decent burial."

Paula and Sasha were more than happy to comply with her wish.

When they reached the drill assembly, Jo inspected it and rolled out the cables. She needed to make some repairs to the damaged cable. Paula and Sasha drove down the road toward the bottom of the cliff.

Jo skinned back the damaged cable and twisted the conductors together. After taping them securely, she powered up the drill assembly and waited for it to complete its diagnostics and charge up. She thought about the fun she had with Paula and Sasha. Perhaps she could continue her relationship with the women. If not, then she'd hope to be successful at drilling and find new interns. *Maybe my next interns will be young women,* she teased herself. *Or better yet, one woman and one man.*

⸻ ✦ ⸻

After a rough ride down through the valley, the Escalade stopped at the base of the cliff. Paula and Sasha warily exited the truck, each armed with a pistol.

The dead Ardonean lay over the rocks and already showed signs of decay. They were befuddled that there was no sign of Gino's body.

Paula and Sasha scanned the area and were stumped by his disappearance. They called out to him several times, wondering if he somehow survived the fall. With no success by the alien carcass, they searched the lower face of the cliff.

Both women thought they heard a faint cry for help. They scanned the base of the cliff further until they discovered a small cave.

"We haven't had much luck with caves lately," complained Paula.

"Do you think he's in there?"

"Shit," barked Paula. "I guess I'll have to find out." She crept toward the cave and bent down to peer inside. Sasha was right behind her with her hand on Paula's hip.

As Paula leaned inside, a man's hand reached out and grabbed the gun. Both women screamed until Gino's head appeared from inside.

"Please don't shoot me," he requested pleadingly.

The women regained their composure and scolded him for scaring them. Gino let go of the gun and slid his body out of the cave. He had a badly broken leg and a dislocated left shoulder.

"We thought you were dead, Gino."

"Gino's still inside," he informed them. "This is Pir you are speaking to."

"We need to get you help fast," Paula explained urgently.

"No, that's not possible. Take me to Jo immediately."

"Oh, she's gonna be happy to see you," quipped Sasha.

The two women tied his leg to a tree limb like a splint and dragged him back to the truck. Carefully they placed him in the bed and drove off.

Jo had just finished positioning the drill against the initial bore in the rock when the women returned. She walked hesitantly toward them, expecting to see Gino's corpse in the back of the Escalade.

Paula got out and placed her hands on Jo's shoulders. In a somber tone, she advised her to brace herself for what she was going to see. Jo took a deep breath as Paula stepped aside. She bravely walked to the rear of the vehicle.

Gino peered at her with an odd and confused look. The real Gino was pleased to see her while their alien ally was concerned about the health of its host.

"Jesus, Gino, look at you!" Jo cried. She climbed in the back of the truck and raised him into a sitting position. Gino winced from the pain but welcomed her affection.

Tears streamed down Jo's cheeks and then a rush of emotion took over her. Her face became bright red and the two of them were engulfed in an opaque mist for several moments.

Paula and Sasha watched in amazement as they realized this was an indication of Jo's new power.

When they visually looked normal again, Gino's leg and shoulder were healed. His mouth opened and the alien exited.

Paula and Sasha realized that Jo had the ability to heal. Jo was relieved to know what power she had and cried over Gino.

"I didn't know you cared so much about me," Gino whispered to Jo.

"You dumb bastard," she replied. "Who else is gonna fuck me silly like you do?" Gino chuckled at her.

Pir levitated briefly and set down on the tailgate. They congregated around their odd ally and awaited instructions. Pir warned them that, if they defeated the Ardoneans, their peers on board the spaceship would come to slay them.

"So how do we destroy the ship?" asked Paula in frustration.

"You have the skills among you to defeat them. My lifespan is curtailed significantly when I transfer in and out of a host."

"You mean you're dying?" asked Sasha.

"Soon. I am the last of my kind that will come to your world. You will be your own guardians when I'm gone."

"I hate drama," complained Jo. "Can't we just nuke the bastards?"

"You'll do what needs to be done. My mission here is finished," Pir explained confidently and levitated away from them into the trees.

"Alright girls; we have work to do!" ordered Jo with renewed vigor as she hurried to the drill assembly. "Get on the generator, Gino," she ordered.

Gino controlled the power to the drill while Jo operated it. Soon the drill assembly was melting through the rock at a slow but steady pace.

Sasha followed Paula to the toppled SUV and helped her retrieve their supplies. Paula took the remaining dynamite and strapped it together.

"What's that for?" asked Sasha curiously.

"We're going to send a going away present to the spaceship."

"And how is that gonna happen?"

Paula grinned deviously. "The same way they got here. All we have to do is figure out how to make it work."

Sasha recalled the pods in the cavern and revealed to Paula how the creatures arrived through the hole in the cavern roof.

Paula then attempted to put together a home-made pressure plate attached to a detonator with a timer. She had her doubts about whether or not it would work but she'd do her best and see what the others thought.

Sasha focused her thoughts on birds from a distance. She summoned them to return to the area and, despite their reluctance, they obeyed. Within an hour, a variety of birds were circling overhead, searching for any sign of the Ardoneans.

As the afternoon wore on, Jo's drill made great headway through the mountainside. Gino had set the generator to maximum power and the rock was soft enough for the drill to shatter it.

"How much further?" Paula shouted to Jo.

Jo glanced at a small screen on her control panel and replied, "We're twenty feet in now. Another five or six feet should do it."

"Time?"

"Two hours."

Paula was concerned that the sun would soon be setting. She went to the trailer and sat alone on the ramp. She prayed that Johnny and Lamar were okay. For some reason, she couldn't understand why their thoughts were sometimes blocked. Was it the creatures? Was it the thickness of the rock? Maybe she didn't focus hard enough.

Sasha joined her and the two discussed where their future was going. Sasha explained her perception of their future as superheroes who would defend mankind against the Ardoneans.

Paula smiled at her and replied, "I like the way you look at things, Sasha - very philosophical."

"Thank you, I think," she replied skeptically.

The two watched Jo's drilling rig extend further into the rock as the sun set lower.

"Look at her," kidded Paula. "She thinks it's a big dick and she's ramming it home."

Jo stood up and turned to her with her hands on her hips, looking insulted. Paula blew her a kiss and gestured with a wave of her hand to continue drilling.

Sasha was amused by her nonchalance. "We'll have to get used to this open telepathy thing, especially if we get Lamar and Johnny back."

"What's this 'if' shit? We will get them back," Paula declared confidently.

Jo motioned for Gino to cut the power and she retracted the drill from the mountainside. Once it fully withdrew, she backed the assembly away from the mountainside.

It was nearly dark and the overhead lamps on the drill assembly provided the only lighting.

Paula and Sasha slept inside the Escalade, each with her head on the door.

"Come on, bitches," ordered Jo. "Let's get real."

The women awoke and joined her. Gino took a pistol from the rear of the Escalade and pursued the women into the tunnel.

---

Johnny imagined having sex with Paula and Jo as Lamar slept next to him. He wondered if he'd ever get the chance to experience a threesome with the girls.

The sound of viscous liquid seeping down the cavern wall onto the stone floor interrupted Johnny's fantasy. He crawled across the ledge through the impeding rocks toward the source of the sound. His heart pounded as he wondered what was happening. Then he realized his vision allowed him to see in the dark. Ahead of him was a dark gray hole on the cavern wall. Molten rock lay to either side of the hole.

"Lamar!" he called excitedly. "Come see this!"

Lamar lay motionless and didn't respond. Johnny hurried back to him and tried to lift him. "Come on, buddy. We're getting out of here."

Lamar barely breathed and was unconscious. Johnny lifted him and pulled him toward the new tunnel. The sound of flapping wings startled him as the remaining Ardoneans descended from above and blocked their exit.

One creature communicated with him, sending threats. Johnny sent threats of his own. He projected thoughts of a virus he and Lamar had that would cause the Ardoneans to die a horrible death with Ebola-like symptoms.

The aliens hissed but refused to back away. Johnny set Lamar down on the ground and stood facing the creatures. He projected thoughts of himself wringing its neck and snapping its head off. Then the alien responded with its own thoughts: thousands of pods landing on Earth; Ardoneans killing humans.

Then Johnny interceded by projecting a nuclear blast that obliterates the entire world. Then there is nothing but blackness. The creatures were stunned and became still.

Jo stepped into the cavern behind the creatures. She remained silent until Paula, Sasha and Gino entered. The three of them trained their pistols on the aliens but were amused by Johnny's doomsday show.

"What the hell you doing, Johnny?" chided Jo. "You need a date that bad."

"Kiss my ass, Jo. Either do something or get the hell out of the way."

The creatures were surprised by their presence and took flight. Paula stepped forward and balled her hands into fists. "Die you bastards," she shouted.

A loud boom filled the cavern and the aliens were thrown across the cavern against the wall. One was crushed but the other was still alive, reeling from the impact.

Sasha and Jo rushed to Lamar's aid. They lifted him and pulled him into the tunnel.

Johnny staggered to Paula and threw his arms around her. "I don't know where you learned that trick but it's pretty fucking impressive … just like you." He hugged her tightly.

Paula was pleased by his complement. She chose the opportunity to warn him that she would use it on him if he screwed with her. He looked baffled by her comment. She placed her arm around his waist and escorted him from the cavern.

Once they exited the tunnel, Jo and Gino started the drill assembly again. Jo drove the assembly forward until she plugged the tunnel with the drill. Gino shut down the generator and Jo turned off the controls. They all climbed into the Escalade and Jo drove them to the cabin. No one spoke during the ride, although Paula and Sasha tried unsuccessfully to give Lamar water. Johnny was exhausted and slept soundly during the ride.

When they reached the cabin, Johnny and Paula lifted Lamar and moved him inside the cabin. Sasha watched over him and fretted as he was ever so pale. His body was covered with gashes and dried blood.

"We have to do something," panicked Sasha. "He's a mess."

Jo knelt over him and studied his wounds.

"We have to get him to a doctor or he'll die," cried Johnny.

Paula embraced Johnny and assured him that Lamar would be fine. Everyone watched as Jo placed her hands on Lamar's chest. The two became opaque as she and Gino did earlier.

"What the hell is she doing?" blurted Johnny.

"She's healing him," replied Paula.

Johnny glanced at her and then at Sasha. "What happened to you girls?" he questioned Paula. "You bounced those things off the wall like a tennis ball and now she's healing Lamar!" Then he noticed Gino in the room and uttered in disbelief," And you're supposed to be dead; you and Jo!"

Paula tried to calm him down. She took him by the hand and led him outside. "We learned a lot about ourselves while we were apart, Johnny. I can't wait to tell you about it later."

Johnny fell to his knees and broke down in tears. "I thought I was going to die and never get to say goodbye. I missed you so much."

Paula knelt down next to him and nestled his head against her. "It's going to be all right. I promise."

Johnny held her tightly until Jo appeared at the door. "Hey, you pussies; you want to see your friend or not?"

Johnny glanced at Paula, stunned, and then hurried inside. Lamar sat on a chair with his hands on his knees. He looked frail and weak but much better than when they left the cavern.

Johnny hugged him tightly. "I thought you were a goner," he said, still worried.

Lamar forced a smile and replied, "I thought we were both goners."

Jo stood by them with arms folded and suggested, "Why don't we get some sleep? Tomorrow is the day we finish that asshole alien once and for all."

Everyone broke up into groups and moved to separate parts of the cabin to sleep. They used chair cushions, sheets and quilts to make suitable sleeping areas on the floors. Jo and Gino slept in the bed since she already took the cabin as her own.

For one night, everyone just slept quietly.

# CHAPTER XI

# THE FUTURE UNFOLDS

When morning came, Jo tidied up the bedroom and collected the linens to be washed. Gino drove into Clearview to pick up breakfast for everyone.

Paula and Johnny sat on the front porch, holding hands while Lamar and Sasha sat on the couch inside the cabin in silence.

Gino returned with a box of breakfast sandwiches and juices. He smiled at Paula as he passed them and entered the cabin. Johnny noticed and glanced at Paula but her reaction was cool.

"It's time, Johnny," announced Paula somberly. "We need to get with the others and come to terms with what we are."

Johnny replied disinterestedly, "And what are we, really?"

Paula stood up with her hands on her hips and chided, "Now's not the time to go limp-dick on me. Let's go." She entered the cabin without him.

Johnny thought for a moment about her comment and chuckled. "Limp-dick, huh?" As he stood, he thought about Paula, Jo and Sasha working together. He fantasized the three of them on several occasions but thought nothing of it. At the door he paused and sensed that Paula did have an affair with one or both of them. *Damn*, he thought. *She got a little from the girls and now she's all lezbo on me.*

When he entered the cabin, the women glared at him. He realized that they heard his thoughts. "I was only kidding," he said innocently and took a seat. "Now, what is it you ladies wish to talk about?"

Paula revealed the powers that the women possessed and, in a roundabout way, how they discovered them. She went on to explain how

Pir, the alien, was responsible for preparing them to be the guardians against the Ardoneans.

When she finished, Johnny raised his hand cynically and asked, "So what's my magic power, a limp dick?"

"No, dick head," she scolded him. "This is serious."

"Where do Johnny and I come in with these powers?" Lamar asked, curious. "We're infected just like you are."

"It took a while before we figured out that Jo's power was healing. Mine was pretty evident while Sasha's was more subtle."

Lamar suggested to Johnny, "Maybe yours is more about mind control. You fucked with that alien pretty good back in the cavern."

Paula was surprised by Lamar's comment, even more convinced that Johnny was responsible for changing her. Jo and Sasha noticed, also interested in his mind control.

"Yeah, in case it gets back to the mother ship," explained Johnny proudly. "If they're smart, they'll get the hell out of our part of the universe and stay out."

Johnny recalled how he projected the world getting nuked to the alien. Then he suggested, "Perhaps you are the glue that holds us together, Lamar. Kind of like the father figure."

"The last thing I want to be is a father figure for you rejects," he joked.

Jo mentioned that Pir warned them about a spaceship that held additional forces. "I think we need to find a way to destroy that ship if we expect to finish this thing off," she suggested.

Paula told them about the dynamite with the pressure-plate switch and timer that she crudely assembled. She asked for the others to inspect it and make sure it could work.

"Very creative, Missy," Lamar complimented her.

"We still have to find out how to use it against them," replied Jo.

"What if we could make them summon the ship down here to Earth?" inquired Sasha. "If Johnny's power is good enough, he can convince them to do that."

"If I was an alien," Johnny responded sarcastically, "the last thing I'd do is bring my mother ship down here, especially if my forces are getting their asses handed to them by women who might be stronger than them."

Lamar chuckled and replied, "Kind of like last time, if I remember correctly."

"So, what then?" Paula challenged him.

"There's only one left," Johnny commented. "The leader."

"So, let's take it alive," Paula responded confidently. "Then we'll figure out what to do with it."

"I like that idea," Lamar said supportively.

"Then let's do this," announced Jo confidently.

Johnny took Paula by the hand and ordered her, "Outside now. We have something that needs to be dealt with."

Paula looked concerned as she stood. She tried to read his thoughts but realized that Johnny could cloak them. He was much more talented than she thought with telepathy. Then she realized that he likely mutated before her and was more advanced with his telepathy. She followed him outside to the rear of the Escalade. "I hope this is important," she said impatiently.

Johnny lowered the tailgate on Jo's pickup and lifted her onto the back bumper. "I can't believe you called me limp dick," he complained.

Paula reached into his pants and felt his rock-hard penis. "I guess you proved me wrong," she replied, feigning disinterest.

"So how was it?" he asked as he nibbled her neck.

"How was what?" she inquired.

"How did you like eating cougar?"

Paula squeezed his testicles and warned, "Keep it up and I'll rip them off."

"You win," Johnny replied with a pained expression.

"I have to ask you something."

"Anything," he blurted anxiously.

"Do you have any secrets you'd like to share with me?"

"Huh? Hell no!"

"You know what I can do to you if you're lying."

Johnny stared at her with a strange expression on his face. "I'd never hurt you; you know that," he assured her.

"Then fuck away," she said with a fiendish smile.

Johnny anxiously removed his pants and climbed on top of her. Eagerly, he plunged himself into her. Paula moaned as he drove himself into her again and again.

"Cougar tasted good," she uttered, while panting.

Johnny paused briefly, stunned by her remark. "You had Jo?"

"Sure did. Now fuck me before I change my mind," warned Paula.

Johnny felt like he could go on for hours, gyrating against her, pressing harder each time. Paula grabbed his ass tightly, nearly leaving handprints.

Johnny leaned forward on both hands and pumped her faster. The back of the vehicle shook up and down in rhythm with Johnny's thrusts. Finally, they both came together with a loud moan and a sigh.

Then they were startled when the others stood around them cheering. Johnny and Paula giggled, despite their embarrassment.

"Now, if you two free spirits are done fucking your brains out, we have some business to take care of," Lamar chastised with a sly grin.

Johnny and Paula dressed while the others climbed inside the Escalade. Jo glanced down at Johnny's penis and winked at him as she walked by.

"Was she really that good?" Johnny asked Paula.

"The best I ever had," she remarked slyly.

Johnny glanced at Jo and then at Paula. She grabbed his head with both hands and kissed him passionately.

---

When they reached the drill site, Paula and Lamar inspected her explosive device. After contemplating the design, he asked, "Where's you get the idea for this?"

Paula shrugged her shoulders and replied, "I'm not sure. It's all we had to work with so I tried to be creative."

Lamar pondered for a moment and then inquired, "How did you foresee using it?"

"Maybe to collapse the cavern and kill those bastards."

Jo promptly charged over and warned, "Nobody collapses that cavern. Those diamonds are mine and there's enough rocks to clear out without blowing anything else up in there."

"Then what do you propose?" asked Lamar.

"You just wait," Jo sternly instructed him. "If you can make that thing work the way it's supposed to, I think I can solve all our problems."

Lamar and Paula tried to read Jo's thoughts as she walked away but she shielded them. The two glanced at each other suspiciously.

"I guess it's a good thing that we can cloak our thoughts when we choose to," remarked Paula. "Some things should be private."

Lamar chuckled and remarked giddily "You're right but, unfortunately, I am sure gonna remember that image of you and Johnny back there, bare-ass naked."

Paula blushed and countered, "I can hardly wait for the day I see you and Sasha doing the funky monkey in some public place."

"I don't do public places," Lamar kidded.

"Only strange hotel rooms, I hear," she teased.

Lamar blushed. "Who told you that story?" he inquired irritably. "I had nothing to do with it."

Paula nodded playfully. "Sure, Lamar. I know you really wanted to join in with Jo and her interns."

"Bah," he grumbled and waved her off. Sasha enjoyed watching Paula torment him.

Jo and Gino started the drill assembly's generator. Jo climbed inside the cab and prepared to withdraw the drill assembly from the tunnel. She held her pistol in one hand and held the steering wheel with the other. Gino was also armed and eyed the tunnel as he waited for Jo to back the drill out.

Johnny instructed Lamar and Sasha to remain outside the cavern and make sure Paula's explosive device was ready when they needed it.

Johnny and Paula stood on either side of the tunnel, with pistols in both their hands. Johnny nodded to Jo. She reversed the crawler and pulled the drill out.

Once the drill was clear of the tunnel, the two of them proceeded inside. By now, their mutated traits had allowed for their vision to adapt to the darkness. Both were crouched low as the tunnel was only about five feet in circumference.

Gino took over in the cab of the drill as Jo entered the tunnel to back up her friends.

Once inside the cavern, they kept their thoughts cloaked to disguise their presence from the creature. That also limited the communication between the three of them. Inside the cavern, an ominous silence sent chills down their spines.

Large rocks were strewn about the cavern floor and the glistening of diamonds and minerals along one wall created a dim but noticeable kaleidoscopic effect.

Paula discovered the partially-eaten body of one of Leon's thugs near one side of the cavern. The smell was awful and she nearly vomited. As she turned to leave, she discovered Johnny's camera lying among the rocks. Chuckling to herself, she picked it up and viewed the pictures. The camera made a slight noise as the lens extended when she turned it on. She then realized that Leon found them through Johnny's pictures. It was evident that it was the west side of Graham's Mountain by the view of the peak in the background.

Johnny found the corpses of the dead aliens laid out in a neat row in the middle of the cavern. They appeared as if they were to be transported back to the ship.

Jo discovered both the small pods and the larger, coffin-shaped pod not far from Johnny. She knelt by the large pod and studied the construction. She discovered a slimy coating that covered the interior surface and four tubes along the sides that were made of a ceramic-like material. Jo surmised that the aliens were sedated with gas which was then replaced by the viscous fluid to allow them to travel long distances. Once the pod landed, the fluid was drained and the pod opened.

The head of the pod had a series of buttons or touch pads on it but they were inoperative now. Jo wondered how they managed to control the pod and soon concluded that they had remote help from their ship.

Paula stowed the camera in her pocket. When she turned around, she was face to face with the Ardonean. Before she could react, it grabbed her arms with its talons and threw her against the cavern wall.

Paula opened her thoughts to the others and warned them. She lay stunned as the creature lunged at her.

Johnny and Jo immediately rushed to her defense. Johnny focused on the creature's head and instilled fear in it through images of him ripping its stomach open and choking it with its own organs.

The Ardonean was disoriented by the images but still pinned Paula down. She tried to summon her power to shove the alien away but she couldn't focus. It was inflicting pain to distract her.

Jo drew her gun and beat it repeatedly over the head. Johnny tried to wrestle the creature off of Paula but with no luck. The Ardonean placed its talons around Paula's neck and choked her.

Johnny focused on Lamar and showed him what was happening. He panicked when he received no response. He kicked the alien in the jaw and staggered it backwards. The alien turned and punched him in the face. Johnny crashed against the wall and collapsed on the ground. His head spun and he felt nauseous.

The alien then turned on Jo, knocking her to the ground. It leaped on her and extended its long tongue from its mouth. Jo shouted for help as the alien attempted to insert its tongue into her mouth to implant its eggs within her.

Johnny focused on the alien and sent images of the tongue exploding and its face burning. Suddenly, the alien shrieked and Johnny's projected thoughts came true. The Ardonean's face flashed briefly with a hot fire and its tongue exploded. It fled from Jo with smoke and red charred flesh on its face.

Paula watched in amazement as she crawled to her knees. She couldn't believe Johnny had that kind of power.

"Shit, Johnny! You almost burnt me!" Jo chastised.

"I guess I'm too hot for you," he kidded weakly as he tried to stand.

"Oh, I see we have a little challenge here," she countered.

"I wouldn't call it little," he replied defensively.

Paula summoned enough strength to exert her power on the alien and sent it crashing against the wall. The alien reeled as it staggered toward the large pod.

"Get it!" shouted Paula. As the alien drew close to its pod, she exerted her power and shoved the pod away from it.

Johnny aimed his pistol at the alien but Jo raced in front of him. "Don't kill it!" she shouted. "We need it alive."

"You're kidding!"

"It's critical. Do not kill it!"

Johnny reluctantly refrained from shooting the creature. "I guess we have to do this the hard way," he complained.

Jo lunged from behind and tackled the alien. The creature thrashed frantically and threw her over its shoulder. Briefly, she lay stunned on the ground.

From behind, Johnny grabbed it by the neck and bull-dogged it to the ground. Jo scrambled to her feet and went to his aid. The two of them held the creature down and waited for support from the others. They glanced around the cavern, while struggling with the alien. There was no sign of Paula.

"Where'd she go?" asked Johnny frantically.

"I don't know," replied Jo uneasily. "None of them are responding to my thoughts." Jo sat on the creature's ass to prevent it from thrashing its legs. She had several gashes in her arms already and Johnny had a deep cut in his shoulder.

Johnny maneuvered himself on top of the alien's neck and pressed its face against the rocky floor. He could see the fear in its mind as it tried to communicate with the ship. There was no response.

"Can we kill it now?" Johnny asked anxiously.

"Just chill the fuck out," Jo ordered him. "We're not killing it."

Johnny was surprised by Jo's determination to keep the creature alive. Then Jo explained, "Gino tells me the others are on the way. We hold on until they arrive."

Johnny felt himself weaken as he still hadn't fully healed from his gunshot wounds and his head still hurt. Frustration overtook him and he shouted, "This is bullshit! What'd they do, go out for pizza or something?"

"Just hold on, Johnny. I know you're hurting."

"Can I ask you something, Jo?"

"No, you can't wear my bra and panties," she mocked him.

The two of them chuckled for a moment, and then Johnny continued, "Did you enjoy making love to Paula?"

Jo nearly got thrown when the Ardonean made another frantic attempt to get free. "Why the fuck would you ask me that now?"

"Just wondering."

"Oh, yes. She said I was better than you," she taunted.

"Get the fuck out!" he blurted in disbelief.

The two were more at ease from their conversation. Now they took pleasure in roughing up the Ardonean and instilling more fear in it.

Lamar, Sasha, Paula and Gino entered the cavern carrying a bundle of dynamite, the timer package and the pressure plate assembly separately but each piece was already connected by wires.

Johnny suddenly realized what their intentions were. He projected thoughts to the alien of returning to its ship and never coming back.

Lamar and Paula inserted the dynamite in the head of the pod. Sasha set the timer device down at the bottom of the pod where the creature couldn't reach it. The wires ran down the middle of the pod.

The alien, unaware of the bomb placement, responded to Johnny that they would keep coming until they conquered his race. Johnny informed the creature that each time they encounter the aliens, they would inflict more casualties on them and, if necessary, they'd chase them all the way back to their world and destroy it.

The Ardonean doubted him until he portrayed images of Hiroshima and Nagasaki. Then he portrayed images of the beach assault on D-Day. The alien was appalled by how violent that humans could be.

Johnny reiterated his offer for peace. The alien replied that its race would never cede to the humans. He responded that he would be humane and allow the creature to return to its ship. He then projected an image of a deep sleep overcoming the creature. It tried to fight his thoughts but he was the more powerful of the two. Soon, the creature became motionless and slept.

Gino gently set the pressure plate in the middle of the pod and tucked in the remaining wires.

Johnny and Jo got off the creature and staggered backwards. Jo dragged the creature to the pod and, with help from the others, they moved the Ardonean delicately onto the pressure plate in the pod.

As soon as they backed away, the pod sensed the Ardonean's presence and illuminated. Within seconds the pod closed, levitated for a moment and then accelerated out of the cavern through the tunnel.

"Well, how about …?" Johnny started to say and then collapsed.

"Get him out to the truck, now!" ordered Jo.

Together, they lifted him and carried him out to her pickup. As soon as they placed him inside, they returned to the cabin.

During the drive, Jo placed her hands over various parts of Johnny's body and sensed his injuries. His loss of blood was the primary concern she had.

Scanning him repeatedly, she tried to focus on his body functions to increase the flow of blood through his heart and stimulate its replenishment. While probing his mind for control of the functions, she found Johnny dreaming of a threesome with her and Paula. Jo was flattered and considered how to address the issue when he was well. She and Paula both thought it odd that they each became aroused at a time like this. Then Paula hinted to Jo that there was more to these frequent arousals. Now Jo understood and knew Johnny had to be behind them.

When they arrived at the cabin, Johnny was moved inside to a bed. Jo explained to the others about the issue of the blood loss and how she would try to accelerate its replenishment. Paula was concerned that Johnny still hadn't regained consciousness but Jo assured her that he was stable.

They gathered on the front porch and fretted whether or not their explosive device would work on the alien ship.

"I thought we'd have seen something by now," Lamar commented dejectedly.

"Maybe it didn't work," replied Sasha. "I mean the wires could have pulled out of the detonator or something if the creature moved."

Jo frowned and returned to check on Johnny. She placed her hands on his chest and sensed that he was doing much better. She telepathically informed Paula about his improvement and suggested they do something for Johnny together. Paula liked the idea and agreed to play along when the time was right.

Jo removed Johnny's clothes and set them aside. She ogled his naked body and considered payback for using his powers of persuasion on them. After running her hands over his body once more, she was confident that he would soon regain consciousness.

From the porch in front of the cabin, the others were stunned by a massive flash in the sky, soon followed by fireworks as debris rained down through the Earth's atmosphere and burnt up. They were relieved that the aliens had finally been defeated.

Paula took Gino by the hand and led him inside the cabin. Lamar and Sasha climbed in the back seat of the Escalade.

In the bedroom, Jo tied Johnny's hands together and his ankles to the bed posts. Johnny awoke and was startled. "Why am I tied up?" he asked frantically.

"I want you to remember this," Paula answered coyly.

Paula and Jo undressed Gino and massaged him until he became aroused. Gino returned the favor, undressing each of the women, while kissing and fondling them.

"Come on, Paula. Untie me," Johnny pleaded as he grew excited.

Paula informed him that Gino would help him with blood flow to aid in his recovery. She kissed Jo hungrily and led her out of the room, leaving only Gino and Johnny.

Together the women projected their own sexual images to Johnny of him and Gino together. They enhanced their images, urging Johnny to enjoy himself with another man. They waited anxiously for Gino to tell them he was finished with Johnny and then returned to the room.

Paula and Jo entered and gazed at Johnny. "How was he?" taunted Paula. "Did you enjoy yourself, Sweetie?"

Johnny was embarrassed, with Gino's semen all over his face and chest. "This was just wrong!" he groaned. "Nobody hears about this. Got it?"

The women laughed hysterically at him. Jo continued to harass him and asked, "So, Johnny, are you a spitter or a swallower?"

"Fuck you, Jo!" he shouted, his ego hurt.

Then Paula and Gino went into the other room.

"Where are they going?" asked Johnny nervously.

Jo strutted toward him and responded, "Paula's got this uncontrollable urge to have Gino in unimaginable ways."

"What about me?"

Jo frowned at him and reminded him of his response at the hospital. "I really don't think you want any of this," she concluded as she fondled herself.

"I didn't mean it that way, Jo," he explained apologetically. You're a beautiful woman. Now, please untie me."

"Not yet," she answered. "I understand you have a problem with cougars."

Johnny apologized and swore he'd never speak ill of older women again. She untied Johnny's hands and then his ankles.

Johnny got up and peered into the living room. Paula was on her knees with Gino immersed in her mouth. As he drew close to coming, she turned her body away from him and positioned herself on all fours. Gino mounted her from behind and rhythmically slid in and out of her, sensing her pleasure as he changed his pace.

Johnny was stunned that Paula would give herself to others so freely. Jo stood behind him and placed her hand on his shoulder. "Remember, Johnny, this is what you wanted. You made a nice girl into a whore." Johnny realized that she was right. This was his doing.

"Besides," she informed him, "not only is Gino hung like a horse; he comes like one as well. Doesn't he?"

"Don't remind me," he muttered as he watched, disappointed.

Paula pondered as she felt Gino penetrate her again and again that she had become such a slut. Gino quickened the pace and excited her more than ever. Her legs weakened and she lay flat on the ground. Gino relentlessly slid on top of her and continued to pound her until he exploded within her. Both let out gasps of satisfaction as she felt Gino dripping out of her.

As they both watched, Jo reminded Johnny that it could have been him.

---

In the Escalade, Lamar questioned Sasha about the sexual effects on Paula and Jo and if they affected her. Sasha revealed to him how she "imagined" her encounter with Jo and Paula, to release her power.

Lamar informed her that his logic tells him that Johnny had a lot to do with it and, for some reason, he didn't think it would happen again after today.

Sasha confessed that it did turn her on and, while rubbing Lamar's crotch, admitted that she was ready for him.

Lamar quipped, "We're just as bad as they are."

"Yes, we are," she replied giddily.

---

Johnny recalled that Pir was right about one thing: they were all in sync now. Pir emerged from the trees and levitated in front of them. "What brings you here?" inquired Lamar. "I think we pretty much took care of everything."

"Not quite," answered Pir. "There is another issue that we need to discuss. My time is short so I will be brief with you and the other guardians."

Lamar cracked a smile at Sasha. "He called us guardians."

"Well, we are, if you think about it," she replied.

"All right, Mr. Pir, let's go inside and get this over with."

Lamar and Sasha entered through the front door, followed by their floating alien ally, Pir.

"I see Pir is back," Johnny commented. "Is everything all right?"

"We're going to discuss that."

They gathered around Pir and waited anxiously to hear him confirm that they successfully destroyed their alien intruders.

First of all, I'd like to commend you on a great job. The alien ship was destroyed. I'm not sure how you did it, but it was very effective. We have not been able to penetrate their force fields to inflict damage to their mother ships. You seemed to have found a way to do it, not once, but twice."

"You said 'ships'" Johnny noted.

"Yes. There are others positioned in various parts of the sector. It will be a long time before they learn of this ship's fate."

"So, we won't see them again in our lifetime," remarked Paula confidently.

"That's one issue we need to discuss. You no longer have a lifetime. You will not age. You will not grow old."

"Hold on there, bubbalooey!" shouted Johnny. "You're telling me that we're going to live forever?"

"Or until you are killed. You will always be guardians on your planet."

"I'm liking this more and more," Johnny quipped.

Pir continued, "You (Lamar) will be the leader and mentor for the group. You will also be the ruling authority on all extraterrestrial matters." Lamar beamed proudly and folded his arms.

"You (Sasha) will be the communicator. You have the powers to telepathically speak to and understand all creatures on Earth and other worlds, should that become necessary."

Sasha and Lamar placed their arms around each other's waists and nestled against each other.

Pir moved to Gino and explained, "You will be the mender of spirit among the group. You will provide them the support they need to function as one."

"What does that mean?" asked Jo, somewhat confused.

Gino replied excitedly, "That means I get to be everyone's sex toy!" He lifted Jo in the air and happily spun her around.

"You (Jo) are the healer and, as you have already learned, it does have its limitations."

Pir approached Paula and Johnny. "You two are the warriors: with both mental and physical powers. Together, all of you can defeat any enemy in the universe but you must do it together."

"And why is that?" asked Sasha. "What if you don't need everyone to handle a situation?"

"Separately, your powers are significantly weaker. Together, they increase a hundred-fold."

"I have some questions," interjected Paula, knowing it was the right time. "Who was the first one to be infected and mutated?"

Everyone grew curious as they wondered why she raised the question. Pir floated over to Johnny and levitated in front of his face. "This man was the first and he did well in the earlier encounter with our forces."

"So, Johnny's been a mutant since the spring event!" she commented.

"That's correct."

With her eyes glowing red, Paula glared at Johnny and clenched her fists. "You let me believe that I infected you and you said nothing!"

Johnny grinned sheepishly and replied, "I couldn't tell any of you that I was infected. I didn't know how you'd react."

"So, you used your power to manipulate me into becoming your whore?"

"It wasn't like that," Johnny said nervously.

Lamar and Sasha were amused by Johnny's defensiveness. They stepped back and watched, knowing what was coming.

"And it was you who blocked us from communicating all that time!"

"Not every time. The alien could do that, too."

Jo got in his face and inquired, "You really used that power to manipulate me as well?"

"I had to," he replied timidly. "You would have killed Paula if I didn't."

Jo grinned and commented sheepishly, "Personally, I rather liked it."

Sasha and Paula glared at her. She smiled and shrugged her shoulders at them.

Sensing the anger in Paula, Johnny backed toward the door. "I was going to tell you all, I swear; as soon as we finished off the aliens!"

"And you manipulated me, too?" asked Sasha angrily.

"Uh, kind of. That was an accident, though."

"You fed off my sympathy, you dick!" Paula shouted.

"Look, it was my burden to carry," he said apologetically. "I wanted to tell you. I really did."

Lamar commented defensively, "I got nothin'."

Pir attempted to quell the situation, "Johnny needed to hone his power just as you needed to hone yours."

"I trusted you and you fucked me!" shouted Paula.

Lamar glanced at Sasha and quipped, "That he did." They chuckled and continued to watch. Sasha became relaxed knowing that Paula was going to give Johnny his due.

"Look, Paula, I was afraid if I said anything that you, or anyone else for that matter, you would kill me."

"You know, Johnny, you are right." Her face became beet red now.

Johnny reached for the doorknob and opened it slightly. "Relax, Paula. It's not that big a deal."

"As I said, you were right, Johnny. I am gonna kill you!" she screamed.

Johnny opened the door and fled the cabin.

Paula reached for her pistol on the table, but Lamar grabbed her arm. "No guns," he ordered.

"Fine," she replied tersely and rushed after him.

Everyone hurried to the door to watch Johnny's misfortune unfold.

As Johnny ran down the trail, Paula stopped and focused her power on him. A small boom filled the air and floored Johnny.

Paula looked back at the plate on the side of the house for the septic system and forced the lid open with her power. She then turned Johnny upside down. He levitated past her toward the septic system until he dangled over the top of the opening.

"Please, Paula! I'll make it up to you!" he pleaded.

"That's enough, Paula," ordered Lamar. "I think he learned his lesson."

Johnny's body descended into the septic tank until only his feet were visible. "Please!" he begged. "I can't breathe!"

"That's enough, Paula," ordered Lamar. "He's no good to you dead."

Paula hesitated and Johnny's body arose from the tank. Everyone watched anxiously, wondering if there was more punishment to come. Johnny's body then flipped upright. He floated toward her with fear in his eyes.

"Come on, Paula," Johnny pleaded. "You know I love you."

Paula still bristled as she sat him down in front of her. She promptly grabbed his testicles through his pants and warned, "If you ever attempt to manipulate me again, I'll rip these off and hang them on the back of my new truck."

Johnny cringed in fear and nodded in agreement.

"What new truck?" asked Lamar curiously.

Paula turned to him with a sadistic smile. "The one that you're going to buy me to replace the one that the animals wrecked."

Johnny nodded to Lamar for him to agree to her request. Lamar offered to arrange for the state to forward her a check as soon as possible.

"Can you let go of my testicles, please?" Johnny pleaded. Paula's eyes returned to normal and she released her hold on him.

Johnny then pointed out that they would need several other vehicles replaced as well.

"I'll speak to DHS about it," replied Lamar confidently. I'm sure they can find it in their 'discretionary' budget." Everyone laughed at his pun.

Pir commented to Lamar, "You humans are a unique breed."

"If you only knew," Lamar remarked, considering how bizarre this was.

"I must leave you now," Pir announced.

"Thank you for all your help," Lamar replied humbly. "I wish we could do something to help you."

"No. My time here is done," Pir explained and levitated into the woods.

Johnny looked around for Gino and Paula. There was no sign of them. "Where'd they go now?" he asked, concerned.

"I can't read their minds," Jo responded in amusement. She enjoyed seeing Johnny become frantic over Paula's lust for Gino. "They're blocking us out."

Johnny grew angry and rushed into the cabin in search of her.

"Damn it! Someone's gonna get hurt!" fretted Lamar as he charged after him into the cabin.

Johnny burst into the bedroom. To his embarrassment, Gino lay naked on the bed and Paula took a picture of the expression on Johnny's face.

Lamar barged in, followed by Joe and Sasha.

"Would you like to join us, Mayor?" she asked Lamar.

"I think he's heard that before," kidded Jo.

"Oh, fuck you all," Lamar shouted and stormed out of the cabin. Everyone laughed.

"I'd better go to him. He's still sensitive about the hotel jokes," Sasha explained giddily and left them.

When evening came, Paula and Johnny sat on the cabin steps. Johnny asked uneasily, "Are we all right?"

Paula smiled at him and answered, "Maybe one day we will. What you did was wrong and I won't let you forget it."

"When did you know?" he asked curiously.

"Oh, I knew for a while that you were manipulating us. That's why I took Gino like I did. Call it payback."

"I was really worried," Johnny confessed.

"About what?"

"I was afraid you were done with me."

"No. I do think I'd like to do both you and Gino from now on."

"Huh?" asked Johnny in utter surprise.

"I think it'll take two men to satisfy me now. Thank you very much for that."

Johnny rolled his eyes and regretted ever starting this game with the women. As if on cue, Gino exited the cabin. Paula stood and took him by the hand. Johnny was stunned until Paula reached for his hand.

"There's a nice soft spot by the stream if you'd like to join us," she offered playfully.

Johnny realized that this was how it was going to be, from now on. He took her hand and the three of them went to the stream.

Pir levitated over the stream a short distance away and heard Paula's moans.

Those humans are definitely the strangest species I have ever met," he remarked and then exploded into blue dust that settled in the water.

· ·•◆•· ·

Sasha and Lamar walked hand in hand down the road. "Finally, things are back to normal," she said happily.

Surprised, Lamar stopped and stared at her. "How can you say that?"

"Well, we shouldn't have to deal with aliens coming back here for a long time."

"So, what do we do until then?"

Sasha lifted her shirt, revealing her breasts. "You mean I have to tell you?"

Lamar smiled and quipped, "Here we go again."

## The End

## Or is it?